## Praise for *Himalayan Dhaba*

"Prose that sings . . . A vision that pierces the clouds at the top of the world and allows us to see beyond ourselves."
—*Statesman Journal* (Salem, Oregon)

"A breathtaking display of enormous talent."
—*The Bellingham Herald*

"Captivating . . . A vibrant, emotionally resonant tale."
—*Publishers Weekly*

"An engaging debut novel . . . A fresh spirit animates this tale, one carefully constructed, simply narrated, and briskly organized."
—*Kirkus Reviews*

"Don't miss it. Mr. Danner is a born storyteller, and writing with rare competence, he has given us a unique and unforgettable world." —Pete Fromm, PNBA Award–winning author of *How All This Started* and *Night Swimming*

"Danner never makes a slip. He is a writer not only of place and person, but also of the soul."
—Pete Sinclair, author of *We Aspired: The Last Innocent Americans*

**Craig Joseph Danner,** a physician's assistant with a degree in creative writing, lives with his wife on a farm in Oregon, where he is at work on his next novel, *The Fires of Edgarville.*

**Visit www.himalayandhaba.com**

# Himalayan Dhaba

## Craig Joseph Danner

A PLUME BOOK

PLUME
Published by the Penguin Group
Penguin Group (USA) Inc., 375 Hudson Street, New York, New York 10014, U.S.A.
Penguin Books Ltd, 80 Strand, London WC2R 0RL, England
Penguin Books Australia Ltd, 250 Camberwell Road, Camberwell, Victoria 3124, Australia
Penguin Books Canada Ltd, 10 Alcorn Avenue, Toronto, Ontario, Canada M4V 3B2
Penguin Books (N.Z.) Ltd, Cnr Rosedale and Airborne Roads, Albany, Auckland 1310, New Zealand

Penguin Books Ltd, Registered Offices: 80 Strand, London WC2R 0RL, England

Published by Plume, a member of Penguin Group (USA) Inc. Previously published in a Dutton edition.
Originally published in 2001 by Crispin/Hammer Publishing Company, Hood River, Oregon.

First Plume Printing, June 2003
10  9  8  7  6  5  4  3  2  1

Ⓟ REGISTERED TRADEMARK—MARCA REGISTRADA

The Library of Congress has catalogued the Crispin/Hammer edition as follows:

Danner, Craig Joseph
Himalayan Dhaba / Craig Joseph Danner.—1st ed.
p.   cm.
ISBN 0-9706405-9-5
ISBN 0-525-94690-X (Dutton hc.)
ISBN 0-452-28387-6 (Plume pbk.)
I. Title.
Library of Congress Control Number: 2001087259
813'.54—dc21

Printed in the United States of America
Set in Bembo
Original Dutton hardcover design by Leonard Telesca

—for Beth

May

# The Patient

She's waiting out a sudden shower of fifty-kilo bags of rice, a gathered clutch of angry chickens flapping like their heads are off. It's raining rolls of razor wire and wooden crates of tangerines, a blood-red set of luggage for a couple on their honeymoon. The driver honked through eighteen hours of blindly climbing hairpin turns; the bus hit every dog that dared to cross the road from Chandigarh. Mary's so exhausted she can barely stand among the crowd—she's praying that her bags are there, the one box in particular. At last she sees her canvas duffel sailing through the mountain air; she waves and yells to get the man to treat her box more carefully. But his ropy muscles flex and stretch across his shirtless arms and back, the sun gleams off the lines of sweat that trickle down his dusty flank. He doesn't look or heed her shout before he drops it to the ground—the box lands in the mud and dust: the sparkling sound of broken glass.

Trying not to get upset, she's swallowing her rising bile: *stupid idiot!* she thinks, though not referring to the man. She feels like everything she's touched has shattered in the past six months; *can't even get a goddamn box of medicines down off a bus*. She knows that things are different here, she's not back home in Baltimore, but seven thousand feet above the plains of Northern India. The sun is beaming overhead, the sky the blue of early May; a soft breeze swings the evergreens, the mountains oh-so-beautiful. But the bus keeps belching diesel smoke and noise so she can't concentrate; three men are shouting in her face, each claiming his hotel is best. She'd like to turn around and leave, go find someplace to sit and cry—she's desperate for a private place to drop her pants around her knees. She has to shift from foot to foot, she hasn't gone since yesterday; the few times that the driver stopped, there wasn't any ladies' room. Every muscle in her back is on the verge of spasming: sudden shooting, stabbing pains enough to take her breath away.

The closest man before her has a cancer growing on his lip; in all her years of practice she has never seen one half as big. Trying not to stare she shouts, "I'm staying at the hospital!" She sees the hope drop from his face, the pearly tumor glistening. The three men turn away as she attempts to gather up her bags; she thought, perhaps, there'd be somebody waiting for her when she came. She feels like she can't focus, like there's nothing under her control: a nauseating moment when she steps in something soft and dull. A half-dozen porters want to help her with her duffel bag, but all she sees are wasted arms on men who must weigh less than her. She doesn't want to feel this way, she thought that she had come prepared: she read the books and travel guides, the passages on culture shock. But she's never been so far from home or traveled overseas before; she's following her husband's ghost that led her to this wretched town. She makes herself meet one man's eyes, a porter with a crooked smile, her random choice because his shirt's the only one not torn with holes.

They are high up in a little town where tourists come to see the snow; the valley walls with peaks of ice are lined with fruiting apple trees. Her map shows that the road ends here, the last real town before the pass—further north are only arid mountains going on and on. But this town's rimmed by forests filled with evergreen deodar trees that rise up from the duff to try to imitate the mountain peaks. The buildings stand two stories high, their walls are mortared brick and stone; the town is just a couple blocks of alleyways and market stalls. The alley that they're walking down is filled with tourists from the plains: long-haired Western travelers and newlyweds with hennaed hands. The hotel signs are lettered in half a dozen languages: *Stay Here for Your Honeymoon* and *Best Place for the Hippie Freaks;* Hindi, English, French, and several others she can't recognize. But Mary doesn't have the time or energy to look about for anything except a place to let her aching bladder down. She'd like a clean, well-lighted place where she could trust them with her bags, a disinfected toilet, and a sink to wash her face and hands.

Nothing looks too promising, the storefronts are all dark inside, the sidewalk lined with metal plates on stoves of hissing kerosene. These sizzling grills are saucer shaped and large enough to sled on snow; she feels the spit of grease from brown samosas fried in smoking oil. She braced herself for beggars, but the impact is still visceral: a woman without legs has propped herself against a crumbling wall. On what's left of her lap she holds a plump and squirming two-year-old who vigorously sucks beneath a coarsely woven woolen shawl. This woman looks at Mary so their eyes meet for the briefest time—Mary has to look away or risk another crying jag. The wallahs in their canvas stalls—all shouting at her constantly—demand that she must stop and buy their cabbages and tangerines. And she'd like to pass this holy man, this baba smeared with human ash, who's blocking half the sidewalk as he browses through the marketplace. His begging bowl is pounded brass, his trident staff is tipped with bone; he hasn't got a stitch of clothes but dreadlocks filled with marigolds. She doesn't try to pass because she'd likely bump him with her bag—afraid she'd have to buy the goat he'd need for cleansing sacrifice. But then she sees a little café up another alleyway, a landmark from the photos that she memorized in Baltimore. It was where her husband took his meals, back a dozen years ago, *Himalayan Dhaba* painted on the sign above the door. It doesn't look much better than the other cafés that she's seen: built from poorly mortared brick, tiny windows thick with grease.

She motions to the porter that she wants him to wait by the door, signing with her hands, hoping he'll stay and guard her box and bags. She drops her backpack on the ground and feels a wave of urgency; she rushes through the café door and almost knocks the waiter down. He's a short and slender walleyed man dressed neatly in a Nehru suit—she's shocked to recognize his face, from another photo Richard kept. The picture shows her husband with his arm around this gentleman: Richard has a goofy smile, the waiter's eyes look here and there. The café is so dark inside she has to strain to look around: the room is twenty feet across, the tables don't look very clean. The café's barely half full with a funny mix of clientele; suddenly she's thinking that she should have looked around some more. Everyone has turned to stare; she feels a dozen sets of eyes: a ragged Western traveler, an Indian in suit and tie. She asks this man her husband knew: please, could she use the ladies' room? He bows to her then wags his head, an answer she can't comprehend.

"*Mé-ré saath aa-i-yé,*" he says and gently takes her arm, leads her down the center of this darkly paneled restaurant. The room is close and filled with smoke, she smells the faintest hint of dope; the waiter guides her through the darkness toward the swinging door in back. He points her to a closet that smells like an open septic tank—ripping at her belt she barely gets her pants down fast enough.

The only light comes through a tiny window high up overhead, and there isn't any toilet but a hole cut in the concrete floor. She's focusing on balance, trying to keep her pants up off the ground—horrified she'll tumble over, unsure where she's supposed to aim. At last her bladder's letting down, her feet not quite spread wide enough; her passport safe around her waist now jabbing in her pancreas. She'd made a promise to herself she wouldn't cry for two more days; tears have come so quickly ever since the day that Richard died. She feels them running down her cheeks, along the crease beside her nose, dripping from her chin into this hole between her hiking boots. She's worried that the porter won't be outside when she's finished here, and worried that she's never going to find the mission hospital. She's not sure why she's doing this, except her husband loved it here— she's thinking she should turn around for safe and sterile Baltimore. But there's nothing for her there now that she's left her home and quit her job, sold her house and practice in a clinic for the very old. She knows she'll find the hospital, it can't be very far away, and if the porter steals her bags she'll buy some other clothes to wear. There isn't any paper so she zips up her wrinkled pants—doesn't trust the water in the pail to give her hands a wash. She wipes her eyes off with her sleeves, takes a breath of fetid air. She shakes her head and wonders *what the hell* she thinks she's doing here.

The alley's paved with graveled rock, the sunlight bouncing off the dust, and Mary has to squint to see, the restaurant was dark as night. The porter is still waiting with her bags beneath the dhaba's sign; she tells him with her red-rimmed eyes that she's feeling better than before. Now that she has peed and cried and hasn't lost all her supplies, this tiny village doesn't seem as awful as at first it had. The porter has a friendly face, his eyes are sparkling with life; she shows him once again the name of Doctor Vikram's hospital. She knows it's likely he can't read, especially her English script; his head moves in a way that Mary can't quite tell is no or yes. So she mimes as if she has a cough, walks like someone with a limp, finally rifles through a bag, pulls out her shiny stethoscope. The porter rolls his eyes and laughs, her destination obvious.

"*Achhaa-ji,*" he says, and picks up Doctor Mary's dusty bags.

He leads her from the restaurant, it isn't very far at all; he takes her down a winding maze of gravel paths and alleyways. As they walk she's looking round, half a world away from home; she watches someone scrub a pot with dirt scraped straight up off the ground. But the sky today is cloudless, and she's almost at her journey's end, anxious to meet Doctor Vikram, another one of Richard's friends. She's having a rare moment of her optimism blossoming: maybe she will like it here, this busy little tourist town. Her husband talked about this place, he worked here when he finished school: spent two months in these mountains just before they met in internship. He'd told her of the hospital, of Doctor Vikram Vargeela, a man from Southern India who runs the place all by himself. Richard called the man a saint, said Vikram had a magic touch—so long as you ignored the surgeon's tendency to preach too much. Rich said the place was beautiful with lovely terraced valley walls, a temple in the forest, and the Himalayas all around. But he didn't mention how it smells, the nasty open-sewer stink, the beggars with their pleading palms and exudative skin disease. This is why she's come here, though, so useless since her husband's death: her love cut down in the prime of life, a stupid biking accident. She cried herself to sleep for weeks, then made herself go back to work; just couldn't care enough about her aging patients' chief complaints. Her partners bought her practice for a price that was quite generous; she banked it with the million from the life insurance Richard kept. She contemplated suicide, but wasn't really serious; she tried to think what Rich would do if *she* had been the one to die. That's when Vikram's card came with his yearly Christmas newsletter, which hinted for donations for his hospital in India. A way to keep her husband near, it felt like such a good idea: *Supplies are low, the wards are full, could use a doctor volunteer.*

The compound has seen better days, with patchy bits of weeds and grass—she recognizes everything from Richard's color photographs. The buildings haven't changed at all, with roofs of rusty village tin, the windows glazed with wavy glass, the walls in need of plastering. She thought that this would feel familiar, as if she'd been up here before, but really it was Rich who worked here back a dozen years ago. Like all the buildings in this town, they're brick and rock and wooden beams—a painted sign in English points the way to the X-ray machine. The wards are both two stories high with wooden stairs and balconies, the courtyard beaten free of grass by years of patients' trampling feet. In the center of the yard there is a stunning, ancient walnut tree: massive trunk and spreading limbs, its canopy blocks out the sky. The porter drops her bags beneath it, speaks to her in Kullui; Mary doesn't know the coins so lets the porter keep the change. The man gives her his crooked smile and brings his hands before his face. Bowing he takes one step back before he turns to take his leave.

The hospital is tiny, with the buildings scattered randomly, dwarfed from east and west by massive Himalayan mountain peaks. She smells the sweet deodar smoke of someone cooking over fire, reminding her of camping in the pines of western Maryland. She wonders where the patients are, the lines that Richard once described—Vikram wrote that there was never time enough to see them all. It is sometime in the afternoon, perhaps the staff has gone to lunch; she set her watch in Delhi, though she could have turned the dial wrong. But *someone* should be hanging round, she knows they are expecting her; she sent a message yesterday: *arriving soon as possible.* The last time Vikram wrote he said there's always so much work to do—the clinic runs four days a week, with surgery the other two. Sunday is his day of rest, he preaches in the little church; she sees the tiny, empty building: a steeple and a crucifix. She tries to think what day it is, she left the States on Saturday; spent one night in the Delhi Hilton's musty air-conditioning. She's guessing that it's Tuesday and it must be close to three o'clock—unlikely Doctor Vikram would take off to play a round of golf. So she leaves her bags beneath the tree with leaves the green of early spring, and wanders through the courtyard, through the echoing dispensary. The only sound she hears is someone's distant whistle off somewhere. She follows it in through a door, a painted sign to *Surgery*.

The hall is almost black inside, the walls are stacked with limp supplies: boxes with their lids cut off, the dust has never been disturbed. She's thinking it's incredible, the storeroom's loaded with antiques: surgical contraptions no one's used in half a century. She takes a cloth mask from a bin and holds it to her mouth and nose, then opens up a door that's marked the entrance to the surgery. It should be draped with braided rope, an old-time surgical museum: an overwhelming ether stink is sickly sweet and volatile. The table has a dozen cranks, a sheet draped over stainless steel; above it hangs an ancient lamp: a giant metal buttercup.

Nobody's there, but still she hears the funny, tuneless whistling—and then a ringing echoed laugh, a soft and high-pitched giggle. It comes out from a little room, the next door that she opens up; she finds a tiny woman, someone Richard once had talked about.

"*Doctor-ji! Namasté!*" At last someone expecting her; she sent a photo of herself and Richard the first time she wrote. Padma can't be four feet tall, her body nearly bent in half: Rich had said he liked her best of all the people working there. Mary is amazed at how she looks just like her photograph: tiny little angel face and eyes benignly mischievous. Her spine has got a nasty twist, perhaps a childhood accident, but Mary's never seen a face as beautiful and radiant. Padma climbs down off a stool, her wrinkled apron stained with red from washing blood off rubber gloves so that they can be used again. She wangs her hands before her face: palms together, fingers straight; a man stands from a wooden bench: he's the source of all the whistling. She wonders if this could be Vikram—pleasant smile and slender hips—but he hasn't got the features of a man from Southern India. His face is more Tibetan-shaped, his eyes a little wide apart; in very broken English he says *Tamding* is his given name. Mary only knows a couple phrases of the dialect, studied from a worthless book, a numbing set of language tapes. She's not sure what his job is but he does what Padma tells him to: he helps her with her bags and shows her to the rooms that she's to have. They cross the dusty courtyard past the one-room missionary school; Tamding might be speaking English, but she doesn't know for sure. He's pointing out the landmarks, making jutting gestures with his chin; Mary only smiles and wonders anxiously where Vikram is.

He leads her to a building that could be a mom-and-pop motel: single-story cinder block with doors all lined up in a row. She's got the last rooms on the end, the farthest from the hospital; Tamding opens up the door and shows her where she's going to live. *This won't do at all,* she thinks, her heart drops down another inch: the walls a shade of green like something growing in a swimming pool. She tries to see her husband here, how Richard thought it wonderful; the bed a musty block of foam, the kitchen doesn't have a stove; she looks into the bathroom: just another hole where she's to go. Tamding brings her bags inside and stacks them neat against the wall, wangs his hands before his face, and goes out backward through the door. She's glad, at least, to be alone, to have some time to recompose; her stomach gripped with anxious fear, she thinks *this was a bad idea.* Richard was the one who dreamed of coming back to India—never was the kind of man who needed to be comfortable. She wants her husband desperately, perhaps she would relax a bit: he'd take her out exploring, wander through the winding marketplace.

She lies down on the bed but can't relax enough to fall asleep; she wonders if the water in the tap is safe to brush her teeth. The only nice thing in the room is a sunny wooden window seat that overlooks an alley with a glimpse of snowy mountain peak. She pulls the curtains back to let some light into this gloomy space, wanders through the tiny kitchen, sniffs a hint of rat perfume. Then on a table by the bed she finds a letter with her name, held down at one corner with a textbook as a paperweight. She looks first at the massive tome, the English title on the spine: *General Practice Guidelines for the Rural District Hospital.* She flips through several pages filled with pictures of advanced disease: liver cysts from parasites she's hoping that she'll never see. She's thinking she won't be much help with everything so different here—Richard was the surgeon, could have operated anywhere. But Mary is an internist, knows medicines and lab reports: a specialist in geriatrics, treating grandpa's gout and stroke. She opens up the envelope, her name spelled in a hasty hand; it takes some time to read the words, decipher Vikram's doctor-scratch.

At first she doesn't understand, she has to guess some of the words; but then it all comes clear why there weren't patients at the hospital. And she thought that she hit bottom when she saw where she's supposed to live, but now she knows her heart can sink at least another couple feet. She's thinking now would be the time to quietly just disappear, leave a note for Vikram on the box of shattered medicines. But then she hears the whistling, the flute of Tamding's puckered lips—he's knocking nonstop on her door until she starts to open it. Breathlessly he's talking in a language she can't understand, motions with his hands so that she knows to quickly follow him. With no idea what's going on, she's led across the hard dirt yard; she's running through a list of what might be the worst that she could find. She's thinking it's a heart attack, a motorcycle accident—someone with a bleeding cut, an artery that's gushing blood. They cross beneath the walnut tree, the speckled light of twitching leaves; he leads her to a room that smells of nasty disinfectant spray. But no one's on the table that is centered in the trauma room, just a woman on a bench, a bundle cradled in her arms. The bundle's covered with a shawl and Mary's trying to catch her breath; the woman looks up briefly but then turns her eyes away. The woman's dressed in local clothes, a pattu made of homespun wool, a scarf ties back her long black hair, silver hoops pierced through her nose.

And Tamding's somehow disappeared so Mary's not sure where he's gone—doesn't even know exactly why he left her standing here. She doesn't have her stethoscope, she isn't in her long white coat; she couldn't even start to ask the questions that a doctor must. She's trying to imagine what required her so urgently; this woman isn't bleeding, isn't writhing round in agony. Mary tries to guess her age—she could be forty-five years old, she could be half of that but Mary finds it difficult to tell. Right then the woman looks at her, the saddest eyes she's ever seen;

now Mary understands what made them call for her so urgently. Her heart skips several beats at first, a lump forms large inside her throat; she motions to the mother that she'd like to take a closer look. The mother pulls the shawl back so that Mary sees the baby's face—Mary has to swallow hard to keep her gasp from being heard.

The baby looks a hundred years, with sagging skin across the face: sunken eyes and fontanel, breathing at too slow a rate. She hasn't got a clue what's wrong: a birth defect or rare disease; she takes the baby from the mom as if she holds a hand grenade. With the baby on the table, she unwraps the musty woolen shawl; the skin hangs down like melted wax: a dying little baby girl. Her eyes are dry and glazed as if she hasn't blinked since she was born; doesn't cry or make a fuss, just stares and slowly gasps for air. In Baltimore there'd be a dozen nurses working frantically: X-ray techs and lab reports and respiratory therapists. All she'd have to do is give the orders to the nursing staff: stand and watch and make sure that the blood gets sent off fast enough. Mary hasn't slept in days, her thinking isn't very clear: this baby is dehydrated, should get some fluids into her. She's thinking meningitis, maybe *H. flu* septicemia: spinal tap and blood cultures; X-ray and a white cell count. She needs an IV right away, she'd like to put her on a vent; she puts an ear against her chest to listen to what noise she makes. She wants to know how long it's been, how old this ancient baby is; she needs to get the baby's weight to calculate the fluid drip. At last she hears the whistling of Tamding coming back this way; he steps in through the door and rattles something off in Kullui. She asks him for an IV drip; he only shrugs and wags his head. It's obvious he doesn't understand a word that Doctor Mary says. At last she hears another set of footsteps from across the yard—she sees a floating nurse's cap come sailing past the window frame.

The nurse who comes in through the door is not a day past seventeen: long black hair done in a braid, a ribbon tied up in a bow. She says her name is Chidda and she'll try to help the best she can; the other nurses are at home, they weren't expecting her so soon. She says she's only worked a month, just graduated nursing school—that Doctor Vikram said he thinks that one day she'll be pretty good. But Mary doesn't have the time, this baby is about to die; already diagnosed the nurse's tendency to rattle on.

"I'm Doctor Mary Davis," she says, cutting off the chattering; starts listing off the things she'll need: an IV and a catheter. She's calculating in her head the dosages that she should give; she needs antibiotics that will cross the blood brain barrier. This infant's running out of time, each breath could be her final gasp, and Mary isn't sure about the doses she's remembering. The nurse just stands in horror when she sees the withered infant girl, so Mary gets the feeling that this nurse won't do her any good. She starts into the list again, anxious that the work begin—mimes the way she'd try to stick a needle in the baby's vein.

"If you can't help, I understand. *Just find somebody else who can!*"

The nurse then turns around and leaves, comes back in with an IV tray; puts it down then backs away, not volunteering for the job. Mary hasn't started IVs since she finished internship; she's used to having IV techs and nurses with experience. She quickly asks for sterile gloves, a swab or two of Betadine; she'll need a couple culture jars, plus red and purple vacuum tubes. Mary's nervous she won't find a vein before the baby dies; asks then for a tourniquet to strap around the baby's thigh. She's slapping at the leg to see if she can raise a purple vein—baby so lethargic that the slapping doesn't make her cry. She looks up at the nurse to see if she has brought the things she needs; nurse is still just standing staring at the walnut tree outside.

"I'm sorry," Chidda says this time, "but everybody else is gone."

The nurse sounds like she's going to cry—she says that she is all alone; when Doctor Vikram left he said that they should close the hospital. They can't get any X-rays since the tech has gone to Chandigarh, off to search for parts to fix the broken autoclave machine. They can't do any cultures since they haven't got a microlab; she thinks the spinal needles are still waiting to be sterilized.

"And we don't have any *bata-deen*. I'm not sure what it is you need."

Mary's hands are shaking, thinks this baby can't be three weeks old; the baby doesn't have the strength to keep on gasping anymore.

"I need something to clean the skin," and Mary's also on the verge; she's slapping at the other leg, still desperate for a decent vein. Chidda brings a cotton ball that's soaked in something horrible; slowly mops the knee and thigh till Mary knocks her hands away. The baby is so deep in shock her veins have all nearly collapsed; with fingers trembling Mary blindly sticks the IV needle in. She knows that there's a big vein somewhere near the outside of the shin; after several tries she finds it: tiny flash of something red.

"Damn it! I need tape!" she screams, her patience finally wearing out; she knows this baby's going to die and everything will be her fault. Vikram's letter said the staff would help her any way they could; all she needs to do is ask: *The nurses are all excellent.* And this was what he'd written in the letter underneath the book: that he would keep her in his prayers, that Richard would be proud of her. *I'm going home to Kerala. My father's taken gravely ill. I'll be back in a month or so. The hospital depends on you.*

She knows that she's not up for this, she hasn't got much in reserve—she came this far to find a ghost to hold her hand and comfort her. She looks down at this tiny girl, while Chidda draws the saline push; this dying baby's face holds all the sadness in the universe. She knows that she will have to stay, if only for a couple days: *She'll live but only if I keep this needle safe inside her vein.*

October

# The Dhaba

Amod has his hands full, serving hot tea to the doctor here, the beer is for the hippies there, chapatis for the honeymooners keeping silent company. The dhaba has been busy since the summer rains let up last month: tourists trying to escape some sticky hot metropolis. He's done this for so many years these rushes have become routine; his hands are full but he is busy thinking about other things. He's worried Doctor Mary doesn't have much of an appetite—she's lost a lot of weight since she first came here back in early May. And now that it's October he is thinking she's not fat enough: needs some extra weight to get her through the coming winter months. She'll order just a lemon tea, some cheese nan if he pushes her; he's counting and she hasn't had a decent meal since Saturday. He knows that she's been working late with Doctor Vikram still away—he sees her in the trauma room while walking home at one or two. He takes this shortcut late at night, he closes once the hippies leave; often stops to chat with Tamding, watchman for the hospital. Tamding tells him all the news, the gossip from the nursing staff: how Doctor Mary's hands will shake while doing simple surgery. He puts the tea before her, and of course she looks at him and smiles: *thank you, Amod-ji,* she says, *your tea is all I want today.* He knows the nurses must be wrong, he knows that Mary's wonderful—the only customer he has who asks him how his day has been. He wishes that he could insist she have some curried peas and rice; maybe she would like to taste the eggplant bharta that they make. But all she ever wants is tea, however many times he asks; he wags his head and turns away: she's got such sad and lonely eyes.

The restaurant is dimly lit, the paneling is walnut brown; the power in the evenings is so weak the lightbulbs cast a pall. There's a candle on each table so the room's filled with a yellow haze; his boss sits in his corner booth and slowly adds the patrons' checks. His boss sits there behind his gut and picks out Western music hits—the tape deck spills out songs as slow and sour as a yogurt drink. Amod doesn't care for it, this syncopated thumping sound; for years he's tried to tune it out, like whiffs of stinking sewer gas.

That hippie man is back again, he's been away a month or so; he wishes that the man would find some other place to deal his dope. He dresses just like all the other ragged Western travelers: blue jeans torn up at the knees, his skin does not look very clean. But he's older than the rest of them, his hair is coarse and streaked with gray—the other Western travelers look barely old enough to shave. They've all got too much time to spare, from Europe and America; they're here because the dope is cheap, to escape the searing Goan beach. But this old guy makes Amod nervous with his lines of scabby needle marks; his hair is long and matted, hangs down halfway past his shoulder blades. The hippie men all look alike with woolen vests and tattooed arms; the young ones all go barefoot, but this older one wears army boots. He puts the beer before this man who acts like Amod isn't there; he gets a face full of the smoke this ancient hippie man exhales. Then Amod is distracted by the honeymooners near the stove: they're out of things to say and so they want their order changed once more.

He goes back to the kitchen where the thumping music's not so loud; he stops the other waiter who with caution loads a dinner tray. They both are dressed in uniform, in black pants with a shiny stripe—their woolen Nehru jackets buttoned stiffly to the very top. Amod is inspecting him, then helps him lift the heavy tray; he pulls the young man's jacket straight and brushes at some vagrant stain.

"Table four needs water," he says, giving him a final nod; he steps aside to let the young man get his tray out through the door. He lets the cook know what he needs, then gathers what's been freshly made: a plate full of biryani and another glass of lemon tea. The kitchen is a mix of smells: fresh spices and the toilet stall; the cook is good but can't help that the plumbing isn't vented well. The door is hinged in two directions, swinging in and out the same; Amod leans his shoulder then to go back where it's dark and loud.

He puts the dinner down before a young blond hippie traveler—the boy looks barely seventeen, a hint of fuzzy lip mustache. He's dressed up in the right attire, in local vest and torn-up jeans; his hair is proper hippie style, with dreadlocks to his shoulder blades. It's strange that he should sit alone, the men all come in threes and fours; Amod saw that when he came in the other hippies turned to look, didn't recognize him so went back to staring off in space. The boy then sat and lit a smoke, the menu got a turned-up nose; in nasal British English he asked if they had some "real food." He ordered the biryani saying all this curry makes him sick; he slid his leather jacket off, a black thing fixed with metal studs: another hippie fashion hit.

Amod goes back to the doctor, hoping she'll want something more—she only smiles and shakes her head: *the lemon tea was really good*. She's trying not to let him see the pages of the book she's got; the pictures in it so grotesque could ruin any appetite. She's wearing such a tired look, her soft brown eyes remote and sad—she's trying not to show it, though, by smiling through her weariness. She's looking almost pretty now her hair is starting to grow out: was cut so short when she first came she could have been a boy of eight. She dresses like a man in woolen sweaters and long baggy pants; her clothes are marked with dark red stains, no time to wash them out herself.

The hippie with the big black boots is signaling he wants his check; he sat alone for several hours and smoked a pack of cigarettes. He comes through every month or so—a habit now for many years—and takes a table by the tandoor, makes his quiet hippie deals. Every local person knows that hippies are all drug addicts—they come to buy the black charas, to smoke and talk and eat and sleep. Amod's looking forward to when hippie season settles down; they migrate when it gets too cold to walk outside without their shoes. The check is finally added up, the dealer never orders much; he's always charged a private tax to pay the boss for rental space. This long-haired man with big black boots gets up and walks across the room; he stops next to the younger hippie sitting eating all alone. He doesn't bother to sit down but offers an extended hand; the young one doesn't shake at first, he's unsure what is going on. But Amod's seen this done before; he's slipping him a stick of hash: just offering a token from his little leather sample bag.

# The Rat

They woke her up again last night—the nurses on the grave-yard shift—to sew a tiny forehead cut, to help them get a baby out. It must be almost six o'clock as she drags home through her universe: the dusty yard between the wards of Himchal Mission Hospital. The sun has not yet risen, but it's dawning on the sleeping town—it's lighting up the mountainsides, the Himalayas shining proud. Grudgingly she loves to be up earlier than anyone: the locals still asleep in bed, some distant roosters hollering, the only time that's all her own to wonder what she's doing here.

Doctor Mary's greeted by a dog whose coat is caked with dirt; a dog named for a Hindu goddess: Kali, black and horrible. The dog has had so many pups her teats drag through the mud and dust; her red tongue hangs out from her mouth like sirloin from a grinder spout. She's seen this big dog snap at kids and chase the men who carry bricks—in Baltimore they wouldn't hesitate to put this dog to sleep. But here the locals leave it be,

her namesake mean and terrible; no Hindu wants to risk the
karma, Buddhists wouldn't think of it. Mary's grown fond of the
beast, this dog the only friend she has; Kali greets her in the yard
like children when their father's home.

Mary's thinking of her husband as she walks back to her
lonely rooms: it's past the anniversary: a year and twenty days
since Richard died and left her on her own. It's six months since
she first arrived and found that Vikram wasn't here; his note said
he would be back soon, but then he wrote he wasn't sure. It's
early in the morning and Mary's been up since the night before;
she wants an hour of sleep before they open up the clinic doors.
She loves the fresh sweet morning air, the silence as the day begins; the only sound she's hearing is the flapping of a raven's
wings. No buses idle in the street, no storefronts blare their ra-
dios—no sound of wretched women pounding gravel out of
larger stones. Most mornings she hears donkeys braying—just
like Richard once described—but now there's only silence: just
the whoosh of feathers overhead. The air is crisp and steams her
breath, a couple weeks till Halloween; the other night the Hin-
dus had Diwali with its fireworks. She smells the sweet deodar
smoke, her hand on top of Kali's head; she's finally lost the image
of a mother's bleeding private parts.

They'd called for her at one A.M., the nurse up on the grave-
yard shift—she heard the watchman's whistling, her heart was in
her throat before he'd even had a chance to knock. Tamding is a
handsome man—a sweet Tibetan refugee—whose constant
whistle only stops when he's about to smile at her. Each night she
lies and waits for him, imagining the worst she can; she's always
tired but hasn't slept well since the day that Richard died. The
nights all have the same routine, the staff calls her for everything:
the cuts and sprains and tummy aches of tourists who ate something strange. But she carries now a constant fear of how in-

competent she is; she knows there's something out there that she won't know how to deal with. She didn't train for this at all, this medicine so primitive; she'd rather order MRIs and blood cultures and scintigrams. But here they bring her little kids who should be in intensive care; treated by the best there is—her husband should be standing there. All she's got are ears and eyes, an X-ray and a microscope, a staff without credentials who were trained by *Doctor Saint* himself. She lugs around this massive book that Vikram left there with his note; she knows this only makes it worse, the staff have lost their confidence. She'd leave this place tomorrow but then who would hear the watchman's song? The whistle seems to circle round, just waiting for an opening. And here is how it goes most nights: already she'll be out of bed and pulling on some dirty clothes—embarrassed by their nervous stink, *but when am I supposed to wash?!* She'll open up her door to find his knuckled fist about to strike; Tamding's pleasant, sing-song voice announcing what she's needed for. He'll sweetly say a baby's stuck, somebody's wound is pumping blood; but always in a pleasant voice, without a hint that she should rush.

This time it wasn't urgent though; the night nurse should have handled it; Vikram's note said they were trained to almost do without his help. But Nishi called her anyway, sent Tamding on a doctor run; Mary stumbled in to find an old man with a tiny cut. The patient was a little drunk, out chopping kindling late at night; he'd swung an ax a bit too dull which bounced and cut him on the brow. He spoke to her in Kullui—unwary of her sewing style—and she barely understood a word but sensed that he'd proposed to her. She couldn't yet give him her hand, but thought a tetanus shot might do; it went into his upper arm, the old man didn't flinch at all: skin as tough as mutton cutlet, the needle was a little dull.

Then Nishi asked the doctor if she'd check a woman laboring: upstairs in the delivery room, the baby not descending much. Delivery's up a wooden flight that's narrow, steep, and treacherous, the doorway built so low that only Padma doesn't have to duck. And Mary *hates* deliveries, they're so damn unpredictable— the women scream, there's so much blood: the shadow of impending doom. She'd only done a few in school, then swore she wouldn't anymore: her nerves got all tied up in knots, with visions of catastrophe. But now that she's been here for months, she's starting to accept her fate; they average three newborns a week: she's almost got the hang of it.

She found the woman lying flat against the wooden labor bed; the family anxious from the noise, her screams of fruitless pushing pain. All the noise made Mary tense, the mothers sometimes lose control; she doesn't have the expertise to know when things are going well. With her hands around the hump, she felt the pregnant belly tense: contractions feeling strong and hard, the baby should have squirted out. The mom had pushed so long that she now barely had the strength to talk; Mary listened for the heartbeat, then she spread the woman's legs apart. Her sweating hand inside a glove, she felt the woman's bulging bag—the shock of water warm and smooth sent shivers up and down her spine. The woman's urine started flowing, also washing Mary's hand, pressed against the baby's head, still between the mother's legs. The baby had been floating there, the cervix hadn't reached complete—and now the baby sank down just like water through an unstopped drain. She knew she had to push the head to slow this sudden exiting: her hand out like she'd catch a melon tumbling from a fruit display. The woman gave a sudden scream—her womb clenched as an angry fist—and Mary tried to hold her ground, but suddenly the head popped out. Too fast, too big, a certain tear: this mother would be sore for weeks. She thought perhaps it was her fault, but really she'd done all she could.

The baby's head was round and smooth, and she suctioned slime out of its mouth; she wrapped a towel around the head, the better to hang on to it. The head turned, then the shoulders popped, the left and then the right came out; the body slithered from the womb, a snake discarding worn-out skin. She clamped and cut and handed off, then didn't want to look again—to see what she knew wasn't there, the X-Y kind of genitals. No woman here would want a girl, no father wants to hear this news: a burden to the family, a dowry to be paid someday. They find out that it's not a son—someone to light their funeral pyre—then scream and wail and beat their heads right there against the labor bed. But Mary wants to place the babies warm against the mothers' chests; snuggle them between their breasts all glistening with labor sweat.

Instead she stood there gloved and gowned between the woman's wide spread legs—tension light on veiny cord, the book said not to pull too hard. Blood was dripping from the mom, big clots spilled out at Mary's feet; she heard the baby's healthy cry, seemed everything was going right. The placenta finally wallowed forth, came past the yawning labia; it lumbered from between the legs like some great uncooked pork roast roll. The smell of iron was powerful, like rusty metal warm and wet; steam rose off this bloody mass as rain dries from a summer storm.

The book said to examine it, this shiny deep magenta sack; to count the vessels in the cord, make sure that it came out intact. But all this blood kept gushing forth from out between the mother's legs. She told the nurse to push pitocin, something obviously wrong. And this was what she'd tried to stop: something torn up deep inside. She shouted at Padma to get a torch, shouted because the ring clamps weren't on the table like she'd asked for them a dozen times. She pushed gauze into the woman's vault.

"Get me those clamps!"

They unrolled on the table: only three. She pushed them up inside, one after another after another. Padma brought a torch, but the batteries were dead, and so blindly Mary grabbed what tissue she could with the ends of the long clamps. She felt her own heart pounding, the pressure rising from her chest, through her neck, until she heard each beat drumming inside her ears. Finally something she did caused the bleeding to slow, the gushing to stop. Half a liter, she guessed, looking at the red-soaked drapes. She took a deep breath, ocean-sized. She apologized to Nishi and Padma: she hadn't meant to yell so loud. Another torch was found, and so she mopped the blood inside the vault—the bleeding stopped, the crisis gone, but now the work had multiplied. She gently loosened all the clamps, to see which one had stemmed the flow; she found what she expected there: the cervix torn at three o'clock. She thought again she has no choice: *I can't run home to Baltimore; if I'd escaped the day before, this mother would be dead by now.*

She knows if she goes right to sleep she'll dream of streams of gushing red, of soaking warm in spa-like pools of steaming silky human heme. The dreams aren't all unpleasant ones, but still she finds them frightening: steeping warm in body fluids, ninety-eight-point-six degrees. So Mary didn't go to sleep—it was nearly morning anyway—but sat there in the duty room, the only place with any heat. She tried to chat in broken Hindi, barely could pronounce the words; Padma was the only one who smiling tried to humor her. But she doesn't know what else to do to make them comfortable with her; she knows she doesn't measure up to Vikram's saintly memory. So she and Padma sat in silence, Padma knitting woolen socks; Tamding only whistled as he kept the tandoor blazing hot.

It's nearly six as she walks home, the black dog following along; the Himalayas all around her look about to burst in flame. These peaks are just the foothills yet the snow is sweet vanilla white; the scattered clouds are glowing pink like cherries on an ice cream scoop. She hears the whoosh of feathered wings flapping through the morning air; Mary watches as a raven flies straight at her overhead.

It drops down from the walnut tree, gliding low across the yard; it's swooping downward toward her so she feels a tingling thrill of fear. The taste of iron is in her mouth, the raven's soaring straight for her; she feels a quick adrenal rush, there's something hanging from its claws. But then it breaks its swooping flight to hover in the air above; a noisy clapping flap of wings, she feels the chilling turbulence. It drops what's in its claws and so her arm goes up in self-defense; something solid hits her shoulder, falling heavy to the ground. She opens up her eyes to find the raven's nowhere to be seen; but at her feet there lies a corpse, its little legs still quivering. She wonders in her sleepless state, what does the raven want from her: to raise this rat up from the dead, try once more for a miracle.

# The Chest

For Amod Sunday's nothing more than just another working day, except the Western tourists come for breakfast in the afternoon. So the morning shift is always slow, starts picking up just after ten; Amod opens up at nine, then asks if Ram will watch the place. He asks the cook for dum alu, an order of the saffron rice, a couple of the garlic nan, a little bit of eggplant stew. It's only quarter after, so he has an hour all his own, and he likes to wander through the town to try to catch what's going on. He puts the food in stainless tins that stack for easy carrying; he's thinking he'll go find a sunny spot to eat his morning meal. He goes out through the back door, down an alley barely shoulder width; it comes out on the main street, just across from where the taxis sit. The town is just a couple blocks, the taxis are for tourist trade: the families from the plains without the wind or legs to carry them. The town's three thousand meters high, the mountain air is rarified—the valley walls are steep and close so all the streets go up and down. It might take twenty minutes to traverse the town from north to south, another ten to walk across the forest to the riverside. Today he's feeling fresh and thinks he'll circumnavigate the town—takes a right out on the street, past sweater shops and restaurants.

He strolls south down the main street till the concrete walk abruptly ends, then west along an alley so there's gravel crunching underfoot. There are several other dhabas, though there's only one as nice as his—the others all have roll-up doors and tables lined with folding chairs. He's never been inside of them, he doesn't know the waiters' names; by habit he works every day; goes walking when the dhaba's closed. He strolls past several little stores, selling music tapes and videos, and yet another shop that's pushing woolens on the tourist trade. But a half a block off main street and the shops start looking dull and dark—selling dreary items only local people want to buy. He stops to watch as someone welds tin sheets to make a tandoor stove; sparks of vibrant orange and red rain down against the wooden floor. The next shop's filled with burlap bags: red and yellow lentil beans, rice and bricks of palm sugar all brown and crawling thick with bees. The alley starts to wind and turn, goes past the Post & Telegraph. He ducks beneath a power line that fell down several weeks ago. This neighborhood is where he lives, a room up on the second floor: a place he's lived all by himself for going now on thirty years. He nods then to his landlady who's sweeping dust off of the stoop; he only sees her now and then, whenever he must pay the rent. The next block is the Buddhist temple, painted brilliant gold and blue; across from this a tiny mosque, the front steps lined with dusty shoes.

He's almost on the edge of town and turns to climb the valley wall: across a crumbling concrete bridge that spans a little mountain stream. The other side is lined with trees, the apple orchards crowd the town: the fruit is ready to be picked; October's nearly halfway through. He takes a path between the fruit trees planted out in terraced rows: the orchard maybe ten years old, the apples looking beautiful. Amod climbs the terraced steps until he's up above the town; he looks down on the scattered buildings: mostly newly built hotels. They're all made out of handmade brick and pillars sprouting rods of steel: they all stop at two stories but they look like they're not finished yet. Their rooftops have small wooden shacks where watchmen go to sleep at night; they all have plastic water tanks and lines to hang the laundry up. All around are massive peaks, their tops are dusted freshly white, and they still seem just as big as when he came so many years ago. He wonders what it's like up there, above the trees and people noise—he's never gone much higher than the spot where he is standing now.

He thinks that he might sit down here and eat his Sunday morning meal—open up his tiffin tins while everything's still nice and warm. It only takes a minute for his racing heart to slow back down; he finds a spot between the trees that looks out at the mountaintops. He's barely gotten comfortable before he sees the slinking dog; he hasn't opened up his tins when several children scramble by. He's learned from bad experience that dogs and kids and he don't mix—the dog will try to steal his food, the children think that he's a freak. They taunt him for his lazy eye, the fact he has no family here; he's found it best to just keep moving when these elements collide. That's why he often walks at night, or when the children are in school; he picks his tins up off the wall to eat back in the restaurant. He starts back down some muddy steps—being careful where he puts his feet—and decides to take the shortcut through the courtyard of the hospital. He's back behind some houses on a pathway made by sheep and goats, comes out on an alley where the drivers wash their gravel trucks. He stops to listen to some play: an argument about a ball; it sounds like two or three young boys are fighting over who's at fault. He can't remember when he ever had such opportunity: to fight with someone over something absolutely trivial. He remembers how his cousins used to beat him for his drifting eye; his uncle would tell neighbors their new bad luck was all Amod's fault. He's been a waiter all his life: a busboy by the age of eight. He didn't go to school because it interfered with work too much.

He walks down to the valley floor where the alley meets a wider street; he figures he should head back since he still needs time to sit and eat. He stops just once to look inside a window that is open wide: briefest glance of some young girl bent mopping off the kitchen floor. He doesn't like to stare too long, in case somebody notices—he's learned to satisfy himself with just a hint of what's inside. He takes the path that leads right through the courtyard of the hospital; stops again because there's someone crying near the treatment room. He's done this for so many years, it's how he educates himself: he watches people living through their windows when he walks about. The hospital is fertile ground; there's often drama going on: he's learned how people cope with grief, how Doctor Vikram operates. It's mostly late at night after he locks the dhaba's wooden door; he doesn't sleep well so he goes for walks through his adopted town. The hospital's the only place that's active when he takes his walks—he listens for the rumble of the generator turning on. It's a sure sign of an accident, or someone's belly getting worse: the nurses busy fixing large syringes filled with who knows what. Today he sees a local woman crying on a wooden bench; a man, could be her husband, pacing back and forth in front of it. Amod's in the courtyard, hidden by the shadow of the tree; he watches Doctor Mary pressing frantically on someone's chest. The treatment room has windows all around to let in lots of light; the table in the middle so there's room to do the dirty work.

The doctor's hands are pressing on the bare chest of a little boy, and every couple moments she bends down as if to kiss the mouth. She pounds again and tells the nurse she isn't working fast enough; he's yards away but Amod hears the anger in the doctor's voice. He's seen this more than once before, when Doctor Vikram was around—but Vikram would just thump the chest and breathe for them a couple times. He'd place his fingers on the neck, then shrug and send the body home; he wouldn't waste the time it took, treating those already gone. The nurses all agree with Vikram: so much other work to do; Amod watches as they leave to let poor Mary work alone. Doctor Mary doesn't stop her violent pounding on the chest; the mother on the bench is wailing, father's arms around her head. The only one who stays to help is Manu from the laundry room, who hasn't spoken since her husband died and left her destitute. When Doctor Mary finally stops, then Manu helps her clean things up: she's ready with a fresh clean cloth to wipe the blood and vomitus. The mother's crying on her knees, the father standing at the door; the doctor gives the boy to him then tries to speak in Kullui. Amod knows what she is trying to say, he hears the sadness break her voice—but even standing yards away he knows her words aren't making sense. Manu helps the mother up, then gently shows them out the door; Amod sees the doctor standing, watching as they walk away. Because it's Sunday morning, all the staff have gathered in the church, and he listens as the sound of singing voices comes across the yard. He watches Mary wipe her hands and pull a sleeve across her mouth; he watches as she tries to brush the wisps of hair back from her face. For the first time he can see how Doctor Mary's totally alone—how no one offers comfort to her when she must be feeling bad. He wishes he could talk to her, could whisper reassuring words, could fold his arms around her so that he could give some strength to her. But of course that's all impossible, he hasn't any strength to give; but in his hand he finds another way to offer nourishment. He pulls back from the shadow so that he can quickly disappear; he knows her door there on the end: he'll leave his set of tiffin tins.

# The Knife

Mary's staring at a man, his penis limp and circumcised, his abdomen so trim and flat: a lovely set of sculpted pecs. She's standing looking over him, deciding where to drag her knife—suddenly she's struck by just how beautiful his body is. She hasn't seen one this nice since her med school days in Baltimore: an adult body, trim and sound, that needs a look around inside. Back home her patients all were old, with sagging obese abdomens; she'd send them off to specialists for triple bypass surgery. But this man is a beauty, with his rippled belly paralyzed; the local men she's worked on have been strong but thin and sinewy. She hates to have to do this to him, ruin his Adonis shape: slice him down the middle to repair his perforated bowel. His quads are big as watermelons, forearms like a carpenter's; his scrotum's tight and meaty as a walnut from the tree outside. And what if she should kill this one? Her record isn't very good. They come in three days after their appendix has already burst. She tries hard not to blame herself for patients who do not survive;

*it's not my fault!* their families drag them in three breaths before they die. The last man that she opened up, his cancer was metastasized—she never would have cut if she had access to a CT scan. Still she took out what she could—her hands shook as she cut and tied—and she thought that he might live a month but he died the night of surgery. She knows she hasn't got the touch of Doctor Vikram Vargeela; the nurses don't know how to hide the fact they have no trust in her. It's more than just a passing thought that maybe she's done something wrong: a knot tied as a granny when it should have been a double square. But what is she supposed to do? There are no other doctors near. It's either do the best she can or leave and close the hospital.

This man presented classically, with fevers for a couple weeks: tired, coughing, frequent stools, then yesterday he got much worse. His neighbors carried him as he passed in and out of consciousness; he barely opened up his eyes when Mary asked him where it hurt. She was thinking typhoid fever, though he was much too weak to talk to her; his X-ray showed clear evidence of free air in his abdomen. She'd have to slice him open to repair his perforated bowel; she'd have to tank his fluids up to get him past his low-grade shock. She isn't trained in surgery, but knew what she'd be looking for: a small bowel perforation caused by typhoid burning through his gut.

She started inauspiciously: some trouble with the breathing tube. She tried hard not to get upset like all the times she tried before. The patient got his sedative, and Sushila got in both IVs; Tamding pushed the paralytic just when Mary asked him to. She taught herself to do this, since they don't use ether in the States— she learned it from a book she found in Vikram's tiny library. The patient's tongue will quiver as the paralytic takes effect; she placed the tongue blade past the lips, the teeth were pearly white and straight. She pushed the tongue off to one side and peered straight down the trachea; the light had worked quite well for once; she gently tried to pass the tube between his flaccid vocal cords. But suddenly they spasmed tight, the cords closed like a shuttered shop; Mary'd never seen this but the book frequently warned of it. She couldn't get the breathing tube in past the cords till they relaxed, and since the man was paralyzed, he couldn't breathe in for himself. The only thing to do was wait—how long since he had had a breath? Thirty seconds, maybe more, without exchanging oxygen. This is why she's so afraid: she knows she's going to kill someone; can tell when someone needs the knife, but not sure if she holds it right. She hasn't yet convinced herself that patients die all by themselves; instead she blames her bad technique, her diagnosis isn't right. She glanced across his hairless chest, the graceful curving of his pecs, his belly smooth and dune-like to his cresting pubic prominence. She counted ten, then looked once more—the cords appeared all limp and pale. She slid the tube in quietly: *a minute, maybe less,* she thought. Quickly she hooked up the tubes and pumped the bellows several times; she watched his chest both rise and fall, the air and ether flowing in. The sweet smell of the ether was so thick it made her headache worse; the cloud of anesthetic gave a touch of sudden nausea. She asked the aide to breathe for him, to pump the bellows up and down; the ether set to ten percent, she left the room to scrub and gown.

Now Mary's looking at this man, his pupils slightly dilated; he's nicely in an ether sleep, she's just begun to prep the skin. All gloved and gowned, she shakes her shoulders, mask taped firmly to her nose; the theater is cold but she's not worrying about herself. She dips a gauze ball in a cup and starts to paint this masterpiece: his broad chest smooth and tapering, his little nipples dark and flat. Starting at his navel she scrubs out the bits of lint and dust; she's working with a cotton ball that's dipped in disinfectant paint. She's never felt like this before, so nonplussed by this body here—he's obviously Indian, his skin a velvet chocolate tan. But he looks like an American brought up on beef and butterfat; no local man could grow like this on mushy yellow dal and rice. The village men are handsome but they barely average five feet five; she's guessing this one's six feet tall; he's got some meat upon his bones. She tries to block these thoughts she has, they're rushing toward forbidden lines: think about this surgery, how likely she will kill this man. She paints his belly three times round, her artist's brush a long ring clamp: the same thing used the other night to save that bleeding mother's life. She looks down at her handiwork, three overlapping galaxies—a trickle of the disinfectant running off and down his side. It tickles her in sympathy, the cold drop inching down his flank, the tiny bulge of belly fat, the handle for a lover's grasp. When last has she seen one of these? It wasn't on a local man: some whiney tourist, overweight, complaining of a tummy ache.

"Sushila, get him covered up. We'll give him hypothermia."

The scalpel's nice and sharp today, it's feeling solid in her hand: nimble and well balanced as she opens up his abdomen. The incision goes from north to south, a red line down a highway map; she hates having to do this to this topographic masterpiece. Her own stomach is tied in knots, her fingers finely trembling; *please don't let me kill him,* she's not sure, though, who she's praying to. She circumnavigates his navel, like a ship around a jutting point; she makes the cut much longer than she knows a real surgeon would. But no one's here to teach her how—she's got to do it all herself: she's nearly memorized the book that shows her how to do this stuff. Now that it's been six months she has almost got the hang of it: the ether still can make her sick, but the scalpel doesn't shake so much. It's going fairly well now that the breathing tube is safely down; the ether took quite quickly and his blood pressure has stabilized. She's cut down through the fascia layer, separated muscle lines; the clamps catch crimson bleeders on the first or maybe second try. She's getting used to all the blood, how things get so damn slippery; she's finally got a mental map of all the major arteries. Sushila's in good form, anticipating all her moves; she's ready with the instruments she thinks that Mary's going to use.

The staff is still not used to her, though better than they were at first: each time she wrote an order down, the nurses would all bob their heads, a gesture she is still unsure means *yes* or *if I get to it*. But last night they called only once for things they could have done themselves; still she didn't get much rest: she doesn't sleep well by herself. She's finally in the abdomen and finds the hole right there on top—the gut with red strawberry spots: *I got the diagnosis right!*

She's still afraid of handling gut, of clamping it and sewing up: a thing that's always done back home by overpaid sub-specialists. But the book has got a diagram that shows a nice inverted stitch; it's no more difficult than something taught in high school quilting class. There are two small holes a foot apart, and she's careful with the bright red gut. The book warns that the typhoid makes it tender as a rose petal. Once she's got the holes repaired, she takes a bowl of warm saline, rinses out his belly, even thinks to change her dirty gloves. She reaches in to satisfy the thought there might be something else: to feel for his appendix, for his spongy spleen and pancreas. Hoping that it's all okay, she starts to close his abdomen.

"How's his pressure?" Mary asks.

"Ninety," is the aide's reply.

She closes him in layers, pulls the fascia cover nice and

tight—the skin is always hardest since the needle's never very sharp. The thread's not always strong enough, just cotton bought in the bazaar: weakened when they sterilize it in the ancient autoclave. The aide has turned the ether off, the patient's started waking up: he's fighting with the breathing tube, the aide's attempt to suction it. Mary's pleased with how this went, the patient closed and stabilized—everything went as it should, she didn't have to yell this time. She steps back from the table as she snaps her bloody rubber gloves, pulls her sweaty gown off as she drops them with the instruments. She reaches for the chart to write the postop orders for the nurse, her hands still damp with nervous sweat, the stress of doing what she must. This only needs a simple note since nothing much went wrong this time, but the pen she has won't write because the cheap ink's thickened by the cold. She sneaks the pen behind her mask to warm the tip up with her tongue, and as she gets the pen to write she realizes something's wrong.

She listens as her patient starts to cough and gag against the tube; the aide has passed a catheter to get the phlegm out of his throat. The gas is quickly wearing off, the patient barely half asleep; to put him out again she'd have to reinsert the breathing tube.

"Sushila, I forgot the drain. I forgot the goddamn fucking drain!"

Sushila turns and looks at her above her poorly fitting mask, and Mary's thinking this time she has killed someone she shouldn't have. The book states plain as day she has to drain the dirty abdomen; standard practice anytime a hole is found in someone's bowel.

"It's too late now," she tells the nurse, "we'll have to watch his temperature."

All she wants now is a bath, to wash the stench out of her

clothes; better she should burn them, maybe, on this patient's funeral pyre. She doesn't realize how deep she's breathing through
her flaring nose; only that she's certain she can't take goddamn
much more of this. She goes back to the order sheet, to try to fix
this last mistake: check his vitals every hour, increase the chloramphenicol.

# The Club

Phillip's staring at some shit, his face pressed flat against the ground: a not-unknown experience of sleeping where he fell down last. He's not sure what has happened and it isn't clear yet where he is; but he knows the shit he's staring at is a pile of human excrement. It isn't goat or donkey dung; it isn't yak or yeti crap; no local dog eats well enough to make a pile as big as that. He knows all this because his sense of smell's the only one that works, his other senses fogged by pain that's ripping through his twisted neck. This smell he knows as India now dominates his nasal sense: the dust embedded in his nose is not his good old British dirt.

*Damn, I hope I had some fun. This bloody neck is killing me.*

As he lies there trying to think, his vision's slowly coming back; he's able now to focus on the other things in front of him. Up close he sees his matted curls, the long blond dreadlocks of his hair, beyond that not too far away, a hand is lying on the ground. This startles him more than the shit: he's not sure if the hand is his—there isn't any feeling there, just dirt ground black beneath the nails and rubbed into the fingerprints. Several woven friendship bracelets are tied around the dirty wrist; he recognizes these because he had to buy them for himself. The fingers, long and delicate, are naked as old dried-up bones—the ring his father gave him isn't wrapped around the middle one. He's worn the ring for three years straight, a present when he turned sixteen, a golden band with precious stones, a thing passed down for centuries.

The ground transmits a bitter cold, he'd shiver but he's frozen stiff; his wrist and arm are bare, he sees his leather jacket's been removed. It's slowly dawning on him why he's lying in the freezing dirt.

*Damn it! Damn it! Damn it! Why's this always happening to me?*

Locals often asked him if he'd sell his jacket for a price, and they'd name something ridiculous: their wages for a couple months, but just a fraction of its cost. One offer was a night alone with some man's younger sister—he was tempted till he noticed she was missing all her teeth in front. Now he's lost the jacket anyway, and spent the night there fucking dirt: the cold is so intense he's sure his useless prick has broken off. He tries to move the naked arm that's lying lifeless on the ground; the thieves just hacked it from his body when they yanked his leather jacket off. Once more he tries to move the arm, his hand, to wiggle anything—but everything is frozen hard with deeply penetrating cold. His lids close down before his eyes, then slowly open up again; they're the only things that move: no legs or toes or shoulder blades.

A panic grabs him round the chest, convinced he must be paralyzed. He tries to take a deep breath in, the muscles of his chest scream out; a half a cup of dust and dirt clog deeply up his nose and mouth. He coughs, which fills the air with dust; each gasp and gag hurts more and more; this cloud of breath, dried shit, and germs is causing him to suffocate. He rocks his shoulders back and forth to raise his face up off the ground—desperately he's reaching for a breath that has some air in it. Finally his arm moves, though it flops like it is unattached, swinging from his shoulder, feeling numb but for a pressure sense. Its weight pulls him onto his back, the severed arm lands next to him, as heavy and as lifeless as a drunken sumo wrestler. The air is fresher facing up, but then the tingling begins: the million pins and needles someone's poking in his flaccid arm.

Inside he knows he's paralyzed, and someone's going to pay for this: *How dare they take the ring and coat of Phillip Glaston Davenport!* He coughs and gasps at air so cold it burns the lining of his lungs—the fear deep in his heart is that nobody's going to give a damn. Looking straight up at the sky, he sees the great deodar trees, the ravens in the branches, glossy black and cawing happily. *Shut UP! I'm trying to think!* but he still can't remember where he is: somewhere in a forest near a river he can barely hear. Turning put him in the sun, it starts to warm his aching neck, but the tingling now is more intense, like he's rolled onto a hill of ants.

He remembers being sick all week with intermittent belly pain, a gassy diarrhea so he stayed close to his hotel room. He walked once to the hospital, that *bitch* there with the stethoscope; he'd heard he'd find a doctor with an accent he could figure out. The place was swarmed with local people, old men with sick withered limbs, little girls with smaller children screaming hanging from their hips. They gave him number eighty-three, said he should sit and wait his turn; he sat there for the longest time—at least a half an hour or so. But he couldn't stand the thought of being coughed on by these wretched hordes, of watching pierce-nosed women blowing snot onto their scarves and sleeves. The children were all looking at him, scabby-skinned and unashamed—their blatant stares were even worse than when they'd cough into his face. Then a wailing sound came from the yard and five big men came rushing in: a body carried in their arms, a girl who looked about his age. Her flimsy sari dripping wet, her long hair trailing to the ground, she looked just like a load of laundry beaten on the river rocks. Another cramp had seized his gut as Phillip watched them pushing past: a sharp but fleeting queasy pain, a little bit of nausea. The door to the exam room opened up then to the urgent cries, and so he stood, joined their parade, and shuffled in behind to where the doctor was supposed to be.

A woman with a stethoscope looked up when they burst in the room, the men holding the dripping girl all stopped, not knowing what to do. The woman was a Westerner, with tangled hair down past her ears—she wasn't big or tall but had the presence of a rugby player. At first he thought she was the nurse, the doctor busy somewhere else, but quickly it was obvious she was the one in charge of things. She paused for just a moment to take in all that was going on, then quickly cleared her table off, barking out in Hindi for the men to put the poor thing down, flat against the thin stained sheet that covers her exam table. The men stepped back as she approached, her stethoscope held like a whip, her hand went to her patient's neck, feeling for what life was left. She grabbed the girl by the hair and pulled so that her head came back; she pinched the nose and bent to put her mouth over the girl's own. Phillip watched the wet girl's chest both rise and fall a couple times. The doctor pulled the sari loose, ripping fabric off her chest—Phillip stared at naked breasts, the dusky nipples both erect. The doctor breathed for her again, then switched to once more pound her chest. He heard her counting through her teeth, then watched her feel her neck again.

"Rambha, her pulse is back. Get some blankets."

The doctor's hand still on her neck, the dead girl seemed to buck and stir, and the doctor breathed for her again, then quickly rolled her on her side. The victim coughed, then gasped, then retched huge quantities of river out, splashing down against the floor, the water mixed with rice and dal. Phillip faced the doctor as he stood there leaning near the door, and as she thumped the girl the doctor stared at him expressionless. He was dressed as he was every day while traveling the Asian trail: his ragged jeans precisely torn, his dreadlocks hung across his face, three golden hoops in his right ear, his leather jacket, black and chrome. He wasn't wearing any shoes, he hadn't thought he'd need them here; his feet were black with dung and dust and freshly specked with vomitus.

"Excuse me. You're the doctor, right? I've got these bloody awful cramps."

He watched her turn away from him, still thumping on the girl's back.

"Rambha, get this asshole out of here, and help me get these wet clothes off. Send Tamding for some chai. I need something to rinse my mouth."

The drugs that Phillip finally got were from a little alley shop: "Doctor Sukdev" painted on a tiny metal swinging sign. The doctor kindly listened to him, signed a wad of small white notes; he told him he should buy these at the little pharmacy next door. He warned him about alcohol, he shouldn't drink while on this stuff—especially the yellow pills, the side effects were memorable.

There's something else he now recalls, a party to the north of town: a drunken mess of Westerners and Indians with cash to burn. He smoked some hash before he went, from a dealer at some restaurant: an old guy with big army boots who suffered bad from ugliness. This same man had invited him, told Phillip he could meet him there, and if he liked this taste of hash he knew where he could get some more. He didn't mean to drink with plenty other things to get him stoned; he'd found the ugly guy in boots and bought a half an ounce of dope. The party wasn't fun at all, he recognized some of the freaks; but still they wouldn't talk to him: just like back at the Goan beach. Even so, by ten o'clock, he was so stoned he could hardly think—the hash was raw against his throat, his stomach had been grumbling. He was sitting in the lobby on a bench with torn upholstery; he was playing with the stuffing when the dealer sat down next to him. There was music coming from the bar, up loud but somehow played too slow. The dealer's name was Antone, seemed Italian by the sound of it. He was older, maybe forty, although Phillip couldn't really tell—his face so pocked and scarred from zits, his arms with scabby needle marks. The smoke spilled thick out of the bar, a fag hung down from Antone's lip, and he sat down next to Phillip on the damaged vinyl, not too close. He breathed in through the cigarette, then exhaled while it dangled down; he offered up his drink to Phillip, showing that he'd be his friend. Phillip took it without thinking, his throat so raw he couldn't talk: the undiluted whiskey tasted acid-like and poisonous. It burned worse than the hashish, and it landed in his empty gut—he'd only eaten once that day: samosas at a wallah's shop. Through all the haze of dope and hash, he forgot what Doctor Sukdev said about the memorable effects of yellow pills and alcohol.

He turned and looked at Antone.

"You look bad," the dealer said.

Phillip didn't answer. It got quiet and the haze cleared. His memory of Antone's face is crystalline and magnified. The skin was pale and leathery, the large pores black with unwashed oil; there was an acrid odor in the air: an awful burning urine smell. Phillip's gut began to churn as his stomach fought against the drink; he had to quickly get outside, knowing he would soon be sick. Getting off the bench he tripped, the gauze-like dopey haze returned, and all he saw before him was the carpet on the lobby floor, the pattern swirling streaks of red, the yellow of a runny dal. The room jerked roughly to the left, and he put a hand out to one side, but everything had moved so there was nothing for his hand to grab.

Phillip stumbled out the front, past the men who guard the club, beyond the circle on the ground made by the light above the door. He soon was on his hands and knees among the dark deodar trees, head inside a thorny bush while retching dry and violently. The burn inside his gut was like his testicles had caught on fire; that someone followed him outside meant nothing through the nausea. He was aware only of wretchedness, of sickness churning through his bowels, his insides turning inside out, and then the pain, the cracking blow, of something hard against his skull.

Phillip's watching the deodar trees now, gently swaying in the breeze—the very tops dance gently in the sparkling early-morning light. Still certain that he's paralyzed, he's managed to turn on his back; the clouds of dust have settled but he still can't move below the waist. His arms, especially the right, seem severed at the shoulder blade, except the pins and needles feeling makes him know they're still attached. If only he could move his toes, he'd know that he will be all right; their numbness is more frightening than the pain that's coursing down his arms. His ankle might have moved an inch, his right foot wiggling in the grass; maybe he's not paralyzed, perhaps he isn't going to die. Suddenly a noise comes crashing from beyond his field of view; he tries to turn, to see who's rushing through the brush to rescue him. But turning causes sudden pain, a high-voltage electric shock, like biting into tinfoil while somebody kicks him in the nuts. The noise keeps coming closer, then a shadow falls across his face—the scuff of heavy feet comes with a random, hollow, bell-like sound. But he only sees deodar trees, these timbers of the Hindu gods, the shuffling ravens, branch to branch; the sky is cloudless overhead.

The feeling comes back all at once from numb to tortured tingling: his legs burn like he's stepped into a raging tandoor to his knees. He screams out loud and screws his eyes up tight against the bright blue sky—he doesn't see the thing now standing heavy looming over him. His eyes both shut with fear, he feels a rancid breath against his face: a dank and musty sickening smell like spit-up from a two-year-old. Something strikes him in the side and bluntly bounces off his ribs; he opens up his eyes again, perhaps they're thinking that he's dead. Hanging there above his head is a cow the size of India: a sacred, bony, scrawny creature, hideous and horrible. Its cud is drooling, dangling toward him from the corner of its lip; it swings just inches from his face, its arc is hypnotizing him. Phillip stops another scream for fear of opening his mouth; his eyes are wide as rupee coins held warm inside a beggar's hand. Then something strikes the cow itself, bouncing off its hollow flank; he reaches out to find it and his hand goes round a throwing rock. *Aiyyee!* he hears from somewhere off, and another rock clobbers the beast. The cow then turns its ugly head, its cud swings lower from its lip, inching even closer to the wincing grimace on his face. The shouts keep getting louder, with the solid sound of running feet, of bare heels slapping rubber thongs, and another rock strikes hard against the bovine's bony breathing box. The cow moves on, off to the right, the bell tied tinkling round its neck. Phillip finally takes a breath, then lets a groan spill from his lips.

The leg pain is much less severe, his arms are nearly normal now, but as he turns to look and see who's saved him from this horrid beast, the pain rips down his neck like he's been skewered with a cattle prod. He has to lie down flat as all the muscles spasm round his throat, and from the left he sees somebody slowly walking up to him. It's just a kid, a village girl, her clothes exactly like the rest: her pattu woven red and blue, a dot stuck square be- tween her brows. Her left hand holds a wooden switch, her right another throwing rock, and she pitches it off at the cow, an ex- pert toss that hits the mark. She stands beside him, looking down, and he thinks he's seen her face before—she speaks to him in Kullui, his sense is that she's unconcerned. Her face is mildly pretty but she certainly could use a bath. Suddenly she smiles at him, her laughter echoes through the trees, revealing in her mer- riment the gap where her front teeth should be. She nudges him a little rough, his bare arm with her rubber thong.

"*Ko-ee taa-zee kha-bar?*" she says, her laughter starting up again.

# The Worm

An old man sits in front of Mary, a village elder, poorly dressed—a quiet smirk across his face, so proud of his accomplishment. Apparently he cannot talk, or doesn't want to, anyway—he doesn't say a word but sits and patiently awaits his turn. He holds a can in his left hand, a lid pressed on its rusty rim; when Mary asks him what is wrong, he pries the lid with blackened nails, then thrusts the can out toward her so that Mary has to look inside. A stench wafts up out of the can and fills the whole room instantly, and Mary learned her lesson once, to never reach out for the can, to only take a quick glance to identify the parasite.

"Close it up, for heaven's sake!"

She knows he doesn't understand, so she gestures at him violently; she reaches for his record card and scribbles his prescription down. While Rambha translates what to do, the patient wangs before his face—he smiles his thanks to Mary as the smell begins to dissipate. He's not up for a second when the bench is quickly filled again, and Mary looks across to find a woman with a septal ring. She's pierced the middle of her nose like many of the villagers: cow-like, Mary thinks, although she's starting to get used to it.

She sits as Rambha translates why this woman walked for three full days: an abscess in her breast that has it swollen twice its normal size. She admires all her patients here, their stoic strength in suffering; their hardships seem unbearable, their villages so far away: all lacking running water much less any modern medicine. No wonder they come in so sick, their problems festering for months—they're hoping if their god is kind their illnesses will disappear. It's not the worst abscess she's seen, and yet it must hurt awfully much; they go behind a curtain where she cleans the skin and lances it.

Mary hears someone come in, her ears pick out a British clip: so many other languages she couldn't hope to comprehend.

"Where's the doctor? No, I can't wait. It's a fucking emergency!"

She doesn't recognize the voice, but knows exactly what she'll find: some Western tourist stubbed his toe while barefoot in the market stalls. Instantly she's so annoyed she has to stop and count to five; her fingers still are deep inside this woman's tender festered breast. She pushes still more gauze inside as Rambha tries to close the door: push the asshole back where he can sit and wait his bloody turn. With both hands unpresentable, her elbows push the drapes aside; she's holding up a bloodstained clamp to face this stubborn intruder. Her face is flushed with anger and a deep set case of weariness—she's hardly halfway through the day, still has a foot to amputate.

"Who the *hell* are you!?" she shouts, her anger finding what she thought: dusty dreadlocks, woolen vest, skin folds black with dirt and grime, shirt exposing naked chest, his feet without their

shoes and socks. She's mad enough to curse him, and yet something makes her check herself: he's standing there without a
slouch, his neck and shoulders straight and stiff, his face so full of
pain and fear, and tears spilling from red-rimmed eyes. His skin
is pale beneath the dirt, not just the normal pale of Brits, but the
shocky shade of chalky white she sees when things are serious.
He is quiet as she stares at him, as she tries to shake her anger off.

"Where do you hurt?" Mary asks, her voice so sudden quiet
calm that Rambha turns to her and looks confused.

"It's my bleedin' neck," he says. He sounds like his voice will
break. "They clubbed me. They took my jacket. . . ."

He's just a boy, Mary thinks.

"It hurts like hell to turn my head."

"Then don't," she says, then turns away, her anger not yet
fully gone; her other patient still behind the curtain with her
clothes half off.

She has to take off bloody gloves to write some orders on a
card; she gives instructions to the aide to take him for some neck
X-rays.


The films brought back are terrible, so over-penetrated dark—
her thought at first is now she'll have to treat his radiation burns.
She's always hated neck X-rays, how difficult they are to read;
she hates that she can be so sure that everything is A-OK, but
what's that little scratch mark there? A crack or just the shoulder blade? She's never totally assured she hasn't somehow missed
something; she's looking at the lateral that vaguely shows his
vertebrae. She holds it to the window, the exam room's only
source of light; the films are fresh out of the wash so water's
dripping down her sleeve. It's nearly noon now and the sun is
shining on the toilet stalls, all whitewashed just across the yard:

a decent light-box substitute. She holds the film close to her face and shivers from the dripping wash, but really isn't looking at the too-dark X-ray anymore. There's a light spot that's the shadow of his broken C-5 vertebra: the boy will need a halo brace or soon he might be paralyzed.

"Where is our young Prince Charming?" she asks Rajiv, who's the X-ray tech; he tells her that he's in the courtyard, dragging on a cigarette. But Mary isn't listening, she's trying hard to think this through—her vision resting outside on the bright wall of the toilet stall. She has not seen one of these before, his C-5 broken into thirds; she doesn't understand why it hasn't slipped and cut his spinal cord. This X-ray isn't difficult, and she doesn't need the ortho books; she knows this one's beyond her scope, somehow she'll have to get some help. All he'd have to do is sneeze, or stumble on some little rock. He needs his neck immobilized by someone with experience.


"Doctor? Ma'am? Please . . . excuse me. . . ."

The clinic's closed now for the day, and she's at the Post & Telegraph, waiting for an open line, her call to ring in Delhi at the local British embassy. She's tired, staring at the floor, at the darkly worn-out softwood boards. At first she doesn't see a thing, just the darkness of the dusty cracks, the shadows reaching from the door, her eyes not focused anywhere. She's thinking about nothing, feeling just an ancient weariness—a nagging touch of headache settled at the soft bridge of her nose. Her backache eases slightly as she rests against the wooden bench, sighing deeply through exhaustion, her mind as dark and empty as the wooden floor she's staring at. The office door is open, letting light inside the noisy room, and a breeze is pushing bits of dust and paper scraps across the floor. Mary slowly notices what else is in her field of view: first the cracks between the boards, then the dirt collected there, the ants all running back and forth, the seam an arid canyon that these little creatures hurry through. The floor is rough and poorly cut, the carpentry all done by hand; the saw marks are unsanded and the nail holes have been left unfilled. The office is so full of noise, the counter thick with customers: each one wanting to be next, a drum-like pounding from the back—the stamps hand-canceled by a man with no expression on his face. The noise does not quite register: the urgent voices, thumping stamp, the flexing metal muscle of the Teletype machine. The footsteps, though, she plainly hears, the odd sound creeping into her: the heavy bump of solid shoes, of someone's slight ataxic gait. A chill comes on a breeze that blows a paper scrap across the floor, something scrawled in Hindi script and dropped when it had no more use. She feels the bench she's hunched on sway as someone sits down next to her—two boots cap off some torn-up jeans that cloak a man's extended legs.

Mary doesn't move her head, but examines what's in front of her; the soles are caked with mud and dung, the eyelets gleaming silver studs. There is something funny Mary cannot put her finger on at first. The man's as ripe as any, with a rich scent of long-unwashed clothes, of cigarettes and bad BO; she smells the now-familiar tang of hashish that the man has smoked. She thinks of Mister Joey who once gardened in her parents' yard, whose smell was old and stronger than the accent he addressed her by. She never could catch all his words, but listened to them anyway—he smelled of earth and garlic clove, like no one else she'd known before. Joey's clothes were worn and layered, she still can see his thick mustache; every fall her mother said he cut the roses back too far. But he would dig out candies from a pocket buried in his clothes, pulled like weeds from garden soil: a roll of linty LifeSavers.

He is dead though, she remembers, far away and twenty years ago; while staring at these stretched out boots, she figures out what's wrong with them. She's looking through exhaustion, through a dullness caused by lack of sleep; it dawns on her that this man is a simple incongruity. Even with their mud-caked soles, these boots are still a shiny black, all buffed and polished crisp and smooth with spit and wax and elbow grease. The boots should be on a Marine, yet this fragrant man is hippie-like: a fossil from the sixties, thinks that bathing is unnatural. It brings her back to here and now, back to the Post & Telegraph; suddenly the room is full of other people making noise: clearing throats, the Teletype, the pounding of the cancel mark. Trying not to move her head she scans this strange anomaly—he's properly in uniform, but not the military kind. She sees these clothes on all of them, the leather, jeans, and undyed wool; the locals call them "hippies," though they're really just young travelers. But this one isn't young at all, the man beside her on the bench: his arms bare to the shoulders with the deltoids blued with old tattoos; his bearded face is deeply pocked, his forearms scarred with needle marks. He's twice as old as Davenport, young Phillip with the broken neck: the whining Brit with belly cramps, a pocketful of business cards. She's got them in her pocket now, one from the British embassy, another from a colonel here: a military attaché. *"An old friend of the family."* He said to phone the embassy: *"Just tell them who you're calling for and they'll take care of everything."*

"Doctor? Ma'am? Please . . . excuse me. . . ."

The man beside her tugs her sleeve, then gestures out across the room: off toward the clerk behind the counter waving a red telephone. She has to break out of her daze to look up at this waving man: she treated him, two months ago, for problems caused by alcohol.

"Doctor, hurry please! I have the embassy!"

The office is now empty, with the post office already closed: the thumping postmark's silent and the Teletype is paralyzed. Mary's footsteps fill the room, she reaches for the telephone: alone but for the addict and the man who'll charge her for the call.

". . . yes . . . he said his name was Davenport . . . Phillip . . . yes . . . said his father's name was . . . that he works for your embassy in . . . really . . . the ambassador . . . well, I guess that should be helpful . . ."

She's looking back across the room, embarrassed by the echoing. She has to shout into the phone, the line abuzz with crackling noise. The fossil-man is staring, so their eyes meet when she looks at him; she raises her eyebrows, rolls her eyes, miming a sarcastic look of how impressed she really is.

". . . no, he can't . . . he's got a broken neck . . . very primitive up here . . . no, he's strapped to a board, with bags of rice to keep him still . . . can you arrange some sort of transport? . . . I see . . . great . . . all the way to London? . . . They can do that? . . . Yes, of course . . . then tomorrow, we'll expect them by midafternoon. . . ."

Mary gives the phone back to the man behind the counter, and she watches as he clicks his stopwatch exactly when he puts it down.

"Seven hundred forty-eight," he says, and so she pulls her change purse out, unrolls a wad of greasy bills, then turns to find the fossil sitting staring like he's in a trance.

# The Plan

It is early in the evening when Antone leaves the Post & Telegraph: quarter after six o'clock, the streets already getting dark. Not really streets, they're alleyways that barely fit a single car, the unplanned paths that separate the cheap hotels and eating stalls. The P&T is deep inside a maze of these ungainly paths, the canyons of bad brickwork walls that smell of open sewer gas. The office fronts an empty lot that opens up the evening sky, and Antone steps beneath the awning, sees the fading purple clouds. In the twilight he can see the outlined tops of all the brick hotels, the rusted rebar sticking out in all directions everywhere. It's evidence of grand ideas, these balconies without their rails, the extra stories never built so everything looks incomplete. In the empty lot in front of him, he's watching several children play, out swinging on some power lines that hang down low across the yard. The lines must have been jerry-rigged while some repairs were being made, and he hears the clanging temple bell, the siren of the setting sun. He's not sure if the lines are dead, but thinks some children might be soon—the thought just briefly in his mind: bad karma, happens constantly.

He turns away from tragedy, attempting to devise a plan while walking through the lefts and rights that lead out to the marketplace. He knows the way, but now it's dark, his big boots pack the gravel path: the alleys made from stones crushed up by poor Nepali refugees. The men carry the heavy stones up steep paths from the riverside, their wives and mothers pound each one to gravel with a metal club. They sit there by the dusty road, pounding hour after hour, barely with enough to eat and never getting anywhere. Antone has been coming here for something over fifteen years, the women always sitting making gravel one piece at a time. But that does not concern him, he is worrying about himself; this town has gotten bigger, not as safe now as it used to be. He hears the crushing gravel sound of footsteps in the alleyway; he stops and listens to make sure they're walking off away from him.

He's thinking about what he's heard, the young boy from the Club House bash: young Phillip with a broken neck, the son of some ambassador. He can see it clear now in his mind, the effect of money on the boy: his teeth too straight, too polished white, the nasal whining in his voice. He should have seen it earlier, the boy too eager to be liked, the ring he wore a sure sign that there's money in the family. Antone turns an alley corner, his steps are slow and measured yet; he has a growing creepy sense—could really use another hit. Years ago he could just walk, but now there's more to think about; he listens when he's all alone, and worries going past someone, unseen but felt, like fear perhaps: the sense of someone's eyes on him. He stops and turns his head to better listen to a noise behind: nothing, nothing there at all but scraps of paper in the wind.

He continues forward, trying to hear beyond the sounds he

makes himself, thinking still about the boy strapped down up at the hospital. They've sent an ambulance to get him, arrives tomorrow afternoon, although he knows in India that things don't always go so smooth. But even if the Brits move quick he should have time to do these tasks: pick his stash up from his room and put some petrol in the jeep. He turns left down another alley, stops as if he's seen a ghost—did he hear a whispered word, the flip of plastic on a heel? He tilts his head to one side with his eyes unfocused, slackened jaw. There, he heard that sound again, just someone walking up some stairs.

Closer to the main road it is easier to see his feet; light spills from a lantern hissing hanging in a hotel room. He is walking faster now that he can see more of the nooks and cracks, the shadows less a threat now that he sees there's no one hiding there. He stops before a produce stall and stands beneath its pressured light, pulls out a pouch hung round his neck to count what little change he's got. Instead of going to the dhaba for a plate of dal and rice, he buys a loaf of sliced white bread and swipes a couple chocolate bars. He's done this to this man before: just stands there waiting patiently, until this one-eyed vendor turns to put his meager change away. Antone doesn't have much cash, no time to make a couple deals—he'll have to fill the jeep halfway and hope it takes him there and back. He's certain he can make the pass, can coast down on the other side, and coming back won't be so bad with one less passenger to haul.

# The Ravens

Mary's watching from her room, the window seat that faces south—the mountains are just shadows now, their shoulders hunched like mourners gathered round a grave, all dressed in black. The ten of them are back again, it seems the same ones every day: the ravens perched up in the trees above the road she looks across. She wonders why these birds are black, why such a sense of wickedness—a seagull isn't evil, but the two birds often act alike. Why aren't the ravens gray or white, some splendid shade of red or blue? Instead they're cloaked as black as night, their feathers laced with glossiness.

She is desperate for a cup of tea, to heat these little tins of food; she isn't all that hungry but she knows she needs the calories. She's seen this trick work for the staff, it's how the aides make morning tea: her space heater tipped toward the wall, the kettle placed above the coils. Her propane tank is empty and she hasn't any firewood; Tamding was to bring some but she doesn't want to ask again. The power's going on and off, the fourth time in almost an hour, and the afternoon is getting dark: the fading light of six o'clock. The tins have barely gotten warm, the kettle doesn't even hum; at this rate she'll be eating sometime after she does evening rounds.

It's cold inside her little room, she's wrapped up in a woolen shawl; she's watching as the ravens fly around outside from branch to branch. They are constantly in motion, always one or two of them in flight; beneath their weight the tree limbs bend, the branches shaking nervously. It's always only ten of them, no other ravens join this group; they jostle for position as they're waiting for the main event.

These tins are still a mystery, they've been showing up for several weeks: the nurses call them tiffins, how they carry lunch from home to work. She finds them just outside her door each evening when she comes back home: these stacking stainless cups that keep the rice out of the vegetables. She has asked the staff, *Who makes the food?* She'd like to thank them properly. The nurses say that they don't know, and the aides don't catch her Kullui. The tins are filled with rice and dal, with folded nan and eggplant stew—the recipes have varied from the simple to elaborate. This food is all she eats these days, she has no energy to cook: the only form of *thanks* she gets for all this hell she's going through. She picks a tin up from the heater, sees the coils have lost their glow; sticks a fork into the food to find out what's in store for her.

The power comes back on again, and she watches as the coils bloom: first dull, then brilliant sunny orange, like safety stripes on workmen's clothes. She had to turn her lights off to send more power to the heating coils, and as the power gains in strength the room takes on an eerie mix of twilight from the sky outside and sunrise from the heater on the floor there by her chilly toes. The kettle starts a rumbling hum, her first bit of encouragement, and she looks up out the window as the waiting ravens croak and shout. They force their squawking cawing out through bleating beaks cracked open wide—their heads bob down with shoulder shrugs like drunken frat boys vomiting. She watches as a large one shreds and eats a plastic shopping bag, its syncopated movements looking polka-like and rhythmic.

The power goes back off again—her kettle's barely put on steam—*goddamn it!* she thinks as she pours, impatient with the fickle heat. The tea bag's bobbing in her cup just hot enough to bleed some brown; she wonders how the locals do it: cope with this annoying town. She's looking at a woman climbing down some stairs across the street; she's descending from her second floor to her shrubless dirt and gravel yard. She's carrying a plastic bucket, colorless in semi-dark—she comes down very carefully as if she's late in pregnancy. Mary wonders what this woman's life is like day after day: cooking dal, cleaning house, sorting stones out of the rice; scolding snot-nosed children, chasing chickens all around the yard. She imagines what the nights are like when all the family's fast asleep; the woman climbs in with her husband on a mattress stuffed with sticks and straw; has quiet sex there with a man who smells of goats and honest sweat. It might be wonderful, she thinks: a simple life without regret. It wouldn't really matter if the power wasn't on at night.

She's thinking of the nursing aide who never speaks to anyone; the staff says Manu hasn't said a word since she came years ago. Penniless and desperate, she landed on the clinic steps—she came the day her husband died, the day her house burned to the ground. Her husband's family sent her off, she hadn't yet produced a son—was just another worthless girl with burns now up and down her arms. Mary feels some kinship since that's also why she landed here: her life destroyed by some old man not watching out for bicyclists. She couldn't stand to stay home feeling haunted by her husband's death; every morning driving past the place they picked him off the street. She thought that she could pull up stakes, go off where she was needed most; maybe she could do some good since pleasure was beyond her now.

She doesn't have to worry about making money anymore; she liquidated all she had, she's almost twice a millionaire. Her lawyer handles everything, an old friend of the family; she gets a letter once a month: the market has been taking off. But she feels like such a vagrant with the only place to call her own just two rooms and a block of foam: a tin stove with no wood to burn. She doesn't have to stay another minute if she doesn't want—could write a hasty hen-scratched note, write *Vikram* on the envelope. But every time she gets that far the letters sound so juvenile: *How could you just abandon me?! You've been so irresponsible!* She hasn't got an appetite for lentils that aren't really warmed; she's sick of drinking tea so weak, this fickle electricity. She thinks that she might try again, gets out her pad and ballpoint pen: *Dear Vikram,* she writes at the top, *you filthy lying sack of shit . . . !*

As she crumples up the note, the heater cycles on and off: the coils aren't even warm before the power fades away again. Mary watches as her neighbor dumps the contents of her pail, the water splashing out over the rock wall that defines her yard. Like greyhounds through the starting gate the ravens all lift off at once, swooping down onto the wall to see what they can find to eat. They land and bounce from rock to rock, sparring like ten featherweights—they fight over the bits of dal and cauliflower cooked to death. She watches them pick through the stones and listens to their shouted caws; she hears the scratch of talons as they scramble through the rocky wall. Then suddenly they all take off, they're finished with their evening meal—the scraps consumed, the woman gone, and Mary hears the harsh beat as their wings go rustling through the air. In darkness it's volcano-like, erupting on a moonless night. The ravens are just ash and smoke, then suddenly—the ravens gone—she can't see anything at all.

# The Timing

Antone takes his finger off the needle mark fresh on his arm, checks the skin to see if it has finally finished oozing blood. He doesn't want to stain his shirt or get it on his jacket sleeve, and he hates the little scabs they form when he doesn't press them long enough. It isn't bleeding anymore, it's looking just like all the rest: a red dot with a blush of pink above the blueness of a vein. He puts his stuff away into a box beneath the driver's seat, a lacquered black Tibetan thing he ripped off from a market shop. He puts his arm back deep into his old black leather jacket sleeve—he feels the best he has in days and that this might work after all.

He tries to start his fickle jeep, an ancient yellow rattletrap—curry-colored British surplus: a bit of humor on their part. He has the top up, black and torn, like a burned chapati stretched too tight; in the dark inside the jeep he puts a black boot on the clutch, another hard onto the gas. The rush is long familiar and he feels connected to the jeep, can sense the gas and air mix as he pumps on the accelerator. His strong and trembleless fingers find the key still sticking in the dash: *Timing,* he is thinking, *timing's absolutely everything.* He feels the mingling molecules, the carbon mixed with oxygen, and he twists on the ignition switch, feels the spark right in his chest, the brief explosion of the gas and air, the pistons beaten, valves are burned, the engine coughing, turning, *yes!* He listens as the engine roars, his right hand slaps the steering wheel, he revs the ancient motor belching smoke into the village square.

He's in a village close to town—a place where he has always stayed—his jeep parked near the public baths, the hot springs he avoids since he once watched a turd float past his nose. The village rent is cheap compared to hotel prices down in town; the village people understand that hippies are a source of cash. The street is safe, the views are nice, and everybody's brother sells; he has an understanding with the woman where he rents his room. The village is above the town, farther up the valley wall—well above the orchards so in spring it's white and pink below. The apple blossoms look like bits of scattered clouds and patchy fog, the river rushes thickly by, some strange and hyperactive snake. In the fall things aren't so soft: the trees are stark, the valley brown, on the lower peaks the snow is gone. He can see down through the leafless orchards, the town is sparkling far below: a couple miles farther south, a bright spot on the valley floor. In the daylight he can see the birds, the ravens circling over town, so thick sometimes they almost hide the wood smoke drifting in the air. *Where do they go at night?* he wonders. You'd think you'd see them in the trees; all outlined in the branches, unlit lanterns waiting for a match. They're in the forest hiding, maybe, huddled in the evergreens.

Antone's staring down the valley, warming up the engine some; staring through a windshield that is cracked in so many places it's a wonder that it's still attached, as if it's held together by the resin from the joints he's smoked. He's watching as the lights of town twinkle on the valley floor, watching as they flare and dim with surges from the power plant. Suddenly they disappear—not all at once like he'd expect to happen when the power's out, but like a sheet's been pulled across his face, or a hand that's reaching swiftly scooping sparkling jacks up off the ground. He feels a chill go up his spine, a deep foreboding sense of cold, although he's still flush with the dope, not conscious that the air has changed. As suddenly as they went out, the lights of town come on again, glowing ember-like at first, then full and bright and glistening. Antone shrugs the feeling off, revs the engine twice again, grinds the gearbox into first, and pulls out from the village square.

The cobblestones are slick and shiny where the hot springs spill across the road; he starts off slowly through the wet, then shifts to second carefully. He once was nearly stoned to death, while swerving through some little town—he clipped two chickens in the road, the locals quickly mobbed his jeep, demanding that he pay the price. He handed over money, but they beat him senseless anyway, and now he drives through villages as carefully as possible. He doesn't gather speed until he exits from the village walls, the stony houses built so close and elbowing the only street. He's several hundred yards away, the town lights don't shine half this far; he notices he cannot see, he hasn't turned the headlights on. He puts a hand out to the dash, groping for the headlight switch—his blush of optimism fades as quickly as his heart can beat. He feels a tingling sense of fear, a python has embraced his lungs, and then his fingers find the knob and so he pulls the damn thing on. The left light is the one that works, the right one has been dead for years; the road is still in front of him, the naked branches of the trees that reach out from the uphill side. He blinks three times. Something is weird. He's seeing spots before his eyes: large and white and rushing him like tracer bullets through the air, like bright stars zipping past him doing warp speed cruising outer space. He puts a big boot on the brake. He isn't going very fast, but the curry-colored jeep still skids across the rutted road, bouncing bad across a hole, oddball bits of junk start flying forward from the space in back: the black Tibetan lacquered box spills out from underneath his seat. The jeep is stopped, the engine dead, and the single headlight fades away—the battery not strong enough to light the glowing monocle. Once the headlight isn't there, the white spots quickly disappear, and Antone sits confused and scared, not sure at all what's going on. He reaches for the window crank and rolls the dirty window down.

Outside the jeep the air is calm. In the stillness he can hear the sound of spots falling before his eyes. Instantly he understands—the bad-trip sense has disappeared—for on his face bent out the window he can feel the gentle landing of large flakes against his skin and hair: snowflakes large as cookies, white as milk and safe as herbal tea. He bends his face back toward the dark and star-obscuring clouds above, then screams to chase the fear, to let the snow fall down against his lips, past rotting teeth and bleeding gums into his widely gaping laughing mouth.

Antone cranks the window shut and starts the jeep up once again. This time he just lets it roll, pops the clutch in second gear, so when the engine catches on the headlight glows back strong once more. Again, the falling spots are there, but they don't frighten him this time. Instead he's startled by an unexpected sharp left-handed curve. He swings the wheel about, the soft white flakes melt on the window glass. He can barely see enough to know he's safely on the road again. He reaches down between his boots and shoves his box beneath the seat; he wonders if there's fuel enough to make the trip across the pass. He'll take the boy to Koksar, where he's sure no one will give a damn, and Meena can take care of him: he'll give her half an ounce of hash.

# The Dark

Phillip's staring at the ceiling, doesn't really have a choice—afraid to even move his eyes to look around this *bloody room*. Six feet up above his head a single bulb hangs from a wire, just off to his left and feeble-flickering its twenty watts. He is waiting for it to go out, waiting for the power to fail, to plunge him into darkness like it always does in India. No telling when it's going to happen, though always when he needs it most: reaching for the toilet paper, suddenly in total darkness, jeans all bunched around his feet, his butt above some stinking hole. He never has his flashlight and the matchbox opens upside down; the matchsticks scatter tunefully as broken glass across the floor. But lying on this board is worse, his head strapped down with sticky tape; his shoulder on the left is wrapped up in an itchy cotton sling. He's certain he is going to die not long after the power fails—lying helpless in the dark and prey to almost anything. He'd gladly trade his jacket now, just to know the *fucking* time, to know the clock is moving and he hasn't died and gone to hell. But someone handy with a stick is wearing both his watch and coat: some chicken-shitted ass who swings a club could kill an elephant. If only that damn nurse would come, he'd even take the fucking bitch: he has to pee so bad he thinks he's just about to wet himself.

The bitch came in an hour ago to say she phoned the embassy—that's *Doctor* Fucking Bitch, he thinks, attempting to amuse himself. He's trying to relax, to somehow calm his poor tin-bitten nerves; instead he trembles from a chill that's worrying his spinal cord. The muscles in his neck are tight as springs under a Tata truck, loaded up with bricks enough to build another tourist trap. He's feeling cold, still hears the doctor's chilling words ring in his ears: *Don't move, or else,* she'd told him, *or you'll never run or walk again.* She used words like *paralysis* and *total quadriplegia*; she told him, even worse than that, *you'll never get it up again.* He would have sat up if he could then, blushing with embarrassment; the message finally through to him: *don't move, or else,* he heard her say. *Fucking bitch, that's what she is: Doctor goddamn Fucking Bitch.*

The lightbulb flickers bright and dim, and his trembling chill ends in a sweat; he hadn't changed his clothes for several days before this big event. The dampness of his skin makes his clothes heavier against his chest, sucking warmth out of his skin like hot air through a kitchen vent. He stares up at the ceiling, at the movement of the flicking light, surprised the bulb itself stays still as light jumps from the filament. He is lying in the treatment room, the nurses haven't moved him yet—they left him there alone except when all those Jesus freaks came in. Maybe there were five of them, they gathered close around his bed; their leader shook his hand till Phillip had to ask him for it back. He was relieved at first to have them here, all Scots from up in Edinburgh, although they're older than himself, and dressed a bit conservative. He was happy just to see someone who understands his dialect; but soon their tone turned serious, they asked him what church he attends, has he come to know his Savior yet, would he mind then if they prayed for him? Before he had a chance to speak, they joined their hands around his board, and in a heavy Scottish brogue they prayed and started witnessing. They prayed for him forever till he couldn't stand it anymore; he couldn't catch half what they said, he can't stand being stared upon, and the last thing that he wanted was their fucking Christian sympathy. He had to raise his voice before they clued in it was time to leave.

The treatment room smells dusty from the plaster used for making casts—the wafting stink of antiseptic used for cleaning people's skin. Back before the clinic closed, the nurses worked around him while he listened to them dress the wounds of people sitting out of view, push needles into hips and thighs of children crying violently. The grown-ups barely whimpered as the dull spike pushed against their skin, just sat and coughed great lusty gobs of blood and mucus in the air.

He knows he's going to die now, staring straight up into emptiness; he's strapped against this awful board awaiting the apocalypse. The frayed cord to the light makes the bulb look like someone being hanged; his eyes follow the cord across the ceiling then half down the wall. Everything is painted white, a dusty shade of almost gray, like chalk rubbed thick against a board and nothing to erase it with. The flicker of the lightbulb stops, it surges bright with candlepower, and instantly the room's as bright as Delhi on a summer day. The ceiling glares so brilliantly, all trace of texture disappears—he has to close his eyes to keep from burning out his retinas. He knows the door is to his right, that's where the nurses wander from; he's thinking that this room could be the last he'll ever walk into. The door blows open, left unlatched the last time someone came and went: it could have been the cleaning lady staring at him silently. He can just make out the top of it, the door out to the courtyard, where he sat and smoked a cigarette while the doctor read his spinal films. A breeze enters the room and starts the lightbulb swinging back and forth; the shadows that it's casting move and cause him to feel motion sick. Somebody's in the room because he hears the scuff of sandaled feet; he can't see who it is at all, he's helpless to protect himself:

"Help! Nurse! Someone get me off this bloody board!"

The light is growing brighter still, the swinging shadows make him sick; the breeze cuts through the blanket Doctor Fucking Bitch laid on his chest. His eyes are closed, he's scared to death, he hears the door squeak on its hinge; he feels the breeze die in the room, can sense the lightbulb slow its swing. Something touches his right arm and grabs him firmly by the wrist; he screams again and tries to buck, to pull his arm away from it. A pain shoots down his neck now like a knife blade sliding through his brain.

*"Sshhh . . . ,"* he hears, like pressured steam escaping from his vented head.

*"Sshhh . . . Mister Pillip, kyaa baat hai?"*

He opens up his eyes to find a nurse's hand has grabbed his arm, the pretty nurse who must be deaf, just stares there with a stupid grin.

"Bloody scared me half to death!"

"Sorry, my English very little," she says, her head directly over him: a halo from the swinging light that's making him feel nausea.

"Don't creep up like that!"

"My English very little. . . ."

"Stop that bloody light from swinging. It's gonna make me puke. . . ."

He sees her looking down on him, she keeps her hand held to his wrist, raising up her eyebrows as her haloed head swings side to side, a gesture that means yes and no and maybe all at the same time.

"I've got to take a piss," he says, and sees her eyebrows raise again.

"You know, piss, pee, take a leak."

He puts his hand beneath the blanket, raises up his covered thumb.

"You know . . . pssssss. . . ."

"*Ahh . . . pishab . . . Achhaa-ji,*" she says. Again, her head wags back and forth.

"Bloody dunce."

"*Aaj raat barf pa-ré-gee.*"

He watches as she puts her little finger in her starboard ear, wiggling it violently while still she's staring down at him.

"Bloody Christ!" he says, and feels a chill snake up his spinal cord, his hand under the blanket holding tight so that his pants stay dry.


Phillip wakes up suddenly, with both eyes open extra wide: he cannot see a thing and so he's certain that he's paralyzed. A panic kindles in his chest, rising gorge into his throat; in front of him there's nothing, not a spark of light to focus on. The room smells like the hospital; there's still the tape on head and chest; the doctor's voice rings in his ears, *don't move, or else,* he hears again. Something happened while he slept and now he's frozen in the dark: all his strength and vision crushed by galloping paralysis. He must have twisted in a dream and sliced his spinal cord in half—all it took was one good cough and now he'll never get it up. That's all he's ever wanted: just the chance to do the nasty deed—every waking moment since his voice dropped in the seventh grade. But now he'll never walk again, never bend to smell a rose, stuck forever with the ache of permanent virginity. He puts a hand before his face, to see if he can see the thing: suddenly it dawns on him he's moving something after all.

He thinks again, then takes a breath, perhaps he's being paranoid; one by one he checks his toes, can wiggle every one of them. The lights must have gone out: it's just the nightly power ritual. His clothes are damp from drenching sweat; the blanket must have fallen off. The bottle's still propped in his crotch, he had to send the nurse away; embarrassed when she had to help him do the buttons of his pants. His neck hurts and his back is stiff, the muscles in his legs are cramped—he's at the mercy of that bloody nurse to button up his pants. There can't be torture worse than this, he'd rather take the bamboo strips, the water dripping on his forehead, every six months dental checks. His whole life has been miserable, his punishments all undeserved: his parents liked his sister best, his nannies were insufferable. His father was a diplomat, they moved on average once a year; he's lived so many places that he doesn't fit in anywhere. And the rudeness everybody hears is just this nasal voice he has: chronic sinus problems and his adenoids have grown too large.

It must be close to morning since this night has gone on several years; he listens to the rumbling of a generator off somewhere. He's thinking he is not alone; he doesn't really hear a thing, but senses someone in the dark—his hair is standing up on end. The damn door must be open, with a chilling breeze against his face: a sudden sense of presense, something filling up the emptiness.

"What?" he says. He's whispering. "Who's there?"

No one answers from the darkness, but he's certain he is not alone; he hears the quiet whistling of air flow through a crooked nose.

"What do you want?" he says; he speaks a little louder now. "Go get the nurse. This bottle's full. . . ."

No answer but the whistling nose, the smell of someone's bad BO, the sound a couple feet away, a footstep scuffs against the floor.

"Go get the nurse," he says again. "Go get the bloody fuck-ing nurse!!"

# The View

It's harder when the power's out to see in through the dirty glass; the light's not always bright enough to see what's going on inside. He knows enough to not stand close, in case the lights come on again—they'd surely see him standing with his nose pressed to the windowpane. So Amod's standing back against one of the old deodar trees, safely in the shadows, though he can't quite make out everything. The doctor's in the children's ward, examining a little girl: a villager from far away whose head is thickly wrapped in gauze. And even in the candlelight and through the steamy windowpanes, he sees the stain grow on the gauze, the darkness that he knows is blood seeps slowly through the bandages. Chidda is the nurse tonight; she's not the most experienced—barely twenty-one and she's disabled by a nervous laugh. There's someone else there in the ward who's helping translate for them both; they're gathered round one of the beds, the girl rests in her mother's lap, an IV drapes down to her arm, the doctor's staring at a book. The windows aren't tight in their frames so he can hear most of the words; he thinks the man that's translating is the one the doctor cut upon. He's someone Amod hadn't seen before they brought him in last week; he can't be from around here, though he speaks in fluent Kullui.

He doesn't hear it very well, but the man's explaining to the mom: something's pressing on the brain, the doctor has to operate. Chidda left the ward already, off to wake the other nurse; she's got a list of instruments the doctor copied from her book. Amod heard about this man, the watchman tells him everything: Doctor Mary cut him open, plugged some holes burned in his gut. When the patient woke up from the shot the doctor gave to help him sleep, he found himself surrounded by the Christians praying over him. Tamding says he had a fit: the shot made him delirious; he screamed like someone terrified, till the doctor chased the Christians out. Tamding says the doctor won't allow the Christians back inside, that they can't pray around a bed unless the patient asks them to.

The doctor's wearing funny clothes, they must have called her from a bath: a fuzzy dress, her rubber boots, a towel wrapped around her head. The air has turned so cold that Amod has to stamp his aching feet. It's almost twelve o'clock at night; the dhaba cook predicted snow. The lights were bright and steady till perhaps half an hour ago, and he saw the little hippie lying freezing in the treatment room. This young man tried to get the nurse to quickly bring a urinal—Chidda looked about to turn around and leave him lying there. The hospital's completely dark now that the power has gone out: just candles in the children's ward, the tandoor in the duty room. A nurse goes by some yards away, walking from the theater: it's Sushila out of bed to help the doctor with the surgery. She tells the doctor that she has the theater prepared for her—the instruments she asked for have been quickly scrubbed and sterilized. The patient who's been translating looks awful in the candlelight; he's sitting on an empty bed, a blanket wrapped around his chest. He can tell the stranger's English is much better than his Kullui, though his voice is weak so Amod can't hear every word the stranger says.

Doctor Mary takes the little girl, who's obviously not awake: her IV bottle on her lap, Sushila holds the door open. The nurse has Doctor Mary's book, the doctor's nice electric torch, which lights the ground in front of them; the doctor carries off the girl to take her into surgery. As they pass the duty room, the doctor calls for Tamding's help, to go and start the generator, which lights up just the theater. The nurse and Doctor Mary go to scrub and prep this little girl, the nursing aide already there to wipe the table down for her. Amod watches Tamding leave to start the ancient motor up, a noisy thing that guzzles fuel: they can't afford to run it much.

Amod's still against the tree, hidden in the shadowed depths, a habit for so many years, a cure for his insomnia. He knows that Chidda's gone to sleep, the stranger's shuffled off to bed; the air is now so chilly that he can't just stand there anymore. He holds a stack of tiffin tins to leave upon the doctor's porch: another habit that he's got, each night after the dhaba's closed. For months he watched her waste away, the doctor once was curved and soft, but after she'd been here awhile her beauty fat was wearing off. He realized by watching that she didn't have the time to cook, and the nurses at the hospital were not too terribly concerned. He's watched them call her late at night for things she shouldn't have to do—Doctor Vikram always made the nurses sew the cuts themselves. Now half the time she's up all night, but no one's taking care of her; he started leaving tiffin tins to try to make her fat again. He leaves them just outside her door, delivered when she isn't home: afraid it's inappropriate, so he doesn't let her know it's him. She puts them back outside her door when she is finished with the food, though often it's still mostly there, she hasn't any appetite. This has gone on several weeks, she always leaves a little note, *Thanks!* it says in Hindi script, though it's not a word that's used too much.

He drops back through the shadows, goes to leave these tins of food for her; the rooms they gave her near the school are not the nicest ones around. He'll pick the tins up later on, replace them with another set, then wander through the town again, to catch a glimpse of other lives. He turns to walk down to her place, when suddenly he hears the dog: old Kali hiding in the dark, she makes a quiet, high-pitched whine. He only pats his pants leg twice, which almost makes no sound at all, and Kali bounces toward him: she's affectionate as usual. He grabs and tugs her floppy ears, rubs between her shoulder blades—she somehow knows instinctively he wants her to stay quiet now. The dog's the other one he feeds, she's had so many sets of pups; if someone didn't give her food, the dog would quickly starve to death. The top tin's always for the dog, just scraps from other people's plates: enough to keep her flanks filled out, to keep her milk from drying up. The only sound's her panting breath, it billows steaming from her mouth; Amod pulls behind her ears, standing with him in the trees, the only friend he's got in town.

He hears the diesel start up from a shed behind the theater, a sound he's heard a thousand times, the sign of an emergency. It starts off with a stumbled beat that drones on into rumbling; they only start it running when they're late at night in surgery. A faint glow spills out from a little window in the theater, too dim to light the shadows here; the other windows, facing west, spill light back on the garbage dump. A shadow turns the corner coming from the generator shed; Amod knows it's Tamding because Kali wants to run to him. He hates the fact she likes the man, since Tamding's just an idiot: raised to be a Buddhist monk, became a

Christian here, instead. He has the strangest fashion sense, wears blue jeans like a Westerner, a wristwatch bigger than his head; he's always bending down to clean his shoes off with his jacket sleeve. Amod still holds Kali's ear, though she doesn't struggle very much—she knows what's in the tiffin tins and that he hasn't fed her yet. Amod hangs on to her ear until the shadow disappears, gone into the theater to watch them do the surgery. Again he turns to walk away, to place this gift outside her door—the doctor will be up all night, and clinic starts at nine A.M. He can't see Kali with him, but he feels the big dog's quiet steps; she's so black that it's like all light gets sucked into her shaggy coat. She walks with him, then stops again, her hearing's better than his own; she turns back toward the yard where something's moving through the open gate. It's so dark he can't make it out, just hears the rumbling diesel ping, but Kali's throat begins to growl, and Amod reaches down to grab the furry scruff around her neck.

Finally he hears it, too, a quiet crushing gravel sound, and then a high-pitched squeak like someone hurting a small animal. But it's just a set of squeaky brakes, some car or truck's rolled in the yard, its engine and its lights are off, not making any noise at all. Kali doesn't like it, he can feel the fur raise on her back, and he has to tighten up his grip to get her growling muffled some. He can't make out the kind of car, too big for an Ambassador, too long for a Marrudi van; it must be some strange foreign job. A rusty door squeaks open but he doesn't hear it shut again, then heavy footsteps cross the yard like someone walking with a limp. A torch spreads light across the ground, and Kali makes a too-loud growl; Amod ducks behind a tree as the dim torch tries to find the dog. The light shines on the duty room, where smoke comes from the chimney pipe; it flashes quickly through the room, though Chidda's in there fast asleep. The next door is the treatment room, where the hippie boy had yelled and whined; he heard him shouting earlier, his neck hurts and he has to pee. It dawns on him that this must be the ambulance from Chandigarh, some silent kind of vehicle much faster than the usual. The buses all take eighteen hours, but the roads are quiet late at night— perhaps they heard that it might snow and didn't stop for anything. The torch is in the treatment room, the hippie kid shouts with surprise, for a second calling for the nurse, but he doesn't shout for very long. In a couple moments Amod's hearing something dragged across the ground, the heavy awkward footsteps of the driver of the ambulance. He wonders why the man's alone, why someone isn't helping him—he'd offer him assistance but has no excuse for being there. He can't make out the details, just the outline of the hippie's board; the driver drags him to the back, then slides him in the ambulance. He finds out why he coasted in, came downhill from the road above: the driver gets behind the wheel, then cranks the noisy engine up. It runs on just two cylinders, the muffler must be full of holes; it must have come in gliding so as not to wake the hospital. Only one dim headlight works, it's shining through a film of dirt; just bright enough to light the bright white snowflakes falling on the ground.

# The Tenderloin

"Sushila! Let's get out of here!"

Mary's standing in the outer room, the one next to the theater—holding in her arms the bundled body of a three-year-old. The little head is wrapped in gauze, with pupils now both equal-sized; the patient and the surgeon both are sleepy from the ether gas.

"Sushila! Come and ring the bell!"

Mary's waiting for the nurse to come and open up the doors, to ring the bell that lets the staff and family know it's over with. They're to come and take this little girl, so the aide can clean the surgery, so Mary can write in the chart, strip off her bloody gown and gloves. The little girl that's in her arms has just been through a long ordeal—she fell sometime the day before, off an unprotected balcony, in a village somewhere up the road, so it took them hours to get her here. Now she's been anesthetized, her little head's been opened up, which took the morning's early hours with Mary reading the instruction book. She's wishing that Sushila would come open up the double doors, call across the courtyard so the family could come claim their girl: rid her of her little charge so both of them can get some sleep— deep and dreamless sleep now that the pressure's off of both their brains.

Sushila finally shuffles past, takes the hand bell from the shelf, reaches for the double doors, and suddenly, in that much time, Mary's not there anymore. For a moment she's in surgery, still drilling through this pretty skull, knowing if she does this right she might just save this little girl. But then she sees the raven perched up on the dark blue sterile drapes that cover up her patient's head, this skull she's drilling burr holes through. She wonders what it's doing there, watches as it flaps its wings, then glides down to the floor and gently folds its wings back up again. She follows as it hops outside, out through the open double doors: blood is dripping from her gloves, the air outside is bright and warm. The raven stretches out its wings, stirs dust up as it takes to flight, rising, flying upward till it settles in the walnut tree. It's not the only one, the big tree's branches densely black with birds: thick as leaves and strangely quiet, hardly making any noise. The courtyard's full of patients, hundreds wanting to be seen by her— they're dressed in rags stained gray with filth, their ugly ailments exposed: leprous limbs and open sores and pregnant swollen abdomens. As she steps around a legless man, the patients all start grabbing her, tugging at her sterile gown; starving children take her hands. As Mary's walking past, a woman plucks a baby off her breast, forces her to take the child; when Mary looks she sees the baby's just a tiny shriveled corpse. *"Save him, Doctor! Save my son!"* Mary turns back toward the doors, to take the corpse to surgery, not knowing what could work to save this lifeless thing she's clinging to. But she can't go inside anymore, her gown and shoes are caked with dirt—suddenly she sees her husband walking out of surgery. He's still dressed in his biking clothes, his Lycra shorts and jersey shirt, cleated shoes with laces loose and dragging through the filth and dust. He hasn't got his helmet on, and blood drips from a nasty wound—he's holding in his arms the bag of groceries she'd sent him for. All the patients gasp with shock and rush to back away from him—his shorts and shirt are ripped and torn, his skin is scraped with bone exposed. Mary knows what's in the bag, the peppercorns and tenderloin; she wanted to make Sunday dinner, just the way his mother had. Her husband doesn't have the strength to hold the bag up anymore— he stumbles on a tiny pebble, the roast goes tumbling to the ground. The birds are on it instantly, the ravens swooping from the tree, a boiling mass of black and noise that rips the store-bought meat apart: fighting over bits of beef and blood-soaked shreds of plastic wrap. Mary has to close her eyes, can't take a second more of this, and then she feels an icy wind, the sharp crack of a ringing bell.

She opens up her eyes and she is back inside the double doors, in the room outside the theater, the bell rings in the nurse's hand. She's staring through the open doors at a world that's turned incredible: everything is white and clean, it must have snowed a foot last night. The courtyard's never looked so bright, but it doesn't shake her awful dream—she must have slept while standing there, the whole thing happened in a blink. She watches as the family rushes toward her from the duty room, the only place they can keep warm; the patients suffer in the cold. The family makes the only set of footprints in the courtyard snow, and she looks up at the walnut tree, its naked branches thickly flocked: just a single raven, the image startlingly black and white. She remembers then the shriveled corpse, the baby she held in her dream: how heavy it had felt for such a dead and dried up little thing. She looks down at her cradling arms, at the bundle she still holds with care, and she almost screams and drops it till she realizes it's the girl, this healthy, precious three-year-old.

The snow is like adrenaline, the flakes as big as dinner plates, and Mary stomps around outside in foot-thick wet and heavy fluff. She loves the snow, the soft white cold, the day shift gang-ing up on her; she's head to toe all caked in white, it's on her face and down her back. The stinging cold is wonderful, the most awake she's felt in months. It melts against her cheeks so that she tastes it when she licks her lips—she's parched and so she swallows it without concern for parasites. She gathers up a load of snow and rushes Sushila who is laughing at her since she slipped, fell butt-first on an icy spot. The early snow is soft and wet; she's soaked and tired and out of breath: laughing so it's hard to breathe, her gloveless hands sting with the cold.

She sees that Tamding's bent and packing snowballs in a lit-tle pile, that Chidda has an armload, so she dashes for the duty room. Slamming closed the door, she laughs, and instantly her glasses fog; she feels their thumping missiles as they strike below the window frame. It's stifling in the little room, the tin-box stove is nearly red; she stomps her feet to let the snow fall off her while she's by the door. There's someone sitting on the bed, wrapped in several layers of wool, and she wipes her glasses on her shirt, still she's laughing out of breath. Then she recognizes Ravi there, her splendid, classic typhoid man: rippled belly flat and smooth, sutures soon to be removed. Even though she missed the drain, she hadn't killed him after all; he spiked a fever once that night, but normalized soon afterward. The next day when she did her rounds, she found out why he's built so well—he said in perfect English that his parents both were emigrants to somewhere up in Canada. She thought then he was free and clear, just weak and sore but still improved, that all she'd have to do was just continue chloramphenicol. But later on that afternoon, his belly pain got worse again, his fever spiked another time—she sat beside his bed for hours, checking on his vital signs.

"Good morning, Doctor Brain Surgeon. I understand it went quite well." He says this very cheerfully—he's sounding better every day.

"Yes. I think she'll be all right. I didn't find an actual bleed. I think her broken skull was pushing on her brain. I was able to lift the piece up some."

"You saved her life. Like mine."

"Stop," she says. "We all get lucky, sometimes. That's all."

"I wish I could have joined your snowball fight. I'd have been on your side."

He really helped her out last night, the duty nurse so frustrating: she'd spent a half an hour trying to get poor Chidda's story straight. She finally woke up Ravi so that he could do the translating; his mother was from Solong, a small village closer to the pass; his father came from Mandi, had leased land there from her grandfather.

"It looks like you'll be here awhile." She says this to him casually, nodding with her head at the thick snow outside the window.

"My cousin thought that it might snow, so he went home yesterday. But he said he'd come back down in a couple days. He says it melts off fast this early in the year."

Mary moves close to the tandoor, holding out her hands to dry, watching through the window as the day shift stopped their snowball fight: white as sheep, a flock of five, walking now in single file. Her hands begin to tingle from the heat that's blasting from the stove, and suddenly she's tired again: exhaustion coming back to life.

"You look beat. When was the last time you got any sleep?"

"I think it was three days ago. The snow kind of woke me up, but it wasn't real. I'm dead."

She rubs her cold and blushing hands, listens to the snowmelt dripping from her sweater's soaking sleeves: droplets on the tandoor dance and sizzle as they disappear. She remembers Baltimore, how it's so hot in summertime, how she'd go with fellow students to the diner after late-night rounds. They talked about the things they saw, their first times in the surgery: tired but excited by the thrill of seeing living gut, the unexpected fried meat smell that lingers after cautery. The diner's grill was open, just behind the counter where they sat, and she sees the cook work in the heat, the windows and the doors are open, the ceiling fan is on full blast, but still it must be ninety-five, even late as two A.M. She sees the sweat form on the cook, watches as it trickle drips, sizzling down onto the grill between the chops and patty melt.

The door opens to the duty room, the cold air wakes her up again, and the day shift tumbles in still laughing wet and out of breath. Rambha is in charge today, and she shakes the snowflakes from her hat, showing off the pink cheeks of her smiling round Tibetan face.

"Doctor, go sleep," she says. "Patients never come when it snows."

Mary smiles at her and nods, but she knows she has to do her rounds, go through the wards from bed to bed and check the progress of them all: to check the young girl's pupil size, make sure Prince Charming gets some food; be there for the ambulance that's coming up from Chandigarh. But her brain's already shutting down, permission granted deep inside—she'd love to go have breakfast, treat dear Ravi to some real food, speak fluent English for an hour and figure out his history. It's too late, though, she's done for now.

"Tell Tamding to come and wake me in a couple hours. And make sure the hippie gets some food, and have him shift his butt around. He'll get bed sores lying on that board."

# The Rounds

Rambha does the rounds today, with Chidda and the nursing aide; she's done it many times before, when Doctor Vikram was around. She knows the set of protocols, has seen it all over the years—the patients want to go home now, afraid that it might snow again. The snow has stopped, the sun is out, and the walking will be wet but warm; they always empty out the wards each fall before the passes close. The nurses often did the rounds when Doctor Vikram was in charge; he trusted them to do their best: explaining he can't do it all. Then Doctor Mary came along, seemed everything they did was wrong—she'd ask them nice to do a task, then suddenly she'd change her mind. The massive book she hauled around did nothing for their confidence; Rambha can't remember Doctor Vikram ever using it. But Sushila said last night that Doctor Mary's work was excellent: she thought for sure the girl would die, but Doctor Mary saved her life. The sky today is brilliant blue, enough to make the weak feel good, and if it snows again tonight, the patients won't get home till the spring. The snow would get too wet and deep to safely carry invalids; she walks into the men's ward with the order book held to her chest.

The first bed is an amputee, three fingers from his lesser hand; she tells him he can go home if he keeps his bandage nice and clean. The next bed is pneumonia and the old man says he's better now; after him a man who "accidentally" drank some pesticide. The only one who can't go home is a young man with a broken hip who has to stay in traction for at least another couple weeks. The typhoid man from Canada still has his line of sutures in—he says he'd rather check out for a hotel with a little heat. So she tells him to come back tomorrow, sometime in the afternoon; if they leave her alone, the doctor could sleep for a couple days. Then she goes into the women's ward, there are just a couple patients here; the wards aren't full since word got out that Doctor Vikram's gone away. She empties out the OB suite, the newborns have all peed and pooped: reassurance that they've got their wiring and plumbing straight. Of course she keeps the little girl who fell and broke her tender skull—she'll need close observation since the pressure could build up again. So that only leaves two inpatients, and no one comes in when it snows; she only hopes that Doctor Mary doesn't get too mad at her.

A policeman walks into the ward, a rag wrapped tight around his knee; he wants some stitches for a cut, he fell while walking home last night. Chidda wants to call the doctor, but the officer, he understands: the doctor's been awake for days, lets Rambha sew his bleeding knee. She sutures in the treatment room, that's where she thought the hippie was; she only finds his chart with the last note inked in at one A.M. She assumes the ambulance arrived before the snow got very deep—she's mad that they would take him without paying for the care he had.

She straightens out the table, picks a used syringe up off the floor; she puts it in the dirty box, to be autoclaved and used again. She stitches shut this wounded knee, wraps it up in sterile gauze, and she doesn't charge the man a thing: a cheap insurance premium.

# The Bull

The drinking didn't start until the dog ran out into the road, a thump against the fender that felt solid as a cricket bat. He saw it in the headlights, tail poking up out of the ditch: a truck was coming toward them, so the dog skipped to the other side, ran smack-dab in front of them. The driver of the ambulance knew better than to try to swerve, much better just to hit the dog than head-on with a Tata truck. The headlights made the dog's eyes flash, then suddenly it was under them, and Kishan turned around to look, still felt the wicked bump it took, couldn't see a thing behind—so dark out on a moonless night.

The driver's a big turbaned Sikh, his black beard tied above his ears—he sits up straighter in his seat, pretends it doesn't bother him. They both are in a hurry, driving north to save some stupid Brit: the driver gets paid by the mile; Doctor Kishan's on his honeymoon. He's barely graduated, and his wedding night was yesterday—he's still feeling hungover from his one day of celebrity. This job came from one of the guests, an unexpected wedding gift: he got the call this afternoon, a month's wage for two days of work, just sitting in an ambulance. He didn't want to leave his bride, they'd only met a couple times, but she insisted that he go because the money seemed impossible. They started off at eight o'clock, an hour since he got the call; his new wife packed his bag for him: a sweater and some extra socks.

Kishan's never been up any farther north than Chandigarh, he's only seen the mountain peaks as shadows through the dusty haze. He didn't have the time to research where the heck they're going: some tiny mountain town to get a tourist strapped onto a board. He doesn't know the driver, yet the man talks like they're best of friends, and ever since they hit the dog, they've passed his bottle back and forth. At first the whiskey bothered him, his queasy stomach still upset, but after just a sip or two it helped him to relax a bit. The driver's steering carelessly, his right hand free to eat and drink: a tiffin tin of dalmut he has clamped between his knees. He doesn't seem to mind the traffic, headlights race past in the dark—he swerves around most animals, the dog was just unfortunate. There's nothing else to look at but the head-lights of the passing trucks, a glimpse every few minutes of a traf-fic sign or farmer's hut. The driver said this trip would take a full day riding on a bus, but driving without stopping he can cut the time down close to half. Kishan's feeling motion sick, glad Sikhs are not allowed to smoke; it's cold out but he has to crack the window for a breath of air.

He's thinking of his wedding day, how they didn't consum-mate last night—felt nervous, so he drank too much: afraid that he can't do it right. He hasn't yet committed sex; he barely dares to masturbate: advice he's got stored in his head from friends with no experience. He's just completed med school, but the sex-ed course was incomplete—just showed them graphic color slides of organs too promiscuous. So he knows all the anatomy, which parts are supposed to fit in where; it's the method that's the mystery, how he's supposed to get from A to B. The thought of learning all this with a wife who barely knows his name is terribly exciting, yet it's terrifying all the same. They climbed in bed in darkness, and his drunken hands touched breasts and butt; he climbed on top too early and he tried to penetrate too fast. She cried in pain and pushed him off, apologizing all at once—he was horrified that he messed up and started feeling sick again. Even though the room was dark, he knows the rusty smell of blood; she bled there not a little bit, slick proof of her virginity. The blood smell mixed with alcohol was too much for his frightened state, and he had to stumble out of bed and kneel before the toilet head.

It's an hour since the dog was killed, the driver's had a couple swigs, and Kishan's feeling better through the dimness of a little buzz. He's tired and he wants to sleep, but the driver's started in again: found out that he's a newlywed, has lots of stories now to tell. The ambulance is dark inside, just the light from the speedometer, and he sometimes sees the driver's face when some passing headlights shine on him. His nose is bluntly prominent, his beard and mustache long and black, combed back and underneath his chin, then up beneath his turban. Kishan's trying to remember if the color has significance: the driver's turban cloth is red, though most of them he sees are white. The driver talks above the engine noise, listing all the sex he's had, with neighbor's wives and prostitutes—positions recommended if his firstborn is to be a boy. Kishan feels uncomfortable, no one's ever talked to him this way; still, his interest has been piqued, though he's sure he can't believe a word. He feels a pressure in his pants, a sudden urge to urinate.

Kishan asks the man to stop, it must be after twelve o'clock—the traffic's down to almost nil, no village lights shine anywhere. They pull off to the shoulder, and Kishan steps out of the ambulance; the driver turns the headlights off but leaves the engine rumbling. It almost takes his breath away, the night sky like a blazing torch; he clearly sees the Milky Way—the moon has not come out tonight. He's standing by the roadside, the driver walks up next to him, and they're both facing the same way, out across a black expanse of field: the night sky bright but not enough to let him make out anything. He's glad that he can't see a thing, he's in a semi-turgid state: the sex talk stimulated him, he hopes that he can start to piss. He has to swivel round his hips to get his penis through his pants, and he can hear the driver's hearty stream now mixing with the roadside dust.

"We haven't got all night," the man scolds as he's zipping up his fly; Kishan hears him turn around and walk back to the ambulance.


He wakes up from a sudden swerve, his head knocked hard against the glass, and he must have been asleep awhile, they've started up the mountainsides. The last thing he remembers they were still flat driving on the plains, the only turns the driver made were swerves around loose goats and cows. He must have slept at least an hour, they're climbing up the steepest grade—they're going round a switchback curve, and the only things that Kishan sees are bushes in the driving lights. The driver straightens out the wheel, shifting to a lower gear, preparing for another curve just fifty yards in front of them. Kishan has to swallow hard, to keep the bile from coming up—not used to mixing sudden curves with sips of rot-gut alcohol. He's feeling something else, as well, some sense of deep anxiety, or maybe it's adrenaline, caused by an awful dream he's had.

"Stop!" he yells out frantically, already opening the door—the driver hits the breaks so hard that Kishan smacks against the dash. The ambulance is hardly stopped when he's outside on his hands and knees, vomiting up alcohol and undigested rice pul-lao. He retches several minutes, there's no other traffic on the road; he's feeling slightly better, but now hardly has the strength to stand.

"We haven't got all night!" he hears the driver calling from the cab, and finally he stands again and climbs back in the ambulance.

The driver doesn't wait for him to even pull his door shut tight, he's quickly into second gear and swinging round another curve. With one hand on the steering wheel, the driver holds the bottle out.

"To get the taste out of your mouth."

Kishan's manhood so impugned, he grabs the bottle from the man, then takes a fairly good-sized sip and manages to swallow it. It only makes things worse for him, just magnifies the motion spin—he's determined, though, to keep it down, to never ask to stop again. He's glad the ambulance is dark, not used to so much alcohol; he's feeling like he's going to cry, instead of here he could be home all snuggled with his brand-new bride. She's been really understanding, helped him get back into bed last night, had washed herself and changed the sheets, removed all the evidence. They'd spent the morning all alone, had breakfast on the patio; she brought some kind of medicine to try to cure his hangover. She didn't seem to mind at all his bad performance late that night, and when they went out for a walk, she volunteered to hold his hand. He so wants her to like him, she has charmed him with her brilliant smile, and though they undressed in the dark, he's pleased with what he saw of her. He wants a happy married life, just like his parents managed it: together nearly thirty years and still can't stand to be apart.

He's feeling somewhat better now, since throwing up the alcohol—the curves aren't quite so awful if he keeps his focus on
the dash. At the rate the driver's going, he'll be back home sometime late tonight, and he's thinking when he climbs in bed, he'll
only cuddle with his wife. He realizes there's no rush, with years
stretched out in front of them; he's overwhelmed with mixed
emotions: sadness, lust, and happiness. Suddenly he's jerked
about, the driver makes an urgent swerve: two beasts are standing
in the road, a bull on top a sacred cow. He looks up off the dash
in time to see the bull's wide-open eye, and the driver hasn't
turned in time, they clip it there on Kishan's side. He empathizes
instantly with their interrupted coital bliss, and they pass then
into darkness as the ambulance keeps skidding by. And the single
working headlight shows the last thing that they ever see: the
empty mountain valley breadth, a space just filled with smoky
mist, the dim lights from a tiny village near the river far below.

# The Trip

The earth moves under Phillip, a vague rumbling from beneath the ground, and a droning clatter rakes his nerves and drags him up toward consciousness. It must be night, it's dark in here, the stupid power still not on, and something has him held down fast: he cannot move his head or legs. The earthquake keeps on rumbling, the clank and tremor worry him—it often hits a fevered pitch, a whining, grinding mesh of gears. Considering the noise and quake, his anxiousness is relative; there must be someone nice and kind out somewhere taking care of him. He tries to wake himself up, though it really isn't sleep he's in: awake but stumbling through a fog; the landmarks don't make any sense. He opens wide his crusty eyes by arching back his brows, but the movement of his forehead is restricted by the sticky tape. His eyes are both stretched open, but he still can't see a bloody thing; it's important that he figure out the ugly noise that bothers him. He's not confused about himself, he's strapped onto a slab of wood, recalls that Doctor Fucking Bitch is trying hard to save his neck. But the earth keeps shaking under him, and how could they let him get so cold? Why hasn't anybody come to let him know what's going on?

Someone strikes a match so that a golden light glows overhead; it comes from somewhere past his feet and shines on what's in front of him. There's just a rusted metal tube that holds some rotting canvas up; the match flare quickly fades so that he can't see any more than that. The match is shaken out so all the shadows dance before they leave; the instant that it dies he gets a whiff of just-lit cigarette. The smell of it is wonderful, familiar as fresh fish and chips, and it all comes clearly to him now, the rumbling and the whining gears: they've got him in the ambulance, he's on his way back home crammed in a death trap rattling his bones. He takes a deep breath full of smoke, a cigarette would be so nice: he'd gladly kiss the driver's feet for just a couple measly drags. He starts to call out for a smoke, but intuition makes him bite his tongue—he doesn't really want to know what kind of person's at the wheel.

Instead, he shuts his eyes and fantasizes that all's well and good: that he is safe and sound and that his parents are both worried sick. Perhaps they'll be in Chandigarh, to hold his hand while flying home, and he wonders how much farther now, how much longer till he's off this board. They must be going uphill, since the blood is pounding in his head; his feet are toward the front end where the driver lit the cigarette. They should be going downhill, though: they're taking him to Chandigarh; but then he thinks somehow he's wrong, perhaps its just a little climb, some valley coming from the side. He lets it slide, his mind falls back into that other, pleasant state: a place he's never been before, but soft and warm and comforting.

★　　★　　★

When Phillip wakes up next it's from the silence ringing in his
ears, the rumbling and the whining gears no longer filling up his
dreams. It's daylight and he clearly sees the canvas torn up overhead, bright spots of early-morning sky shine blue through little
rotting holes. He wonders if they're almost there, why such a
shit-trap ambulance; why does it seem so goddamn cold? *Why
can't they get some fucking heat back here?* He's cold, so cold it's hard
to think, his arms and legs held down with weights: his head feels
like a rotting scrap of filth a dog might roll upon. His right leg's
tingling with sleep; these straps and bags annoying him: put there
by that doctor-bitch to keep his neck aligned and straight. He
wants real bad to rip them off, to get up off this skinny board, to
go find someplace warm to sit, some coffee and a cigarette. The
silence fills the space left by the absent rattle-grind of gears—the
wind beats on the canvas top, the scratch of blowing sand and
dust, the echo of strong howling gusts out rushing round in
emptiness. Where are all the other sounds? The hordes of people
running round? He still must be in India, they wouldn't drive this
thing back home; but India is never still: pathetic people everywhere. There's only rushing wind outside, the smell of dust in
freezing air; a lonely chill runs up his spine, it's aching where he
broke his neck, and he doesn't want to move because his fear of
death is bottomless. All he really wants is to fall deeply back
asleep again, so when he finally wakes next time, the world might
make a little sense.

But he doesn't get to fall asleep. The gravel scuff of heavy
steps sounds just above the howling wind: the stomp-drag of a
pair of boots worn by somebody with a limp. The driver's door
is opened up, the dust swirls in around his face; above his head
the canvas snaps and billows like an angry bull.

"Phillip! Are you awake yet back there?"

The strange accent surprises him: not British and not Indian; he recognizes something, like he's heard it several times before.

"Shut the door! I'm bloody cold in here! How much longer before Chandigarh?"

He's so annoyed he wants to cry; why can't things go the way he wants? He's hungry and his neck hurts and his right leg's aching with a cramp.

"And for God's sake can't you feed a guy? It's not like I can do it for myself . . ."

The driver's door swings banging shut, a cheap and tinny squeaking sound; the scuffing boots kick gravel as they limp around the ambulance. The driver's fiddling with the top, suddenly it's all pulled back, and Phillip stares up at a face that's smiling upside down at him.

"Sorry about last night," the man says, "but there wasn't any other way."

These features staring upside down are not the friendliest he's seen; it's mostly nose and forehead and the narrow space between the eyes; past them in the air above float tiny bits of dust and snow. The driver's cheeks are deeply pocked, unfathomably cleft and scarred.

"You don't remember me," he said.

"Antone. From the restaurant. It was your bloody drink that did me in."

Antone reaches past him, down beneath the board that Phillip's on, he pulls out an old sleeping sack, a musty Dacron traveler's bag, the loft all beaten down and flat from years of grease and sweat and dirt.

"This might help," Antone says to him. "I wasn't thinking it would snow."

Phillip's in a quandary, confused about what's happening. Nothing's making any sense, especially how cold it is.

"How much longer before Chandigarh?" but he's not sure now he wants to know, suddenly afraid of Antone, afraid to ask what's going on.

"Depends," Antone slowly replies, "how quickly they get me the cash."

# The Pass

At the pass he turns the engine off and lets the jeep roll to a stop, the fuel gauge reading quarter full; perhaps it's even less than that. Antone figures he can coast the jeep down all the way from here; but what he's really worried about is snow out past his wiper blades. The flakes are small and dry, the air much colder at this altitude; it's snowing hard enough there's half an inch already on the road. The wind is really howling now, with patches of the road blown clear; the snow looks spilled, like someone dropped a bag of flour on the floor. The boy is still passed out in back, still sleeping strapped down to his board; Antone opens up the door and puts his big boots on the ground. He stands and stretches quickly, four long hours driving to the pass; he's glad his leather jacket does a good job cutting out the wind, he feels it blowing stiffly through the holes ripped in his thready jeans. A shiver makes his shoulders clench up fist-like just below his neck—he's thinking he could use a fix, but instead he walks out on the road to stretch his tired and crampy legs and look for signs that all this nasty weather won't stay bad for long.

His plan seemed elegant enough, but things just won't cooperate; he didn't figure it would snow, or that he might run out of gas. He's trying to think this further past the easy part of grabbing him: the power went off just in time, he found him on the second try, he only had to walk right in and drag him out across the yard.

*Nurse!* was all the fight he got, he snuck up on him in the dark: the boy strapped down and on display like some dead presidential guy. He was taped across his forehead, with an arm tied in a cotton sling, so Antone grabbed his other hand, the boy not sure what was happening. Antone's done this countless times, when customers are too afraid: squeeze the upper arm until he finds a nicely bulging vein. He knew the nurse might hear the screams, but Phillip passed out instantly; the trick is not to give too much, sometimes the shit can be too strong. It wasn't really snowing then, and he's sure he didn't leave a trail; his captive went to neverland and never said another word. But now, four hours later, they are up on top a mountain pass; it's been snowing since this morning and the wind would keep a raven home.

Antone walks out farther, trying to see way down the other side; it looks a little better there, perhaps the weather still might clear. The snow is blowing on his back, the wind is coming from the south—he's trying to decide if this is foolishness or what. He looks into another world, the endless Himalayan range: mountain after mountain miles high and not a single tree. He'll leave the boy in Koksar with a girl who's got no place to go: drive two hours farther down the hill, then back again this afternoon. If only it won't snow too much, in the little time that's in between, he'll be in Chandigarh tomorrow, phoning up the embassy.

He wonders what this kid is worth, he's never done this work before, and he's not sure how he'll get the cash, or if the embassy's the place to call. But he'll think about these things tomorrow, since first he's got to dump the boy; he's got to hurry or get stuck for months on this side of the pass. He thinks again about a fix, then shrugs and turns back to the jeep; the snowflakes freeze onto his beard and almost stick his lashes closed. It's colder and the air is thin; it's tiresome to think too hard: much easier to just keep driving, figure as he goes along.

# The Stewpot

Meena stands out in the road, her scarred hands holding throwing rocks: she's aiming at the stupid ravens sitting on a building ledge. Even though her hands were burned, the little fingers webbed and curled, she still can handle throwing rocks as well as anybody can. Her aim is good today, the birds all scatter with her second stone—their startled wings flap black as doors that men slam when they're mad at her. The ravens don't fly off too far, so Meena keeps on throwing stones: she lets a curse fly with each rock, her teeth clenched tightly frustrated. She's damning them to come back next as something even worse than this, as maggots or as rabid dogs, as pinworms in a pile of shit.

"Toilet cleaners!" she screams at them; the ravens fly a couple yards: the town's so small there aren't too many places where the birds can land. Her last stone's thrown with so much force she feels it soaring on and on: past the ravens on the wall, rushing to the mountaintops. They are gods, these mountains all around, broadly shouldered jagged peaks that stand so close together they're like riders in an open truck, clothed in only snow and clouds, jostling with every bump. She'd gladly curse them too, if she could find something to curse about, but they're just beasts like sacred cows, the forms of ancient incarnates: of sinners or of holy saints, no one ever told her which. Her stone lands fifty yards away, hardly raising any dust, snuggling with the other rocks out on the road that leads from town.

The Koksar ravens aren't as big as all those on the Kullu side, the ravens just across the pass, where food scraps are more plentiful. They fly the same, they're just as black, their heads bob up and down alike; but they're hardly half the others' size, these ravens on the inner side. The Kullu valley's wet and lush with apple trees and evergreens; but this side of the pass is bare, all monochromic gravel gray and white with piles of dusty snow. The only color is the sky, the blue when clouds aren't in the way; the river is a silty mess, a glacial milky sewer for the snowfields on the mountaintops. The ravens fly about its edge, pick at things between the rocks, then off again to land upon the mudflat rooftops of the town, on top of buildings made of stone.

Standing in the road she feels the wind unchecked by tree or bush, so Meena shrugs to pull her pattu closer up around her neck. She pushes back her braided hair, scratches at the itchy part—that's all the time it takes to make her mangled fingers throb and ache. The wind is never ending here, like life itself, she often thinks; the only thing that changes is the day to night and back again. She's been in Koksar seven years, her father left her stranded here: a deal made with some of the men; she cooks the food and cleans the mess. She doesn't really mind the cold, it's the wind that is her enemy; the wind is like a lonely knife that constantly is cutting her.

Today the weather's not so bad, she turns a circle where she stands, looking at the mountaintops: the white and gray are crisp and bright, the blue sky bordering their peaks. All around the sky is clear except above the southern pass; the snow clouds always gather where the moisture from the ocean stops. Already she's forgotten all about the crows that got her goat, the ravens that she hates so bad she'd gladly wring each neck by hand. Her hatred comes because she knows that only men come back as crows— nobody ever told her that, she figured it out on her own, that women couldn't look that way, that only men could be so rude. But now she strains to hear something: a quiet hum above the breeze, the whining rub of rubber tire rolling on the gravel road. She turns to see what's coming down, descending from the snowy pass, gliding like a raven, coasting toward her with its engine off. She catches just a speck of jeep, the gravel crunch beneath its wheels; it's maybe half an hour away, though hardly half a mile from here. She watches for a little while, an arm held up to shield her eyes; the wind is gusting all around, she catches glimpses of the jeep on sharp outsides of hairpin turns.

"He's back," she says, and breaks a smile.

There's a racket coming from her left, from the building where she does her chores, the mess hall where the men sit down to eat what she has cooked for them. The men are inside making noise, a crew of five to watch the town; the tents have all been taken up now that the roadwork's finally done. Each year, in spring, they start again, digging out the snowed-in pass, pecking like so many chicks, picks and shovels trying to break the shell around the mountaintops. But now, in fall, they've all gone home, the snow's about to close the pass—the storms will make the journey folly, winds like tidal waves of air that flood and drown the unprepared. Meena cooks for six today, two meals a day that taste the same; she's always cooking rice and dal, some pickle when she's called upon. The racket coming from inside is five men calling out for more—she stands and listens through the wood: the wind above the sound of metal plates against the table-tops, the slapping flap of shuffling cards, a cork pulled from a bot-tle neck. It's hardly half till noon when Meena pushes through the solid door: the room filled with a smoky warmth, the smell of kerosene and chang, the sour stink of unwashed men she can't stand for a minute more.

"He's back," she says. "Get your filthy food yourself."

She pushes past the metal plates, held out at arm's length toward her chest, going toward the corner room she keeps near where she cooks the food. Someone grabs her by the arm, a man just bigger than herself, his other hand is now a fist that smashes one side of her face. Blood starts coming from her ear, and the other men are laughing hard; one of them is shuffling cards. Meena doesn't move at all, just waits till she can see again. The man is standing straddle-legged above the bench that he was on, and Meena puts her knee so quick and solid up between his legs, that even though it's padded by the thickness of the clothes he wears, the blow does what she wants it to and quickly takes his breath away. He slowly sits back on the bench and Meena only backs away until she's in the corner with the tandoor and the cooking pots. The other men don't say a thing, she's always taken it before, but then the laughing starts again: the strangest thing they ever saw. Meena backs into a pot, still looking at the man she kicked, whose hands are cupped around his groin, who's try-ing not to moan too loud. She takes the lid off of the pot, hawks and spits into the stew, then slams the lid back down in place; the men are laughing harder now, like ravens cawing from the trees, egging on two fighting birds.

In her room she gathers up her things: not much, she's got an extra blouse, a sweater with some holes in it, a couple scarves to wrap her head, some metal bangles for her wrist, a silver piece that fits her nose. She's hurrying to be out in the road before the jeep arrives, so certain that it's Antone back to keep the promise made to her. She's lived on this for months and months, that he was coming back for her—he promised last time he was here, in trade for several extra beers, a place saved closer to the stove. He hadn't tried to sleep with her, like all the others passing through, just smoked and drank and made his deals and promised he'd come back for her. She only wants to leave this place, to climb into the jeep and flee, to turn the thing around before the pass is covered up with snow. She rolls her things into a shawl that's red and rimmed with indigo, then gets down on her hands and knees to pull a rock out of the wall. Behind the rock she keeps a stocking half filled up with bills and coins, the kind devalued years ago, a thousand make a rupee now. She doesn't think she's rich, but maybe has enough to go somewhere: a rule the boss made years ago, they have to pay her every time they come and have their way with her.

Before she gets up off her knees, she hears the thin door opening; she turns expecting Antone but it's just the man that clobbered her. The blood is drying at her ear, the spinning stars have gone away; the man walks with his legs apart, an angry look across his face. He leaves the door wide open to her room that's just outside the mess; she sees the men behind him find positions not to miss a thing. She watches as this bastard opens up the pin that binds his pants, and she gets up off her knees and swings to hit him with her heavy sock.

"Filthy pig!" she screams at him, the sock connects against his head, she feels like something there gives way, although it barely makes him flinch. He grabs her by the wrist, his other hand pulls on her long black braid, and he turns her face away from him, he pulls her head back by her hair. Her wrist is bent behind her back, her shoulder threatening to snap; he pushes her across the bed, her face against the rocky wall. He pulls her pattu up too far, and every time he makes a thrust, her face is ground into the wall; the blood that's oozing from her skin makes a stain that looks like Hanuman, the legendary monkey prince, rising from the temple flames.

He sits beside her when he's done, she doesn't move or start to cry; he reaches back to touch the spot she cracked him with the sock of coins. He stands and closes up his pants, has trouble with the safety pin, and before he leaves the room he pulls a rupee coin out of his pouch and throws it on the littered bed.

# The Sleep

When Mary finally wakes up it is six o'clock and almost dark; the window-filtered light inside glows rosy tinted warm and soft. It's spring light seen through flowering trees, and she is cozy cuddled up in bed, which makes her think the wind she hears is balmy soft and huggable while it's rattling her window-panes. She isn't really all awake, the sleep she slept was like a drug, and she isn't trying hard to wake because the sense of peace and safety is so strong wrapped deep inside her bed. She's dreaming of a nice hot shower, gushing like a waterfall, right between her shoulder blades, pounding hard against the knot that's been there for the longest time. The humid, soapy smell is strong; she hears the sounds bounce off the tile; she puts her face into a towel that's fat and soft and oh-so-clean: the distant scent of laundry soap, how nice it is to stand there warm and naked by the foggy mirror. She's toweling off her long wet hair, her figure fleshing out now as the steam clears from the silvered glass—she likes the way she looks these days: a little on the skinny side. She hears her husband's whistle slipping underneath the bathroom door, dressing in the bedroom to a song that only he can hear. It's a sound she's heard a thousand times, a song that's never twice the same, she can see him pulling on his socks, standing by the closet door: unconscious of his nakedness, he always dresses randomly. But the whistle doesn't sound quite right, he almost never goes that high; suddenly she can't breathe in, like something's grabbed around her chest, she's fallen in a mountain lake, fighting just to catch a breath. She jumps out of her narrow bed, the concrete cold against her feet, still wearing the same clothes she had on last night and the night before: damp still from the snowball fight, the shower she just dreamed about. She struggles for full consciousness, pulls out of her sweet reverie; she knows exactly where she is: confused about the time is all. The rosy light is dawn or dusk, she can't tell if it's day or night—either way she's slept too late and God knows how many have died: the young girl with the fractured skull, whose brain she had to open up, or some eclamptic pregnant mom who's seizing in the birthing room for lack of something in her vein.

The whistle that she woke to is now fading as she clears her head: just Tamding going past her door, to work or maybe going home. She finally gets her breath back now she knows that he's not calling her, but she keeps on looking for her boots: an urgency she can't deflect. Her room is dark enough she barks her shin against the wooden bed, the sharp edge of the bed rail cutting hard against her tibia. The pain that stabs her is as pure as shots of vodka taken straight, no tonic mixed to mask the taste or cut the burning in her throat. Tears well in her eyes, and then she sits down somewhere near her bed; she was going to put her boots on but instead decides to cry a bit. She hasn't cried in weeks, she thinks, so long now since her husband died; but the vodka shot of pain has broken through to disinhibit her.

The tears dislodge the crusty bits out from the corners of her sleepy eyes, and she lets the drops fall down her cheeks, feels them dripping off her chin. She rubs her shin bone with her hand, still trying to put her boots back on: the rubber-bottomed felt-lined boots she bought back home and brought along. Again she feels her chest tighten, like something squeezing on her lungs; a spasm grabs the muscles in the space beneath her clavicles, forcing breath out through her nose: her teeth are clenched, her lips are closed, not wanting anyone to hear.

After a minute, she feels she can stand, and she knows that it is evening now: the rosy light has disappeared completely from the window frame. She feels her way into the bath: a cold room with a concrete floor, a tap without a sink or drain, a hole for her to squat above. She's glad she doesn't have to go outside each time she has to pee; her bladder is so full she thought she'd lost it when she sobbed before. She turns the knob to light the bulb but finds the power is still out; careful not to slip and fall she pulls her pants down to her knees. Her eyes are still brimmed full of tears, so as she aims above the hole she tries to find the humor here: a trick that sometimes works for her. She's looking down from far above, can see right through the roofs and walls: she's seven thousand feet up on some Himalayan mountainside. All around are massive peaks dressed brightly by the passing storm; she sees the people walk through town, young women herding sheep and goats, honeymooners making love, men and boys out shoveling snow. And there she is inside her loo, squatting with her pants half down, her tail end stuck out in the air, so cold it must be turning blue.

She imagines this is so absurd she cannot help but giggle some, how mortifying it would be if someone were to see her here. The chuckle turns into a laugh, the laugh into a coarse guffaw—what would her mother think to see her doctor-daughter squatting there. For the world she couldn't stop this laugh, the tears still pouring from her eyes, and she hears the rubber-drumming sound she makes when she pees on her boots. Her stream sometimes goes to the left, and she couldn't find it funnier: in danger now of falling down, the tears so thick in both her eyes she couldn't see now if she tried.

She likes the snow feel underfoot, it's heavy snow and packs down nice; she's trying not to rush as she runs off to check the duty room. Snow like this, so wet and thick, takes Mary back to Baltimore: the storms can drop a couple feet, accumulating overnight: the constant traffic has to stop, the snow turns all the gray to white. The city noise is muffled by the blanket over everything, and her walk to work takes her right through the roughest-looking neighborhood. It's the only time she ever thinks that Baltimore is beautiful, when the snow covers the dirt and gray, the few trees flock to twice their size, their branches thick and sparkling white. She lives a couple miles away, the snow makes it seem twice as far; she has to get up early, search for woolen socks in bottom drawers. Few people get up early, most sleep in until the streets are plowed; just now and then she sees somebody sweeping snow off of the stoop, brushing fluff off of their car while standing in a steaming cloud of bright white idling exhaust. The snow makes people smile at her, unlike most other days she walks, as if God made it snow to wipe suspicion out of everyone. She smiles at them and nods her head, shows teeth as white as all this snow; she lets herself relax a bit, the kids out in the schoolyard play so hard that they don't notice her. "Hey white girl!" they shout most days, calling through the rusty cyclone fence—the older boys call out how much they'd like to get inside her pants. But the prison even looks benign beneath a half

foot of snow; she's walking past the coffee shop, the regulars excited, standing drinking out of paper cups. She can see the hospital from here, the blocks and blocks of brick and glass, the old
wing with its dome all white, the little desk where Osler sat. The
steps that sweep up to the doors are shoveled by the janitors, the
cleaning people always there, polishing the hallway floors with
quiet humming buff machines. The snow is nearly virgin on the
sidewalk where she climbs the hill: she's following a lonely set of
footprints to the ER door. The snow stopped falling earlier, and
hints of sun and bright blue sky now glimmer through the breaking clouds. She loves it when things look this way, the white and
blue and gray and sun; she tries to keep her feet inside the footprints out in front of her. They're widely spaced and not too
straight, like someone who was stumbling, and it is then she sees
the bright red spots, the only contrast to the white. At first they're
only here and there, and then they show more frequently: this is
more than just a kitchen slip, an accident while still asleep: slic-
ing bagels or a cantaloupe. The blood red on the brilliant white
is sparklingly beautiful, the patterns look like Rorschach prints,
where someone might see butterflies or people kissing on a
bench. The blood leads to the ER door, a knife wound or a bul-
let hole, and she stops and reaches out to scoop a drop up in her
mittened hand. She's not thinking about viruses or binding sites
of oxygen, but wondering whose body used to hold this in its
pumping veins. How fresh and delicate it is, how angry someone
must have been: to want to cause a mortal wound, leave someone whose blood this once was to stumble all alone out through
the fresh and lovely virgin snow.

And now she is a doctor running through the snow in India,
racing to the treatment room to see how many patients died.
She's struggling with a sense of awful urgency and dread: that
made her rush to find her boots, that makes her feel responsible.

She should be sprinting full speed through the snow up to the children's ward, rushing up the narrow stairs to see who's in the birthing room. She knows this is ridiculous, they've gone for years without her help; yet Mary cannot help herself, can't push away the sense that all the burden rests on her alone—that no one else here gives a damn, or they would not have let her sleep so long.

The snow's about ten inches now, settled in the sun all day; Mary looks up overhead, trying hard to slow herself. Off to her right there's still a hint of purple in the evening sky, and straight above are twinkling stars, the constellations bright and sharp. It was something Richard used to do, he'd wake her up at four A.M.: drag her out into the yard, point out the constellations that weren't visible at other times. He had the night sky memorized, could always point out Hercules, amazing her not that he knew, but that the distant moon and stars so moved something inside of him. The Milky Way is out because the power isn't on in town; she slows, then stops, to stare up at what she and Richard used to share. She is standing in the playground and the trees around have lost their leaves; the starlight bounces off the snow so that the light comes from the ground. She's looking up at Gemini, she finds Orion's belt and sword, but can't recall much more than this, just the Dippers and the Northern Star.

At first she doesn't see him there, standing underneath the trees; she looks up at the sky and hears the quiet of the settling snow. So when he moves she's startled by the icy crunch beneath his boots, and for an instant she is taken back, her husband's foot-steps late at night, out in her parents' big backyard: for a moment he is standing there, to point out some faint galaxy. But when she turns to look she finds she's in a Himalayan town, pausing on her way to work, rushing off to take care of a nonexistent urgency. It's Ravi underneath the trees, coming from the hospital.

"I was hoping you'd be up by now," he said. "I'm off to find a dhaba. Thought I'd talk you into joining me."

"I'd love to, but I slept too late. I haven't done my rounds today."

"Or yesterday, you sleepy head. You slept a full day and a half."

Mary takes a few steps back—she knows this is impossible: she's never in her life been even vaguely irresponsible. But he tells her there's no need to rush, the nurses have done all her work: they discharged all the patients who live farther than an hour's walk. There's just the man in traction and the pretty little three-year-old: an angel playing in the snow just two days after surgery. Mary's totally confused, convinced the man's delirious; her instinct is to touch his forehead, do a couple neuro tests. He says she slept since yesterday, a nurse came once to check on her—he heard them say she mumbled but they couldn't make her stay awake. She's mortified she'd slept so long: doctors can't indulge that way; what if someone discharged should have stayed in bed a few more days? And how will she forgive herself if someone dies while walking home? Did they give them medicine? Enough to last through months of cold? She turns to rush off anyway, to find out what the damage is; a knot of fear inside her gut, a quick jab of adrenaline. But if he's right, there's nothing now that can't wait for another hour; Ravi stands there in the darkness, pointing upward at the stars.

"Andromeda is out tonight."

Mary doesn't want to look, can't follow where his finger points.

"Let's eat," she says and turns around, her first step leading back to town.

# The Joint

Phillip thinks he hears the unoiled squeaking of a wooden door, the empty sound that greets a stranger, first time in a local bar. But he can't be sure because the dusty wind is picking up again, and with his one free hand he's pulled the sleeping bag around his head. He hears the engine pinging as the cold air steals away its heat, and somewhere up above his head he hears the squawk of ravens he imagines flying back and forth. But then there's not another sound for what seems like eternity: the engine pings grow spaced apart until they have completely stopped, the wind picks up a steady pace, the ravens sound monotonous. A single caw flies back and forth across the dust and gravel road, sounding like two stubborn children shouting in an argument. He listens hard for Antone's boots, hoping that he'll be right back; the cramping in his gut returns: he'd taken just a single dose of all that medicine he'd bought. He wants to smoke a cigarette, if only just to calm his nerves, to feel the rush of confidence, to soothe his gnawing belly pains. He'd smoked a couple hours before, when they'd finally started driving down: Antone didn't stop the jeep, but poured tobacco from a bag and rolled it all with just one hand. But one smoke doesn't last too long, and he fought a growing sense of fear—he couldn't tell what's going on, and Antone wouldn't say a thing. He wants to rip off the tape that's got him stuck down to the board, to find whoever's fault this is and really tell the bugger off.

He's been trying hard to reason where this ugly creep is taking him, or what he meant about the cash, and why the hell it's colder now and not the other way around. It's been hours since he woke up, since he struggled from the queerest sleep, to wake up rattled badly in the back of some old ambulance. All that Antone told him was he wants to get some cash somewhere: drive all over India just looking for a cash machine.

There hasn't been another sound for what seems like a week at least, just the ravens' cawing back and forth: *did not, did too, did not, did too,* until he thinks he'll go insane. He's about to reach his free arm up to try to rip the tape apart, afraid his guts are going to leak, his asshole muscle wearing out. He still is scared about his neck—*or else,* said Doctor Fucking Bitch—when suddenly he hears the sound of something scratching overhead, trying hard to tear right through the jeep's old rotting fabric top. He starts grabbing at the sticky tape, desperate to get undone: *fuck this stupid neck!* when something else lands on the ambulance. This time it lands upon the hood and he's clueless what the hell it is—the scratching is like fingernails against the chalky finish paint. He tenses up and tries to hide beneath the stinking sleeping bag, when an electric shock reminds him of the state his spinal cord is in. The jolt speeds down his neck right through his back until it hits his toes, and his panic makes him scream in pain and fear so that the ravens caw and fly up off the top and bonnet of the jeep.

The ravens' chorus builds into a screaming cacophony; the caws and shrieks are so severe they'd make a stray dog wince and howl. Phillip has his one free arm curled up and wrapped around his face, trying to protect himself from God-knows-what unfriendly beasts out looking for something to eat. He hears somebody else join in, a woman's voice all full of tears, of breaking rage in every word; he only understands a few because it's Hindi she is shouting and it's just the curses that he's learned. As she comes up close he hears the wailing ravens move away, the broken steps he knows are Antone's, limping on the gravel road. There are others all with lighter feet, and Antone pulls the window back; he sticks his head inside the jeep, dangling a cigarette.

"You're staying here with Meena," and he takes the fag out of his mouth; he puts it between Phillip's lips and tells him he should take a hit. He's so hungry for a cigarette, he inhales almost instantly; surprised to find that it's a joint, rolled with potent local stuff: the very thing he came here for, that got him in this awful mess.

At first he has to cough and hack, a thing that hurts his broken neck, but then he takes another drag and holds it in as best he can. His eyes held shut against the smoke, he feels his hunger dissipate; his one free hand comes up to take the joint out from between his lips. He looks up once again to watch as Antone flares his nostrils wide, straining as he pulls the board that Phillip's strapped and lying on. They flare so wide that from his viewpoint looking up at Antone's nose, Phillip sees that both the holes are filled with thick and bushy hair. He wants to laugh out loud at this—his guts are not as crampy now. This is better grass than any shit he's ever had before. The rush comes almost instantly, like something strong and smooth as glass; he feels it as they start to slide his board and him out of the jeep. Antone pulls from near his head, and someone else is at his feet; the

woman's voice keeps raging like a chainsaw through a hard-
wood tree. And as they pull him from the jeep, his view is Antone's pointy chin, his hairy nostrils flaring wide, above him
scattered clouds and sky. There are mountains all around, their
shiny peaks are all that Phillip sees: they're covered with the
brightest snow, the sight of them confuses him. He can't see
who has got his feet, but they aren't as careful as he'd like; they
tip him slightly to the side and he screaming thinks he's going
to slide right off onto the gravel ground, certain he won't feel
it when his body finally crashes down. But Doctor Fucking
Bitch had taped him carefully around the waist, so when he tips
all that he does is slide two inches to the left.

"Whooooaa!" is what he says, like he is on some wild amusement ride, and for a moment he can see the south side of the little town. There's the top half of three squatting buildings made
of death-gray mortared stone, the edges of their flat roofs lined
with ravens black and wailing still. It strikes him what is happening is that he's at his funeral: he's dead and this is all he gets, a
hearse that's just a beat-up jeep, with unseen men to carry him,
his casket just a plywood slab: the rat-birds sing his requiem.


It's dark inside and all he sees are brown beams of the ceiling
joists, with several unlit lanterns hanging down from bent and
rusted nails. The smell inside is generous with dust and smoke
and kerosene, and he hears them moving things around as they
carry him across the room. He's glad, at least, he's not outside: his
sleeping bag lost in the wind; he feels the warm and smelly air
climb down inside his dirty clothes. He takes another deep drag
from the joint he still has in his hand; it could be worse than
being dead: they could have left him in the jeep.

As he is moved across the room, his eyes adjusting to the

dark, soon he sees the details of construction of the beams and joists. The joists are not all put in straight, the beams are black with grease and soot; tender strands of cobweb hang like spittle from an old man's face. The mortar in the roof is mud which oozes from between the boards like frosting on a chocolate cake; he still can hear the woman's cries, she's come in from the cold outside. Her anger makes the phlegm catch somewhere deep down in her vocal cords, so every time she takes a breath to push the heavy curses out he hears a gurgle in her throat like someone drowning in a lake. The words she screams are only noise, but the gurgling he's heard before: something that his sister did whenever she was angriest. She'd scream about her early curfews, how she'd date the boys she liked; he couldn't keep from laughing, though he knew those weren't the issues now. He tries to stifle it with smoke, by taking yet another hit, by holding it as best he can. But then the snickers flutter out, rasping through his stuffy nose, a long-neglected squeaking hinge, so finally he's lost control: the laughter bursts out from his lips like sulfur from a fumarole. It is hours since they came inside, and they've only gone across the room—he's never felt more stoned before, it's like some kind of miracle. He hears another squeaking hinge, which makes him laugh again out loud; it hurts because his head is taped, which only makes it funnier. They take him past the noisy door, into a room that's lower still; the ceiling joists slant downward so they're practically on top of him. They put his board on something soft, then leave him suddenly alone; his pallbearers have disappeared out past the rice bags round his head. He still can hear the gargled phlegm, her screams are from the other room, when Antone comes back in again.

"You'll be home in a couple days," he says.

"Antone, what the fuck is going on?"

"She's just upset," is all he says. Phillip doesn't understand.

The woman walks up next to Antone. She isn't screaming anymore, but the tears are running down her cheeks; the two stand so close over him he feels her tears drop on his clothes. The woman has these twisted hands gripped tight around the fellow's arm, and she does it very slowly: Phillip watches as she begs and pleads, her mouth pulled down like she is tasting something awful bitter-sour, her chin is quiver-spasming, then slowly bobbing up and down. He can't find a position, though, to get too good a look at her: can only see beneath her chin, the stud that's pierced in through her nose. Her hair is long and black, unlike his sister's, which is brown or blonde, but their dark eyebrows are similar, their noses have the same straight line, and he thinks she might be pretty if her face weren't all bent out of shape.

Phillip watches Antone reach to pry her claw-like hands off him, then feels the matted sleeping bag land limp and heavy on his legs. Antone turns and leaves the room, at least as far as he can see, and Phillip hears the high-pierced squeak of hinge as Antone slams a door.

Then suddenly it's quiet; he can hear the ravens on the roof, and then the rumbling burst of Antone starting up his ancient jeep. The engine coughs out clumsily, it sputter-spits and clears its throat; it idles just a second before roaring up the dusty road. Then in the other room he hears the scoot of chairs across the floor, like people sitting down for cards, the sound of liquor being poured.

He notices a smell beneath the others in this little room; distinctive but he can't say what, and he tries to toke his joint again. He brings it up between his lips, sucks on it for all he's worth, wants to feel that high again but nothing's coming out of it. He thought that he'd been left alone, that the woman had gone slamming out, but he hears her take a deep breath with a sob stuck on the end of it. Her crying starts up once again, this time she does it quietly. She must be sitting on the floor, because he can't see her from where he is, but he knows she's over to his right, and he holds his cold joint out to her.

"Excuse me. Do you think that I could have a light?"

Suddenly she's standing up, towering above his head, and he's never seen a face like hers: the bulging eyes are cried-out red, swollen all around the rims, and an anger flashes from them so her nostrils flare like Antone's did. There's something that he'd missed before, the right side of her face is bruised—it's scraped and caked with dried up blood, a wound that can't be very old. She says something in gibberish, the tone implies she's cursing him: he wishes she'd speak English so he'd know what she is trying to say. She knocks the joint out of his hand, then brings a raging fist down in the middle of his narrow chest: it pulls the wind right up and out of both his flattened lungs at once.

His breathing muscles won't respond; stars are dancing past his face; he can't suck any air inside; he thinks he's going to suffocate. He feels the sudden need to sit, like he's about to puke and faint; he has to grab the binding tape and rip so he can breathe again. He tries to force his forehead up, his fingers tearing at the tape, but all this does is make the muscles spasm in his neck again. The pain shoots straight down to his toes, and at last he gets some air inside; he's stoned enough to make himself relax about the way it feels. It feels so good to breathe again that he concentrates on that awhile: the full expansion of his chest, just deeply breathing in and out, like water endless from a tap.

He slows his frantic breathing down until his hands stop tingling; again he notices the smells, how close it is inside the room. The overwhelming smell is smoke, and then the scent of cigarettes: there's kerosene and greasy food, the sour stink of unwashed bodies sewn into their winter clothes. But there's

something else inside the room he feels that he should recognize—
he thinks this must be where she sleeps, exploring with his fingertips. He's on a bed that's not too soft, the blanket is a scratchy
wool; the mattress has a wooden frame he gets a little splinter
from. And while his hand is searching through the crumpled
blanket under him, he touches something wet and cold: his fingers stained with sex and blood.

# The Bear

Ravi holds the door as Mary steps inside the dhaba's warmth; she feels his hand touch lightly just below the small part of her back. It's a feeling she's familiar with, a thing her husband used to do: a gentlemanly ushering, felt through the thickness of her coat. But somehow this is different, feels a little inappropriate: it reminds her that this part of her is intimate and feminine. She ducks as she goes through the door, not because the frame is low, but every time she comes inside she feels she's entering a den: a warm and smelly place where furry animals might hibernate. The dhaba isn't loud inside, the power is still out in town—candles are the only light, the flames are tall and flickering. She and Ravi stand inside, and the warm air slides inside her clothes, like arms with skin that's silky smooth, with hands caressing breast and thigh. The warmth is coming from the stove, placed in the middle of the room: a tandoor that's not just a tin box like the one back in her room, but something tall and iron-cast, proudly radiating heat. This tandoor is cylindrical, a foot across and four feet tall, a round lid on the very top, its handle is a figurine: a naked lady, Barbie-like, with arms held high in silver plate.

Her eyes do not need to adjust, because it's just as dark inside as out; she watches as the waiter walks up toward them from across the room, his shadow cast upon the walls and ceiling from the candlelight. He stops before the two of them, he offers her a pleasant smile, bowing with his palms together, menus pressed between his hands.

"*Namasté, Doctor-ji,*" he says.

"*Namasté,* Amod. How are you tonight?"

He puts them at a table in his section of the little room, pulls out the heavy chair for her, puts down another candle from an empty table next to them.

"The usual?" he says in English, addressing only Mary.

"I'm not sure what I'll have tonight. We'll need a minute to decide."

Mary watches Amod as he puts the menu in her hands: he doesn't say another word, just shakes his head the way they do, like all the nurses on the staff: side to side, expressionless, like he's suddenly annoyed with her.

"I've never been in here before," Ravi says.

"The dum alu is kind of nice," she replies, still watching Amod's back as he goes through the swinging kitchen door.

She looks around the room and thinks it's nicer when the power's down: the customers don't talk so loud, the music isn't blaring out. Everyone is talking like they're worried someone else might hear, their voices kept down soft and low with Amod's footsteps echoing. It's a dark, romantic place right now, a place you'd see on movie screens; she's feeling quite exotic, sitting with this handsome leading man. Mary looks at Ravi, who is squinting in the darkened room, his menu close up to his face, he's tipping it to catch whatever light drips from the candlesticks. She notices a bald spot that she only noticed once before, forgotten at the time when she had trouble with the breathing tube. She tries to focus on deciding what she wants to eat tonight, but the bald spot has distracted her, this sign of his maturity. Now that she has noticed it she's wondering how old he is—she never bothered asking since his body looked like twenty-five. He looks up as she's looking and she doesn't glance away in time; Ravi laughs self-consciously, not knowing what she's staring at.

"The menu doesn't look too bad," he says. "There's quite a few Bengali things."

"Maybe you should order, then. I haven't tried too much of it."

When Amod walks away this time, he's got their order memorized, although it's not as they had asked: he'd argued over everything. *Rice goes better with that dish, this curry and that spice don't mix,* and every order Ravi gave, the waiter turned it back to her. Mary noticed long ago poor Amod's exotropia: his left eye doesn't always look exactly where his right one stares. Every time he looked at her, she felt the gaze from his good eye, but when he looked at Ravi she could tell he was staring at the wall. Ravi didn't seem to mind the way Amod was treating him, accepted each change Amod made, however condescendingly; Ravi'd smile across the table and then quickly wink an eye at her.

Mary watches Amod as he once more pushes through the door: a dapper man, a little short, his Nehru jacket fits him nice. She looks across at Ravi, who is glancing round the smoky room, and she remembers what he looked like when he wasn't wearing anything. His belly flat, a muscled chest, a strong but gently curving neck—his arms and legs are well defined and tapered very gracefully. Suddenly she's conscious of a far-off place between her legs; a warm flush passes through her as she feels her veins all dilate. She's never once had dinner with a patient she has doctored on; has always kept a distance between doctoring and social life. But Ravi is the first person she's come across in months and months who doesn't just speak English, but who speaks in North American. She's trying to deny the fact she's gazed upon his naked flesh, just wants to reminisce about the way things are back in the States: she'll never take for granted, now, how nice hot running water is.

"A penny for your thoughts," he says, and she has to shake herself and laugh.

"They'd cost you more than that," she says, then takes a sip of lemon tea, hiding back behind the glass, feeling after all these months her English isn't sounding right.

Ravi has a handsome face, his forehead broad and masculine, a full beard growing on his chin; he hasn't shaved since he got sick. He's looking so much better now; it's twelve days since she fixed his gut; he smiles a lot, which shows his teeth: a handsome set of pearly whites. She thinks about his vocal cords, all strung up tight and spasming.

"So," he says, distracting her, "what brings you to this neck of the woods? You don't seem like the mission type. . . ."

She's taken back a little; she's not been asked that since she came: Why is it that she's staying here and doing all this awful work? Nobody on the clinic staff has asked her what she's doing here.

"Well . . . I'm not sure that I really know . . . ," then suddenly she blurts it out: she tells him about Doctor Vikram, that she's been here almost seven months; in all that time she hasn't had a second to think for herself. She tells him how her first day here somebody almost died on her: a baby brought in sick as shit in a too-young mother's trembling arms. She wasn't going to stay because the doctor who had asked her here had left the week before she came, with no one here to teach her things. And if the baby hadn't lived she would have turned around for home; instead she managed somehow to extract it from the reaper's grasp. Then she *couldn't* leave because she had this baby in the children's ward, when suddenly a line had formed outside the narrow clinic door. She tells him how the nurses never offer to do anything; they look at her like she's insane whenever she just asks for things. She tells him how her husband always planned to bring her here one day, after they had raised some kids, saved a nest egg for themselves. But her husband up and died . . .

"I'm sorry . . ."

"No. It's okay, I mean . . . It's been over a year . . ."

They are silent for the longest time; both watching candles dribbling wax, the shadows dancing on the walls as Amod serves the other guests.

"How 'bout yourself?" she finally asks, embarrassed by her self-display.

"My mother's family lives up here. In Solong, up the road a ways. I've got cousins here my own age." She listens as he tells her how he finally got his Ph.D.: a horticulture specialist in new organic farm techniques. His mother just spoke Kullui, so he learned to speak it as a child: forty years in Canada, she'd only leave the house to walk the three blocks to the grocery store. He came to meet his cousins and to practice speaking Kullui, and check out all their orchards, preach against the evil pesticides.

"I'm afraid it's hopeless on that front. To them the stuff's a miracle. They want to drench the fruit in it. Try explaining parts per million to a man who barely knows his age . . ."

She's listening to what he says, but she can't stop glancing at his arm: he's playing with a dinner fork, and every time he twiddles it, the muscles in his forearm flex. She always loved her husband's arms, he'd wrap them round her from behind: *they're standing in a grocery store, she feels his teeth against her neck, in front of blushing cans of food, embarrassed box of cereal.* She'd always have to draw the line or Rich would carry things too far: protest just enough to keep the scene from being scandalous. When she is in her doctor mode, she often feels androgynous, but not when she was in his arms; she loved the reassuring strength of being wrapped up in testosterone. She was embarrassed every time she felt such pretty-little-girlishness: Richard so much bigger that his arms seemed twice as strong as hers, protected by his warm embrace, proprietary lustiness. Suddenly she notices that someone's standing to her left, and she turns her head to find she's staring right at Amod's covered crotch: his slender waist and narrow hips; he's putting food in front of them. He's grudgingly obsequious, a little man in waiter's clothes—but something strikes her deep inside, a chord of sexuality. She looks up at his face as he slowly puts the dishes down, arranging each one just so with the candlesticks on either side. He isn't looking back at her, but concentrating on his task; he bows, hopes they enjoy their meal, and backs away a foot or two.

"Amod, this looks beautiful. I'm starving." She looks at him, and so he smiles a little bit, and shakes his head then back and forth and turns and walks away from them. He's never been this way before, he's always such a friendly man; Mary wonders what it is: *some problem with his wife and kids, perhaps the weather bothers him.*

"I'm forty-two," he answers her, and she knows that she has just been rude; the question came out suddenly, as unplanned as a touch of gas. She thought he might be thirty-one, a good deal younger than herself, as young as twenty-eight, perhaps: she's thinking of his abdomen, so lean and rippled flat and smooth. But he does have lines around his eyes, like those who spend time in the sun; she sees him in a farmer's field, black dirt beneath his fingernails. He's wearing something sexy: faded blue jeans and a flannel shirt.

"Which ones are which?" she finally asks, to get her mind on neutral ground; the dishes on the table in the darkness all look wonderful.

"The curry has the bits of meat," he says while tilting back a dish, the dim light from a candle shining off the ghee all red and slick. Mary is surprised to be as interested as she is; the food looks like a royal feast, unlike most nights she looks at it. This all feels so damn *sensual,* the steam drifting through candlelight; already she can taste the silky eggplant slide between her lips. She hasn't had an appetite for maybe a millennium, and Ravi says he's starving, too, his first real food in several weeks. But he's acting like a gentleman, insisting that she start in first, pointing to the rice pullao, the chutney that goes well with it. She can't remember when she last was stimulated so by food, or when she last spent time with someone other than her husband's ghost. Her appetite is overwhelming, she starts to help herself to rice, she's got the spoon in her right hand, when Amod walks back in the room; he's carrying some sticks of wood.

She follows with her eyes as he walks over to the tandoor stove; she sees him reaching for the lid, the naked lady figurine. Amod is still acting weird, and he grabs the lady round the waist, the wood still in his other arm, but her body's much too hot for him. He pulls his hand back suddenly, the lady crashes to the floor, the stove explodes volcano-like, though it's only light that spews like ash, now flashing on the ceiling so that all the shadows disappear. Anybody else would swear, but Amod only shakes his hand, then brings it quickly to his mouth so he can spit and cool the burn. Everyone has turned to look; it's quiet like it never is; he shoves the wood down in the stove and picks the silver statue up, his hand pulled up into his sleeve. The lady goes back up on top, the light is swallowed up inside, and Mary just can't help herself; she pushes back her chair and goes to look at Amod's awful burn.

At first he doesn't want to show, but she decides she must insist; she almost has to pry his fingers open from his clenching fist. Already she finds blisters there, can see the dead skin in the dark, and she wishes they had Silvadene but it's not stocked in the pharmacy.

"Let's get some snow on this," she says, but then she hears an awful sound—she stops dead in the silent room, with everybody listening. The only one to move is Ravi as he stands up from his chair: the horrid sound she's hearing now is whistling from the alleyway. She wants to put poor Amod's hand out in some little drift of snow, take Amod to the treatment room and dress his wound in something clean. And she wants the feel of Ravi's hands all up and down her naked back, to be all warm in bed somewhere, and feel his weight on top of her. She hasn't had a bite to eat, and there's all this food just waiting there: saliva gushing in her mouth, she feels her stomach grumbling. But the whistle stops outside the door, which opens with a gust of wind: the candle flames are blown about, so the shadows dance around the room as wildly as a dizzy spell. Tamding's standing in the door, and for a moment she must blink her eyes; she knows it's him but still it's like a grizzly bear has walked inside. The wind still blows the lights about, and she's not sure that she's seeing right: his shoulders are all broad and square, his chest is tapered to a V, he's covered with a golden fur, his penis rigid in his hand.

She's startled by the size of him, and blinks again to clear her eyes; he's wearing some new awful coat: a padded shouldered furry thing he's bought because of all the snow; his "penis" is a foot-long flashlight, held abruptly at his side.

"*I'm sorry, Doctor-ji,*" he says, "*but Sushila needs you right away.*"

# The Miracle

The day shift left two pregnant women flat out lying on their backs, and Sushila just assumes that all their laboring is going right. She's got some other things to do, so she lets the pregnant women wait—their sisters and their mothers there to squat and keep them company. The labor beds are wooden planks with inch-thick pads to soften things, with spaces cut between the legs, and poles to hang their callused feet. Sushila is in charge tonight, this long shift lasts from eight to eight, with Tamding and a nurse's aide, all glad now for the early snow: the workload drops so drastically. It shouldn't take these mothers long to push their brand-new babies out; they've both had lots of kids before, which makes things go much easier. If things go well, perhaps she'll get a couple hours' sleep tonight.

She walks across the courtyard, in the path that's beaten through the snow; the stars are out so bright she doesn't need a torch to see the way. She stomps into the duty room to get the snow off her boots; Tamding's sitting by the stove, and Padma's got her knitting out, working on another sock. There are just two patients left besides the women in the birthing room; she knows she should get back to them, to listen to their fetal hearts. But instead she asks that Padma go, so she herself can see the little one: the girl who's got the broken head whose brain she saw two nights ago when Doctor Mary saved her life.

With the duty book beneath her arm she stomps out in the snow again, noticing how cold it is, with the sky as clear as chicken broth: the fat and foam skimmed off the top. The children's ward is not too far, just fifteen yards across the way; she's careful walking in the snow because she knows how clumsy she can be. She thinks about the first week Doctor Mary came to work with them: made Sushila far more nervous than Doctor Vikram ever did. Doctor Vikram had his ways, had taught her everything she knows; he taught her how to be a nurse: she'd only been an aide before. Then suddenly he's leaving, saying someone else will take his place: a doctor coming from the States who's trained in every specialty. He says this just before he leaves, and then this woman wanders in, asking where would Vikram be, that he's supposed to teach her things. And when she learned he'd gone away, she almost turned around to leave; but a family brought a baby in that Doctor Mary tried to save. The baby lingered for a week, the Doctor hovering about—she made the staff so nervous since they couldn't get her orders straight. These babies come in all the time, so often past the point of hope; Doctor Vikram only tried if it was something obvious. The families have no money and refuse to go to Chandigarh; Vikram said it's better not to waste the little that they have. But this doctor ordered chest X-rays and medicines they didn't have; asked for things this family couldn't pay for in a hundred years. She wanted them to run and call a helicopter ambulance; wondered could they take this blood down to the nearest microlab. These villagers think Chandigarh is farther than the moon and stars; would never leave the valley even if they could afford the ride. Rambha finally sent them home before they wasted more supplies: a heart defect or rare disease that even Vikram could do nothing for. Rambha told the doctor that the baby's father changed his mind; they took the late-night bus down to the hospital in Chandigarh. But they really made the long walk home, a gasping bundle in their arms; some village near the pass where they're more used to watching babies die.

Now Sushila's reaching for the door into the children's ward, when she hears the sound that Padma makes when she's calling for her urgently. It's a high-pitched sound that's not a scream, but melodious and very loud: a system used in villages where people don't have telephones. Sushila takes a few steps back, some meters out into the yard; Padma's just a little thing: she's up there on the second floor, her head out of a window just outside the tiny birthing room.

"They're coming! Both of them!" she laughs, then quickly pops her head inside.

Sushila's pulse picks up because she knows that sometimes things go wrong, and two at once is one too much: there's only one nurse on at night. She calls across to Tamding, who's still sitting in the duty room: *Go and start the generator, make some electricity*. She climbs the stairs one at a time, there's no sense getting all worn out; she's glad that Padma's on with her: there's laughter from the birthing room. Padma has a pretty face, with eyes that sparkle when she smiles: an aide who finds the stressful things the easiest to laugh about.

"Heeehooo!" comes from the birthing room: it's Padma's call for her to rush; Sushila hurries toward the dual screams of labor pains. She passes husbands in the hall, bumping into both of them; there isn't any light to see, the power hasn't come on yet.

In the birthing room the lamps cast out the golden light of kerosene, and in the corner there's a tin of heating coal that's glowing red. The red's the color she has seen on throats of little hummingbirds; the lamplight yellow fills the room like sunshine through a hurricane. So when Sushila pushes through the door it's like another world: for just a flash she feels the premonition of a miracle. The light is so ethereal, a reddish, golden yellow hue; the women are both laboring: their crying is continuous. The women are still on their backs, their feet up in the stirrup loops; Padma's standing on a box, counting fetal heartbeats through a metal cone pressed to her ear. The moms' two perinea are both naked, staring at the room; Sushila sees one mother's baby's curly head about to crown.

Padma has things all set up, so Sushila grabs a sterile gown, then stretches on a pair of gloves—she has to place a hand because the head is coming much too fast. She presses on the perineum, waiting for the wave to pass, then with her hands she stretches things, trying to prevent a tear. She knows she won't have time to sew this mother back up nice and neat, because from where she stands she sees the other mother pushing now. The one she's with lets out a scream, contracting stronger than before; she looks up at this mother's face: a grimace and distended veins; for all she's worth, the mother pushes till the baby's head pops out. Padma's got the suction ready, slides it in the baby's mouth; Sushila feels the baby turn, its body in the birth canal. She glances at the other mother screaming two yards to her right, she's horrified to see the second baby's feet are coming first. She knows there's nothing she can do until she gets this first one out, and it feels as if the shoulder's stuck: she has to fit a finger in and hook it round the baby's arm. She's praying in her head to Jesus, asking him to intervene; she hears the rumbling sputter of the generator kicking in. Suddenly the lights come on, so bright it seems unnatural; it's like they're suddenly exposed, she's standing there without her clothes. She's shrunk to half her normal size, as if she were a six-year-old; she wishes someone else were here to take responsibility.

The shoulder really isn't stuck, just needs some gentle traction down; a towel wrapped around the head, the shoulder slides out as it should. Sushila's fighting panic, now this baby's coming out just fine; but the other mother's screaming still, and the legs are out up to the butt. Padma's still beside her, doesn't know yet what is going wrong; she lets a laughing squeal out when she sees this first one's genitals.

"A boy!" she screams, and suddenly the lucky ones are all around, laughing getting in the way; the mother's got a beaming smile because she's finally made a little male: now she has a son to light the pyre at her funeral. The healthy baby slithers out to Sushila's trembling arms; she snaps two clamps around the cord, then cuts and hands the baby off.

"Padma! Get the doctor quick!" and she brushes past the mother's knees, snapping off her bloody gloves, lets them drop but doesn't bother looking for another pair. She pulls the curtain all around the second mother laboring, so that the laughing family cannot see this woman's tragedy. She knows she should put on new gloves, but there isn't any time to spare, because when a baby comes out wrong the cord gets pressed on by the skull. This baby isn't getting any oxygen up to the brain; she's got to get the baby out, or watch it slowly suffocate. The mother's still a maniac, she's bearing down with all her strength; Sushila reaches naked fingers up inside to feel the head. It's still up in the uterus because the cervix hasn't reached complete: the head is trapped inside the mother's not-yet-ready uterus. The mother gives another push, and manages the shoulders out; Sushila still hears Padma laughing, celebrating it's a boy.

"Padma! Get the doctor now!"

Padma peeks inside the curtain, gleeful look still on her face: what she sees is just the baby's body hanging from the neck, its head still swallowed up inside, its skin a mottled purple-blue. Sushila looks at her and sees that Padma finally understands; suddenly the aide is gone, her footsteps running down the hall, she's calling out for Tamding's help. The party going on next door is just a curtain width away; Sushila's horrified by such an awful incongruity. She is trying to get a finger in, to slide it in the baby's mouth, to try to pull the little chin in tight against the baby's chest. She is fighting with herself because her instinct is to tug and pull; she knows that this won't help but can't think what else she's supposed to do. Her hands are trembling badly and her sense of time is slowing down; she knows the baby's going to die: won't be a miracle this time.

The baby's body has gone limp, and under all the mucous slime the skin's a pretty shade of beige, like porcelain set out to tan: a broken piece of pottery. She'd like to get down on her knees and pray in Lord-God-Jesus' name; she doesn't know what else to do, and maybe it would keep her thoughts from going where she knows they will. She's listening to several things: the mother with her healthy son, his crying out with gusty wails, the laughing of the relatives. But this mom is still laboring, her womb still traps her baby's head; she screams each time her womb contracts; the head's the baby's biggest part. And Sushila can't glance up because it's now been much too long a time: can't look between the mother's knees and tell her that her baby died.

# The Moment

Mary's boots don't have much grip, so she's careful on the icy steps: God knows what she's going to find upstairs in the delivery room. Tamding almost never runs to call her when the nurses ask, and he's never had to find her when she's dining in a restaurant. So Mary's heart is pounding from her run across the frozen yard, pounding with the sense that this disaster must be all her fault. She never should have slept so long; she should have come and done her rounds; the nurses are all nice but she knows that she can't rely on them. She's moving very quickly but it's taking years to climb the stairs; she hears each piston turning as the generator rumbles on. The stairs are dark and treacherous since no one shoveled off the snow; the night is clear and numbs her cheeks—her coat's back in the restaurant. She imagines she could slip and fall, go sliding backward down the stairs; could break her neck just like that snotty British kid the other day. She'd forgotten all about the boy, now worries what's become of him; the ambulance would have arrived sometime while she was fast asleep. *But what about the ice and snow? Could they have made it up this far? What if someone slipped while they were taking him across the yard?* She's worried that she tied him wrong, his head not strapped down tight enough; she should have told the nurse to pack his X-rays in an envelope.

At last she tops the stairs and grabs the door into the OB ward: it's roughly hewn from hand-sawed planks, the bottom scrapes across the floor. It's so bright in the room that Mary has to squint and shield her eyes—the ceiling slopes down steeply so she ducks her head to get inside. The lights are charged with power from the generator in the shed; usually she sees this room in barely twenty watts of light. It should be full of mothers with their newborn babies sucking breast; family members at their feet and everybody gossiping. But the room is bright and empty, Rambha must have sent the women home: *but did she check their babies' hips? the moms' episiotomies?* It smells of disinfectant and that funny odor babies make: the musty sweet and sour of meconium and mother's milk. It smells of dust and woolen clothes, the ghost of spicy rice and dal; she hears a healthy baby cry come wailing from the birthing room. She notes the proud voice of a dad, concludes the baby must be male: they act as if a baby boy's some kind of blessed miracle. If this baby cries so loud there can't be too much wrong with it—she's rushing through the list of other reasons they might call her for. The mother could be hemorrhaging or seizing with eclampsia; she could have torn so badly that the nurse needs help repairing her. But what's coming through the labor door is joyous celebration noise: perhaps the nurse had just been scared, the emergency is over now. So she stops outside the second door, doesn't want to open it; thinks about the dinner she and Ravi were about to share. Still she's gasping hard for breath, the long run from the restaurant; mortified with guilt and shame at having made them look for her.

Even if it's all for naught, she acted irresponsibly: If someone died while she was gone she knows she'd always blame herself.

She let a man seduce her from her duty to the hospital; let herself believe the world does not always depend on her. But she finally had a touch of luck: she saved that little three-year-old; she went to bed for two full days and the world did not come crashing down. She's been so lonely all this time, the nurses haven't warmed to her; how could she refuse the chance to sit with someone comfortable? She hasn't eaten for two days, the food tonight looked wonderful: the first real appetite she's had since Richard crashed his bicycle. Maybe she thought it was time for Fate to cast a smile on her; she's tired of feeling numb and cold: like winter since her husband died. It's probably all for the best that Tamding called her when he did; how would she have dealt with all these feelings welling up within? She's totally confused about what happened in the restaurant: Ravi is a sweetheart, and poor Amod is a basket case. She doesn't ever want to be attracted to another man; she wants her love for Richard to remain the everlasting kind.

Her breathing has slowed down and so she pushes on this second door: to let the nurse know that she's here, discover what had scared them so. The lights inside are glaring bright, the baby's in the father's arms: he's strutting with the child he hopes will feed him thirty years from now. The mom is lying back in bed, her sister gently strokes her hair; she's sweaty-pale-exhausted like she gave birth to a tourist bus. The aide has left the bloody sheets, the dirty tray of instruments: the mother's feet still dangle in the stirrups clamped onto the bed. It all looks so damn normal that she wonders why they called for her: the nurses each have seen at least two hundred such deliveries. She doesn't know who's on tonight, which nurse cried out so urgently—maybe it was Chidda who is not yet dry behind the ears. Padma peaks out from behind the curtain round the second bed; the expression on her face tells Mary something's more than serious.

*"Doctor-ji,"* is all she says, and Mary's only more confused: *What could be so awful with the mom and baby doing well?* Everything slows down as Mary's mind attempts to grasp the scene: one moment everything is fine, the next her heart has disappeared. Her fingers touch the curtain that is drawn around the second bed: its coarsely woven flowered print contrasting with the sight of blood. Just before she pulls it back to see what they had called her for, a scream tears from behind the curtain, yanks the breath from Mary's lungs. She's heard this very sound before, a year ago in Baltimore: it filled the street where she knelt down beside a crumpled bicycle. Haunted by this awful sound at night when Tamding doesn't call, she knows exactly what it means the instant that it rings her ears. She slips behind the curtain to find Sushila trembling; she's in between the widespread legs of a second mom delivering. Mary has to shut down all her human sensitivity—slam the door shut on the mortal grief exploding in her brain. No matter what her feelings are, she has to be the doctor now; Mary's got to focus on this tragedy in front of her. She asks how long it's been this way, the baby obviously dead; she doesn't put on gloves or gown, just takes her place between the legs. She asks what Sushila's done to try to get the baby out; requests that Padma move the other family to another room.

"Five milligrams of morphine. Two milligrams diazepam. I need a pair of sterile gloves and another tray of instruments."

She doesn't want to notice that Sushila's eyes are spilling tears; she wants to send this mother quickly off to never-never land. For just the shortest moment Mary contemplates her heinous crime; she's done what she has always feared: through negligence she killed someone. She shouldn't have been off where Tamding had to run and search for her; she should have left here months ago, forced Vikram to come back again. She'd like a little morphine too, to dull what she is feeling now: roll up her sleeve and find a vein, then push a fatal overdose. She knows what she's supposed to do, she's read the chapter twenty times: she's looking through the sterile tray for scissors that can cut through bone. She has to save the mother now, or hang two lives around her neck; she watches as her fingers search through rows of shiny instruments. They linger on the ring clamps that once helped her save a woman's life; she's had to ask the nurses more than once to always keep them close. She looks up at Sushila so their eyes meet momentarily; she cannot find the voice to tell her: *Thank you for remembering.*

# The Fix

Antone's thinking this is not the best idea he's ever had—if he had stopped to think it through he'd still be somewhere safe and warm. But he thought that he had fuel enough to get the jeep over the pass; that he could coast back into town and take the bus to Chandigarh. If he'd had time he would have siphoned petrol from some idle truck; Koksar, though, was empty but for Meena's nasty hissy fit. He didn't plan on Meena being such a bitch all set to go, making such a bloody scene so that he had no choice then but to get back in the jeep and leave. It's starting to get late now and the wind is blowing through his jeans, he's glad about his big black boots: the snow is halfway to his knees. He didn't think that it might snow, or that it should come down so fast; he would have made it if he hadn't had to drive through blowing drifts, with all that shifting down the gears and caution going round the curves. He's thinking it's a mile or so of climbing to the very top, and he'd like to cut the switchbacks, which would knock the distance down by half. But even this is much

too steep: he's breathless from the altitude, he's taking little baby
steps at almost thirteen thousand feet. He's wishing that he didn't
leave his sleeping bag with what's-his-name: the whining Brit
tied to the board, so spoiled he couldn't wipe his nose. The Brit
is warm and dry right now, with Meena serving rice and dal,
while Antone's in the freezing cold: his leather jacket's all he's got,
besides his lacquered box of stuff.

The storm had moved in from the south, creeping up the valley
floor, settling on top of the pass so that it still seemed nice below.
But as the jeep climbed farther up, the thinner air was thick with
snow: a wind whipped straight in Antone's face and stung his
frozen ears and nose. Now he's huddled down into his jacket
with the zipper pulled up to his chin, and before he left the jeep
he rummaged through the junk strewn in the back. There he
found a greasy cap, a single dirty cotton sock; he's got it on his
right hand as a glove to keep his fingers warm. He wipes the sock
across his face to get the ice out of his beard; he's wondering how
cold it is—his toes and feet are numb again. He covers up his
nose and mouth, and breathes into this dirty sock, so that the
warm air from his chest can help revitalize his face. A tingle blossoms on his nose and spreads across his ravaged cheeks: a biting,
burning feeling that brings tears into his squinting eyes. He isn't
used to exercise, he isn't used to feeling pain, and it's now been
several hours since he's had a decent needle fix. Why didn't he
prepare one back before he left his gasless jeep? Here he couldn't
light a joint, much less prepare a clean syringe. With the visibil-
ity so poor he sees no shelter from the wind; he only sees what's
on the road, the ten feet out in front of him.

He's finally trying to make a plan, to turn the wheels round
in his head; it's feeling more and more like work instead of just a

kidnapping. He thought this would be easy, all he had to do was grab the kid, put him where they wouldn't look, then slide down into Chandigarh and phone them at the embassy. He wasn't going to ask for much—a couple thousand lakh—so they wouldn't hesitate while calculating what the boy was worth.

And now he's stuck without his jeep, outside at thirteen thousand feet—he hasn't slept since yesterday, and it's a three days' walk down into town. The air is cold and dry; it hurts his throat and chest when he inhales; each step he takes feels like he's had to sprint about a quarter mile. He thinks about just turning back, with Koksar so much closer here; he knows this is the safer thing, but cannot face the thought of being stuck there through the winter months, always within spitting range of a woman who now hates his guts. Suddenly the wind lets up, his face stops stinging quite so much; something flashes black and fast out past the corner of his eye. He stops and looks from side to side; there isn't anything to see, just whirling bits of ice and snow, the gray north face of boulders still protected from the biting wind. His jeep is far behind him, swallowed up inside this howling storm; his footprints even disappear not more than twenty feet behind. The black thing flashes past again, somewhere off and to the right, but when he turns there's nothing there, just white and little bits of rock.

The wind picks up again, so when he turns to start back up the road the ice sticks in his beard once more. He's glad the road is obvious, cut level to the steep incline; he doesn't have to look too far ahead to see he isn't lost. He's thinking of a place to rest, to find a spot out of the wind, and he wonders if they might be there, the men who run the chai shops near the summit of the pass. Their tables sit on terraces, with views clear down to Chandigarh, and they trade on all the tourists who bus up here just to see the snow. Punjabis come with turbans on, Bengalis eating much too loud, all arguing about the price of chai up at this altitude. But the buses won't be running now, six months before they'll plow again—there's little hope he'll find more than a shack to hide inside tonight. A shack would be a blessing since he's feeling he could use a fix: a needle and a cup of tea; a nap to get his head on straight. He should have fixed one in the jeep but thought the pass was not so far; his feet and hands and nose are numb: long hours he's been walking now.

He wants to figure out a plan then let his brain rest for a while, but nothing seems too obvious now that he doesn't have a car. He's broke, and all he's got to sell is what's left in his lacquered box: enough that he could deal some bags for bus fare down to Chandigarh. He wonders why he didn't think before about a place to stay; it might take days to get the cash, he'll have to pay his rent somehow. And phoning up the embassy's like talking to the bloody cops; they'll try some kind of hero stuff, machine guns and big helicopters loudly whirling overhead, breaking down his hotel door, traced right through the telephone. He's never tried this kind of thing, never more than corner stuff: dime bags and small bricks of hash, negotiating sales in smoky dhabas with the music loud. He sees the black thing once again, another flicker to his right, and he turns to try to catch it but it's disappeared into the clouds.

For a moment he is wondering if the light has gotten brighter, and he takes his eyes from off the snow and looks above his head. The snow's still falling but the wind has lightened up a little, and the clouds above aren't half as dark and threatening as they were before. He watches as the clouds part like the curtains pulled across a stage, and for a fraction of a second he sees the shadowed outline of the sun. For that instant it's just like he's had a needle stuck into his arm, the brightness hurts his eyes, but then the rush comes washing over him. Maybe things are going to change, perhaps the weather's going to clear; all he needs to get things straight is to find a place out of the wind and fix up something for a vein. He's hungry but he's sure that this will pass once he has had some stuff, and then the black thing's there again, this time it's right before his eyes. A raven flying through the clouds comes landing right in front of him; it shakes the snow from folding wings a few feet farther up the road. The raven turns to him and caws, starts bleating like a nervous sheep; its head is bobbing up and down, and the brightness of the thinning clouds turns dark like switching off electric lights. He turns back to the sun but it's been covered thick with ugly clouds, as angry as he's ever seen: like thunderheads although he's not heard thunder in a long, long time.

The fantasy he's having now is sitting on a Goan beach, he's listening to wind and waves, and though he's never liked the sun, he's sitting in a sunny chaise and someone's bringing him a beer. The wind is coming from the south, it's full of warmth and moisture now; the waves make rhythmic lazy sounds, not like a driven stormy crash, but like they're drunk and stumbling through a hot and sunny afternoon. The beer comes in a glass, and as he sips it he squints at the beach, the sun is bright and glaring, shining off the waves and clean white sand. It hurts to look across the beach even with sunglasses on; he puts the beer up to his forehead, to shield his eyes and cool his skin. The chill it gives him sends a little shiver up and down his spine so that the warming breeze feels even nicer wrapped all over him. This is all so nice he wonders what to add next to the scene, and though he's never cared for sex, he gets a thrill from watching it. So a couple comes walking along, the waves reach up and splash their feet—they're hardly wearing anything: a bit of string around her waist. He makes her the aggressive one, her hand slides in her partner's pants; in no time they are in the sand and she's on top and straddling. He's looking at her untanned buttocks jiggle as she gallops on, thinking this is kind of tame, maybe he should add some more. So another man walks up the beach, already naked and erect; he joins them in a three-way Antone's not quite sure could work. He's never cared for intercourse, with so much risk of STDs; relationships are too much work, and he doesn't like to pay for it. But he watches as they roll about, and the waves keep splashing all around, and every time one crests the sun glares off it right into his eyes. He's squinting even harder now; his glass of beer is warming up; instead of squawking seagulls he sees ravens flying overhead. A wave crests and he's blinded by the glare off of the froth and foam, and when his eyes adjust again he sees the ravens in the sand, now clustered round the triangle and pecking them from time to time. The blinding glare has given him a headache right between the eyes, and his beer has gotten so warm that he doesn't want it anymore. The waves are coming faster so the glare is almost constant; it makes him so uncomfortable he turns to face the other way.

When he looks again it's not the sun but snow that's blinding him, and he's tripped and fallen in a drift so deep he has to thrash about, struggle to regain his feet. He stands up from his dream and tries to make sure he's on solid ground; he stomps his boots to shake the stubborn blood back down into his toes. From all around the squawk of ravens beats against his frostbit ears; he brushes off his senseless face with the frozen sock around his hand. He doesn't feel it cut his nose, but sees the blood drip in the snow; the wind is blowing twice as strong; the distance he can see is down to less than half a dozen yards. The ravens' cawing frightens him—it's muffled by the howling wind; he can't think what they're doing up here shouting at him in a storm. He looks around to catch a glimpse of where the birds are squawking from, but only if he squints does he imagine something flying by.

He steps out of the drift, which isn't easy with his feet so numb; he's pretty sure he's on the road because the ground is solid underfoot. He wonders if he's near the top, because the climbing doesn't feel so steep; above the sound of wind and ravens suddenly he hears a voice. It isn't clear at first, just a vague mumbling noise from far away, but if he's near the pass the chai shops should be somewhere to the right. He stops to listen harder, thinking that he might be saved at last; it's not just one but several voices rushing at him in the wind. He takes a few steps forward, then tries crying out for someone's help, but the wind is blasting in his face so when he opens up his mouth the words get forced back in and down his throat. He takes a few more steps, then stops, afraid of going off the road; what if it's not real people but a trick played by this nasty storm?

He knows if he goes off the road, he'll never get it back again, and then he would be doubly lost and might as well curl up and die. But the voices come through clear sometimes; he should be on the pass by now; he thinks he'll walk a few more steps and maybe he will see something. Sure enough the voices get much clearer farther to the right, and though he still can't see a thing, he's certain that he's right this time; he can almost make out certain words of Kullui the voices speak. He can't be more than minutes from a dry shack and a cup of tea; but suddenly his body starts to go through heroin withdrawal. He's been so long without a fix, his every muscle throbs and burns; he needs to puke and take a shit; a shiver grabs him by the neck. He almost can't move forward even though he knows he needs to rush; it's hard to move his aching legs through all the snow and jagged rocks. But the voices keep urging him on; he knows they can't be very far; even when he's certain that he cannot take another step, he thinks he sees a shack ahead, right where the clouds hide everything.

He's thinking he's made a mistake, he never should have left the road—the voices disappear again, and the shack he'd swear he saw is gone. He wonders if it's not too late to turn around and find the road, but the wind is howling so hard that his tracks were covered instantly. He's about to go back anyway, when the voices come back clear again; he turns toward them and this time he is certain that it's really there. It's a stone hut with a wooden door, a stove pipe sticking through the wall; someone must be there inside, the smoke spills horizontally. He's feeling like he's going to die; he hasn't felt his face in hours; but not ten yards away there's someone sitting cozy by the fire. The voices are in Kullui: he doesn't understand a word; sometimes there's a laugh or two, and he wonders why they're up here still. The moment that he puts a frozen hand up to the wooden door, the voices stop their chattering; he has to lean his shoulder on the door to make it open up.

Inside the hut it's dark because the window has been boarded shut; he can't see anything, just feels the nausea of drug withdrawal. He senses that the shack is crowded, though the men aren't making noise; they seem to move out of his way; he stumbles on an empty bench. He tries to get his rucksack off, to get into his lacquered box; he's cursing at the frozen knot, his fingers like an elephant's. All of this he's doing blind inside the darkness of the shack, the only light comes from the crack beneath the ill-fit wooden door. He carefully pries off the lid, afraid that everything might spill, so mad to get a fix he doesn't care if everybody knows. It's quiet in the room, with just the sound of wind and shuffling feet; he's focused only on his task: to get this fucking candle lit. The lighter that he's used for years is cold and thick inside his hand; his thumb can't turn the flint wheel with the force it needs to make a spark. Then someone else lights up a match, and he doesn't bother to look up, just holds the shaking candle out. It takes another minute, but he manages a full syringe, and it doesn't take him long to quickly find and slide it in a vein: a fat one on his left hand that he's saved for years for times like this.

The rush does not come all at once, perhaps because his arm's so cold; he closes up his eyes to wait, certain that the pain will leave. He's listening to shuffling feet, to bodies shifting nervously, to a funny itchy-scratchy noise, to an airy sound like flapping wings. Above all this the wind howls through the slated roof and rough-hewn walls; someone tries to clear his throat, which makes a bird-like cawing sound. His rush is creeping slowly on: at last the pain turns wonderful; he opens up his eyes to see who's making all that awful noise. The candle is the only light, he holds it up to fill the room; his eyes are trying to adjust: it's dark and he's not seeing right. For a single moment Antone's brain achieves an equilibrium: the fix has calmed his drug withdrawal, but hasn't reached its pinnacle. While his mind is vaguely clear, he looks around the tiny shack; all he sees are dirt and boards and snow blown in beneath the door. And as his rush finally arrives, he sees that no one else is there: perhaps an angel sent by God had helped him fix his heroin.

# The Bottle

The dope that Phillip smoked was good, and the high seems to go on and on—he's staring at the ceiling while he listens to men playing cards. The time seems strange when he's so high, it's almost like he sees it move, and since that's all there is to do he's watching it float round the room. It doesn't take too long before the hunger pains begin to kick, and he thinks about what he could eat, perhaps a couple bags of chips or snack cakes dressed in plastic wrap. But time starts getting on his nerves; he forgets that he was scared before; he calls out for something to eat: *For God's sake, can't somebody hear?*

"Hey! I'm hungry! Someone get some food for me!"

After he has yelled awhile, the door squeaks on a rusty hinge; it swings in just an inch or two, then quickly closes up again.

"Jesus fucking Christ, you guys! Have a little sympathy!" But he only hears the shuffling cards, so he yells until his voice gives out. And then, of course, his mouth is dry, he hasn't had a drink in years, which only makes him realize how bad he has to pee again. There is nothing he can do about it, lying strapped onto his board, except to shift his butt around and clamp his penis with his hand. It is cold inside the little room; he's glad he has the sleeping bag; the only window he can see is two feet up above the bed. The view is just a patch of sky, all gray with blowing ice and snow, with every now and then a flash of raven battling the wind.

When he wakes he has to orient, to figure out what place he's in; *home* is what he thinks at first, but the wind there doesn't howl like this. The fact he cannot move his head brings back the nightmare fast enough: he's still strapped to a wooden board and waiting for an ambulance. The room has changed from gray to black, he must have slept for several hours—the high he hid in earlier is gone because he's scared again. The room is dank and cold, the only sound outside is blowing wind; inside there's just a whistling breath, the cardplayers have gone to bed. A thrill of fear spreads up his spine from the extra set of breathing sounds. Who else is in the room, about to stab his heart or strangle him? His breath held tight inside his chest, he concentrates his aural sense: a squeak comes somewhere from his right, something moves down by his feet. His free arm raises to his head, attempting to protect himself. It must have been a rat, but then it makes a very non-rat noise: the sound of spoken Kullui, a muffled female voice he recognizes as the battered girl's. The words don't make a lick of sense, but the tone is full of angry pain, like she's screaming dark obscenities from a coffin buried under him.

Meena's on the floor beside him, talking in her fitful sleep; it's dark and quiet and Phillip wants to die and get it over with. *Where the hell is Koksar?* The name does not ring any bells. The only clues so far have been the mountaintops and building tops and snow and ice and raven wings. It's cold and hard to catch a breath; the sleeping bag's obscenely rank; he's hungry, scared, and thirsty and he really, really has to pee. Meena's not too far away, he reaches out and nudges her; he'll wake her up to let her know she's not a very gracious host.

"Excuse me," he says quietly, then louder when she doesn't move. Because she's lying on the floor, he's only guessing where she is; her shoulder is his target but his hand shakes one of Meena's breasts.

"Excuse me, but I have to pee," and suddenly she's off the floor, fists are flailing violently, curses ringing in his ears. Every word drips hate and bile, she doesn't pull a single punch; she smacks his wounded shoulder till his agony is evident. The room fills with his cry of pain, her curses finally peter out; she steps away until her back is pressed against the wall.

"I'm sorry," he says urgently, "I was only trying to wake you up."

Her angry breathing slows as she stands motionless beside the door; the only light comes from the moon that's filtered through the windowpane. It's mostly shining on the bed, so the light he sees her by is dim; he only sees her head and shoulder from his board across the room. She speaks again, this time her voice has dropped about an octave, her tone is drawn out flat and gray as some old unwashed tablecloth. She takes two steps across the room and stands there towering over him, staring down into his face, her own face scraped and filled with rage. The words she says don't mean a thing, but her tone of voice is threatening.

"I'm sorry," he tells her again, "but I've been holding it since yesterday."

★     ★     ★

The bottle that she finds for him originally held alcohol, and it still holds half an inch or so of something in the bottom. The smell makes Phillip's stomach sick, reminding him of Antone's drink; the bottleneck is much too small: he has to ask for something else. She finally brings a glass that's hardly bigger than a coffee cup; he has to have her turn around, and he's only got one hand to use, so he holds the glass between his thighs and tries to let his bladder down. At last he's got it coming out, but the glass is such a little thing—he's scared he'll overflow the rim, and of course it's like the dam has burst. To stop the flow he has to pinch, his sphincter muscle's tired out; he can't let go to test the depth, to tell if it is full or not. Mortified, he has to ask the girl to turn around and help: to reach her awful hands inside and carefully remove the glass. And though he hasn't spilled a drop, the smell of urine fills the room; it's suddenly ten years before: transformed into a boy of eight. He'd wake to smell the soaking sheets, they took him to see specialists; they tried the buzzers and alarms, not drinking after dinnertime. His parents told his nanny she should check him every night at two, to change things if he wet again, the plastic sheet made so much noise. He slept in just pajama tops, the bottoms cut up into rags; his nanny stated loudly that she wouldn't wash them anymore. He'd wake up to the crinkling sheets, to the bad smell of his nanny's breath, to the damp cold of his soaking bed, to the feeling of her warm dry hands down groping in between his legs. She'd tell him he's a lazy shit, he feared her nightly rough routine; she'd cuff him hard to wake him up, but there was something else embarrassing. He knew it must be sick and wrong, and his hatred for her was intense, but he liked it when her callused hands would brush against his private parts.

Now this wretched girl is reaching in to take the glass away; he's looking up to see her face, to check out what expression's

there. In the darkness he can't see much with the moonlight
shining from behind; he mostly sees stray wisps of hair just backlit on one side of her. Her touch is sure and gentle, and she looks
as if she doesn't care; she holds the glass up to the light, the liquor
bottle next to it. The liquids look identical, the moonlight casts a
golden hue; she smiles while concentrating as she pours the urine
through the bottle's hole. The spilling noise makes his need
worse, he has to hold his penis clamped; at last she gives him back
the glass, placing it between his legs. It takes three times to empty
him, to get the bottle almost full; Meena looks at him and smiles:
her expressive face is satisfied. The cork squeaks on the bottle top,
and Phillip's feeling such relief not just because his bladder's dry,
but because he managed to stay small. He's quick to cover up
again, sleeping bag pulled to his nose; Meena leaves the room to
put the bottle back where it belongs. He hears the wooden door
pulled shut, she's lying back down on the floor, and his free hand
has the bag held tight in defense not just from the cold.

# The Embrace

A mod knows which room she's in, her candle makes the window glow, and he's standing closer than his normal caution would advise him to. But he's thinking of the other man, who tried to dine with her tonight, afraid he might be with her now that she's come back from the hospital. An Indian in Western dress, his Kullui was rather stiff; Amod didn't know his name but recognized him as the man that Doctor Mary cut upon. Amod spoke to him a moment, once the doctor had gone running out; this stranger didn't catch the joke that Amod told in Kullu slang. So this man who was the doctor's guest is not from anywhere near here; the man stayed after the doctor left and finished off the food he'd served them, not just his but everything. Amod worries that this man's now sitting in the doctor's room, visiting so late after she ran to some emergency. Amod hates it when it snows because he doesn't like to leave a trail, and the windows all get frosted so it's difficult to see inside. Every time it starts to snow, the power goes out instantly, and days go by without even a hint of electricity. So even with the windows clear there isn't anything to see, the rooms lit up with lamps set low to save on precious kerosene. But the doctor's room is lit up like a temple on a holy day, though the window that he's looking through is nothing but a glowing haze, translucent as an icicle.

All he's seen so far is someone's shadow crossing toward the loo, and he can't get close enough to tell if it's just a radio he hears, or two people laughing quietly. He'd have to walk up to her door, or leave fresh prints across the snow to stand under her windowsill, and neither's what he wants to do; he'd rather watch here from the trees, or go hear what news Tamding has of the excitement that she's just been through. He wonders what they called her for, for Tamding to run breathlessly, to hear them start the generator—a certain sign of something wrong. Amod's feet are in the snow, he's standing out among the trees, hoping Doctor Mary sits alone next to the radio. He's carrying some tiffin tins because the doctor didn't eat; at first he thought he'd knock this time, and not just leave them by the door. He wants so bad to let her know that he's been looking out for her. What if this other man is there? What reason could he give for coming so late to her room alone? Perhaps he'll go see Tamding first, he's never very hard to find: unless the generator's on, he's sleeping by the tandoor stove.

Amod starts to walk away; he bends to grab a little snow to soothe the burning in his hand, when suddenly his foot breaks through the crust of ice that coats the snow. In a flash he's fallen on his face, the tins slide clattering about, and even though they're full of food the noise they make is rudely loud. He's glad that it's so late at night, with no one there to see him fall, but then he hears the doctor's door, her voice sounding a little scared.

"Who's there?" she says in English, then she translates into Kullui. *"Are you all right?"* she asks before he gets a chance to say his name.

*"It's only Amod, Doctor-ji,"* he tells her, wiping snow off of his face, *"From the dhaba. I'm fine. I just tripped in the snow."*

Amod stands and sees her pulling on her clumsy rubber boots; before she puts her coat on she starts scrambling toward him through the snow. To keep from falling down again, he reaches out to grab a branch—he grabs it with his burned hand so the pain shoots up and down his arm. If he had a second more he could have hidden any signs of pain, but she is right there next to him, asking if he is all right and forcing him to bare his palm. With his other hand he's brushing snow off of his heavy coat; he's looking round to find his tins, hoping she won't make a fuss.

"Oh Amod! That's a nasty burn. I forgot how bad you hurt yourself . . ." and she keeps on talking to him but her English comes out much too fast; it's then she looks and notices the tins all scattered in the snow: his offerings of curried goat, the saffroned rice and spicy dal. Even in the cold the smell is fresh and strong and wonderful.

"What a shame," she says. "You spilled all of your leftovers."

He knows, though, by her tone of voice, the wheels are turning in her head: she knows what he was doing, that it isn't just by accident he's walking by so late at night. She starts to gather up the tins, and he helps her with his one good hand. He thinks she tells him something like, "The crows will think they're at a feast," and then she says in Kullui, *"Come on, let's get your hand cleaned up."*

She takes him by the upper arm, turns him toward her open door, and the man who was her dinner guest is standing there without his shoes: a candle held up in his hand that's casting such a feeble light it doesn't help them see at all.

"Ravi, you remember Amod."

"Of course. From the dhaba."

The man puts out his hand to shake, and Amod's glad he

burned his left; it doesn't help that he's so short: he's barely to this
stranger's chin. Amod feels uncomfortable, intruding where he
doesn't fit; this man stands like he owns the place: the threshold
of the doctor's room.

"Amod, this is Ravi Varghese . . ." and that's all that Amod
understands, just something about villages and traveling from
Canada. The man lets go of Amod's hand, and Amod gives a little bow; Ravi does so in return: all confident and casual. The
doctor brings them both inside, she steps out of her rubber boots,
and suddenly she's disappeared to find her box of bandages.
Amod stands there in his coat, still stuck with bits of ice and
snow: his feet in rubber overshoes, a puddle forming under him.
The room looks different from inside, both cluttered up and dirt-
ier, with clothes and books strewn all about, and even with the
candles lit it's cave-like and uncomfortable: stiflingly hot because
the tandoor's burning in a rage.

*"Take your coat off,"* Ravi says to him, *"the fire's finally getting
hot."* Amod's not sure if he should, because the doctor didn't ask
him to; he's smelling something funny mixed with the wood
smoke from the leaky stove. He knows he won't be staying long,
that he may never be back in her room, so he's trying hard to take
it in, to remember what it's like inside. The only furniture she has
is the tandoor and two folding chairs, two wooden produce boxes
and a table with some dirty bowls. She's strung a line above the
stove, and from it hangs a couple socks, a skirt she wears on sunny
days, a bath towel, and some underwear. They're wasting so much
firewood by keeping it too warm inside; the funny smell he noticed is like food but not from India. Then on the table by the
door he sees a picture of himself—he's out before the dhaba with
a stranger standing much too close. He doesn't understand why
she should have his image under glass; the picture must be ten
years old, his hair was still completely black. No one's ever cared

enough to frame his photograph before—maybe this explains why Doctor Mary is so nice to him. This is totally confusing: what deep feelings for him does she have? He's always thought her friendship was some Western form of social grace. He hears the doctor in the back, in the bedroom he would love to see: What other pictures might she have? He wouldn't enter on a dare. But Ravi just goes right on in, taps lightly on the bedroom door, and speaks to her in English words that Amod doesn't understand.

On the tandoor there's a cookpot which is set off to the edge; Amod steps into the room though he still has his black galoshes on. He takes the lid off of the pot, and a little bit of smoke comes out; inside the pot is some strange form of food he's never seen before. It's noodles colored citrus orange; the smell is burning cheesy sweet; he pulls his good hand in his sleeve and puts the pot down on the floor. Suddenly the doctor screams, a jolly laughing startled cry; she's found the box of bandages, but her shout sounds just like *maksenchis!* The doctor rushes from her room, to Amod standing by the stove; she sees the pot down on the floor and bends to open up the lid. More smoke spills out into the room, the air thick from the leaky stove; Doctor Mary waves her hands, trying to fan the smoke around. Ravi tries to pick it up, but drops it because the handle's hot; he grabs a T-shirt from a chair to dump the pot out in the snow.

"I've ruined it," the doctor says, the bandage box still in her hand, and Amod feels against his face the cold air from the open door, refreshing from the smoke and heat of standing too near to the stove. Ravi comes back in the room, and leaves the wooden door ajar.

*"It's something from America,"* Ravi says to him in Kullui. *"I found it in the market. I think it's surplus from some climbing expedition. I thought she might enjoy it since it's been so long since she's been home."*

Ravi says something in English, and it must have been some kind of joke, because the doctor starts to laugh out loud, still waving at the smoky air. Her laugh becomes a little loud, as if she's had too much to drink; she is pawing through the bandages and spilling things onto the floor. He wonders what this stranger brought that's put her in this funny mood; he's never seen her laugh like this: she's bordering hysterical. She finds what she is looking for, a jar from deep inside the box, and she spreads a cream across his palm and wraps it in a stretchy gauze. She isn't acting like herself, she's lost her sense of dignity; it's like she's suddenly become a love-struck giggling teenage girl. He feels cheated of this intimacy, because the doctor's laughing at a joke made by some man she hardly knows, and for months now Amod's brought her food, but he's never made her laugh like this. He stands at last inside her room—how tenderly she holds his hand—yet all he wants to do is get away from here as fast he can.

"*Dhanjavad, Doctor-ji,*" he says, his head moving from side to side, expressing that he wants to leave, when suddenly her laughing stops. He glances at her long enough to see that she is looking at the tiffins in his other hand.

"*Dhanjavad* to you, *Amod-ji,*" and then she says in English things he doesn't really catch, though from the tone he understands: she's thanking him for being kind. Suddenly he's in her arms, she's giving him a tender hug. He isn't used to this at all, his face is pressed against her chest; he doesn't know how to respond, aware that they are not alone. And while he's wrapped up in her arms, the laughter goes out of the room. He feels instead her sadness and a shudder as she starts to cry.

# The Butcher

The next morning is sunny bright, the sky as crisp as salad greens, and Mary wakes up with the light much earlier than usual. She'd like to stay snug warm in bed and fall back into dreamless sleep; she'd like it if she could forget that awful birthing accident. But, if anything, she's more determined now than she has ever been to find a way to make up for her medical incompetence. She knows it wasn't all her fault: she can't be everywhere at once; even if she'd been right there, the baby would have come out wrong. It's never been her practice to check all the women laboring: the one thing that the nurses almost always take care of on their own. But if she had done an exam, she might have noticed something wrong; if only she had ultrasound she might have found out soon enough. But all of this is moot because there's just a single doctor here, and almost all the nurses have done dozens more deliveries. There isn't any ultrasound, and she couldn't read it if there were—she's trained in geriatrics, not in peri- and neonatal care. Her knowledge of deliveries has mostly come from Vikram's book; she's been dreading all along the day she'll have to deal with Caesar's ghost.

Climbing from her foam-block bed she does her morning rituals: splashes water on her face and scrubs the fuzzies off her teeth. Peeking through the window it's so bright out she can barely see; the sun glares off the windowpane, and she wonders just what time it is. She goes back to her bedroom with her feet cold on the concrete floor; she must be running late because her watch has lost a couple hours. Searching for clean clothes to wear, her shirts all smell of nervous sweat, her underwear is full of holes, her pants are stained with blood and filth. She'd gladly pay for washing help but doesn't know how she should ask: afraid she'll rub it in how much she's better off than all of them. But she's got to take care of herself: it isn't someone else's job; Amod bringing all that food is something she can't justify. How can she forgive herself for the way she acted late last night? Laughing too hard at a joke then crying like an idiot. She's got to get a better grip, stop taking everything so hard; she's got to stop resenting all the work the nurses ask of her.

She browses through her kitchen space, a cupboard made with a metal screen: a piece of bread that's green with mold, a paper sack of oatmeal. She's learned to throw her scraps outside to let the ravens fight it out; she takes the bread she let go bad to toss out as she goes to work. It's not until she gets outside that she thinks about the pot she burned; how nice it was of Ravi to have brought the box of macs and cheese. She sees the burned pot in the snow; the ravens haven't found it yet; they're busy eating something else, out underneath one of the trees. A dozen ravens scratch the ground; the snow's so bright it hurts her eyes; she holds the piece of moldy bread to block the ultraviolet light. For a moment they all turn and stare, the ravens fighting on the ground; she's holding something more to eat: the birds are quickly interested. She remembers Amod falling down, with his tiffins clattering around, the food spilled underneath the trees; that's what the birds are eating now. *Poor little man,* and she can't help but wonder what his kindness means; what made him bring her all that food, if not the goodness of his heart? Perhaps it's just a benefit for working as a volunteer; but she's sure they would have said something, the nurses would have let her know. His burned hand could be third degree, and she told him to come back today, to let her change the bandages: can't buy the cream she brought from home. Her hug last night embarrassed him: not culturally appropriate; but she felt so overwhelmed after she cut that tragic baby out.

The morning is so quiet, just the ravens scavenging for food, and she's wondering what day it is because she often loses track of time. Most days she hears the kids in school, but often there's a holiday, though no one seems to know what for: she asks but they just shake their heads. She loves the sound of crunching snow packed underneath her rubber boots; the way the snow clings to the trees, and that everything is white and blue: her breath comes out in steaming clouds. She follows in the path that has been beaten through the snow; she is thinking that it's Tuesday, since the hippie kid came Saturday: the night she did the surgery on the girl who'd fallen off the balcony. Mary wonders how he is, Prince Charming with his broken neck; she hopes they got him out okay, no trouble driving through the snow. She peeks into the children's ward, the windows steamed with breath and fog; the room is mostly empty beds, a sight she isn't used to yet.

The girl she did the burr holes on is sleeping in her mother's arms, her head still wrapped up in the gauze; Mary doesn't want to wake her: obviously doing fine. Mary walks across the clinic yard and wonders where the patients are; they're usually lined up by now, although they never form a line. It must just be the snow that's keeping all of them away, that no one wants to walk through half a foot of slush to get to town. But even still there should be some, if only just the folks from town; and the nurses should be somewhere near, so she walks up to the duty room. She smells the smoke that's coming from the rusty pipe stuck through the wall; the windows are all frosted so she can't see anyone inside. She stamps her feet, then leans her shoulder on the ill-fit wooden door; inside the staff is sound asleep: Sushila and the nurse's aide, with Tamding sitting by the stove shoving sticks of wood in through the lid. These three were all on late last night; Mary's suddenly confused; Tamding doesn't say a word, but smiles a sleepy pleasant smile.

*"What time is it?"* she tries to say, whispering in Kullui—she gets her point across by pointing at her clockless wrist. Tamding nods and checks his watch, a thing the size of Everest; he holds his fingers up for six, then wags his head they way they do. The day shift doesn't come till eight, the clinic doesn't start till nine; everything makes sense now: how still and quiet it has been. And now with three full hours to kill, she's nothing if not wide awake; she shakes her head like Tamding did and backs out quiet through the door. She could start doing rounds, but there are just her turbaned little girl, the two moms in the labor rooms, though only one well-baby check.

Hunger makes her stomach growl, the blue sky is so beautiful; she'd go back to her room and eat but she knows there's only oatmeal. She realizes then that there is nothing that she has to do: the first time since she's come here she has time that isn't occupied. For a moment she is at a loss: What else is there to do but work? Could try to write some letters home, which she hasn't done for several weeks, but she doesn't want to spoil her mood by writing about what's gone on. She could go back home and wash some clothes, scrub out the awful nervous stink, but she has to do it all by hand, and the water makes her fingers ache. She'll just go off for a walk, then see what town is like dressed up in snow; she takes three steps then turns around: tells Tamding where she's going to be.

Kali's in the courtyard, bounding toward her through the snow: clumps of ice caked in her fur, her tail the flocked bough of a tree. Mary whispers loudly to her, urging her on through the drifts, glad there's someone else awake, pleased that she'll have company. Kali almost knocks her down, and they wrestle momentarily; Mary's glad for mittens since she's sure the dog has parasites. Kali finally settles down, eager to go for a walk; Mary's thankful for her boots, the path is not too smoothly packed. The drifts are almost to her knees, the smell of smoke is in the air: the sweet scent of deodar wood, of people trying to stay warm. The hillsides are magnificent, the apple trees still have their leaves; their branches covered thick with ice, the sun is shining from behind, which gives them all a halo glow. Above the hills are mountain peaks like angels in some masterpiece: their wings at twenty thousand feet, the guardians above the town. The sky above the mountains is so blue it takes her breath away—the dust that blows up from the plains was scrubbed out by the clouds of snow.

She walks along an alleyway, the shops are all still closed up tight; the only sounds are ravens' caws and dogs barking from off a ways. The town looks better in the snow, the dusty streets are white and clean, just like her mother's living room: *The carpet's not for walking on!* But Mary takes some pleasure in a certain mild perversity that makes her want to walk across the snow where no one else has been. As a child she spelled out words with letters twice as big as elephants; she'd boldly state she loved some boy or words she wasn't supposed to say, because she knew no one would see but birds and people up in planes. She'd like to write something right now, but the alley's not a perfect place: it isn't wide enough, and someone's walked up through the middle part.

There's something that she'd like to write if only she can find the place; she's walking toward the market, where the buildings are two stories high, with business signs of painted tin in English and in Kullui. One sign reads *Best Place for the Freaks,* a lure to bring the hippies in; she thinks again about the boy she sent off on a plywood board: how scared he must have been to be so injured in so strange a place. She turns off of the alleyway which opens up onto the road—the only sign of life is an old butcher hanging up a goat. The carcass is skinned white and red, its head cut off and in a pile; when he's got it hanging up, the butcher offers her a smile, waves to her with bloody hands, she wangs back to him in return.

*"Namasté, Doctor-ji!"* he shouts, so happy that the sun is bright. The greeting takes her by surprise because she's never bought from him before, hasn't treated him for anything; and yet he knows she's *Doctor-ji* and not some tourist passing through. She wonders why this bloody butcher recognizes who she is; gossip from the nursing staff: *This doctor is incompetent.*

Kali's chasing ravens on the far side of a parking lot: it's empty but for snow because the buses can't get into town. The dog can't stand the ravens, the birds have been her nemeses; she's always chasing them but they are smarter than she'll ever be. Mary wonders at the birds, they're tricky and mischievous: there isn't any food around, they're only out to taunt the dog. And Kali's such a stupid beast, running out across the snow—the ravens stay just out of reach, a tail's length from jaws of death.

"Get 'em, Kali! Get 'em!" she cries, knowing Kali can't run fast; the snow up to the dog's chest, and yet she runs like she's gone crazy, angered by the ravens' cheekiness. Mary's heard they mate for life, like geese and other kinds of birds, and she wonders if it's really true; she's not convinced they aren't all males; they're not the least bit feminine. Kali finally settles down, too tired to chase them anymore, and half the lot of virgin snow is trampled from her running round.

Mary turns around again to look back at the brilliant town: the sun now shining on her back, her rubber boots deep in the snow. She is walking through the one half of the lot that Kali's not disturbed: the perfect place to stomp out words that no one else will ever read. But she can't think what she wants to write; perhaps she'll spell her husband's name, or draw a giant broken heart: FORGIVE ME, all in capitals. She starts the first line of the word, because she knows no one will see; but then a window opens in the room above the butcher's shop. Someone's head pops out to catch a deep breath of the morning air, and suddenly she feels too shy, caught playing in this virgin snow, her thoughts exposed to all the world.

# The Sadhu

Meena wakes before the boy, this stranger with the soft green eyes, who takes up more than half the bed, even on his skinny board. The sun is out this morning, she can see it on the mountaintops—she wonders as she looks outside if the snow will melt enough today so Antone can come back for her. But it isn't going to happen, once it snows the passes never melt; they're cut off from the outside world until the plows start up again in spring. Sometimes she really hates the snow, though other times it's beautiful; the mountains look much better dressed, and it's really just her life she hates. Why couldn't she be somewhere else, or this time have been born a man? She wonders what that would be like, having power over someone else: the way these men can order her, and do to her just what they want, anytime they get the urge.

Meena fastens up her pattu, puts a shawl around her shoulders, slips her feet into cheap rubber boots: galoshes made in Chandigarh, where it never really gets too cold. She has to get the fire going, then put some rice out for her god, then fetch some water from the stream and make the men their morning meal: the usual of rice and dal. In her room she has a piece of mirror, a shard of glass already old, so that the silver on the back is badly scratched and oxidized, so bad she barely sees herself: the scratches gouged into her cheek, the purple swelling underneath, her hair black as a raven's coat, pulled back to stay out of her way. Her face might have been beautiful, her eyes might have been full of fire, but she couldn't be less interested; in this cloudy shard of broken glass she's checking for infection in the damage that she knows is there.

She's very good at lighting fires, she's been doing it since she was four: back when she burned her hands so bad while caring for a two-year-old. The tandoor's in a raging blaze before she grabs the water cans; no one here would ever dream of helping her do anything. The day outside is so bright, for a moment she can barely see, and though the cans are empty, they are awkward for her five-foot frame. The snow is almost half a foot, the drifts are almost to her knees; her right arm still hurts from the last time she was thrown against a wall. Squinting, she heads for the stream, her eyes adjusting to the light; she drags her black galoshes as she looks up at the mountainsides. Today they are magnificent, like the gods that they're supposed to be; the new snow covers everything except the steep cliffs of the valley walls. The sun has not yet risen high enough to reach the valley floor, but is sliding down the mountainsides so that the tops are bright with sun on snow, as if the light was coming from within and is enough to light all India. But the brightness off the snow is not enough to offer any warmth, and she shivers as she walks and puts her water cans down by the stream. She's afraid at first it's frozen, too, but there's still some water flowing from the pipe that sticks out from the rocks. The snow helps hold the cans upright, and she sets one underneath the pipe, and as the can begins to fill it makes her want to urinate. She takes a couple steps away and squats behind a drift of snow, her decency protected by her pattu up an inch or two. The urine makes her burn around the sores that she got yesterday, skin chafed by the man that she had kicked so hard between the legs.

It's taking longer now than usual for the little stream to fill the can, because the water's only dribbling from the pipe that must be clogged with ice. Her shoulders shiver violently, she wraps her arms around herself; it's then the ravens find her there, hoping for something to eat, or just to pass the time away. Koksar has no shrubs or trees, and the snow's too soft to hold the birds—the ravens fly around her head, two birds perch on the water pipe. She really hates their awful noise, their cawing like an aching tooth: a pain that never goes away; and she can't decide if ravens are what men become after they die, or if men are ravens incarnate. She packs a snowball with her crippled hands, wants to knock the ravens off the pipe; but her aim is not so good today, and the ravens hardly have to duck.

She doesn't wait to fill the can, can't stand the ravens flapping round, and her hands are now all wet and cold; she pulls the half-full can away, sets down the other empty one. It takes two hands to move the can and lift it higher than the snow; she holds it up in front of her as she heads back toward the kitchen house. The ravens follow as she walks, flying ten feet overhead; one lands in the tracks she made while walking toward the little stream. It stands between her and the house, its wings spread out for balance as it dances in the still soft snow. She hates it when they get so close, she's not sure what they're going to do—she stops and stands a few yards off, afraid now of this ugly raven flapping in her path. It doesn't volunteer to move, and the water can is heavy and her hands are starting to go numb; she's at a loss for how to cope with this bird all dark and sinister, trying hard to stare her down. It opens up its beak and caws, so startling it makes her scream, because the sound it makes is human, like her mother calling out her name. She's hearing *Meena! Meena!* from the bird, and her own scream scares the beast away, so close she feels and hears the rush of wind made by its flapping wings.

Adrenaline pumps through her veins, her heart pounds deep inside her chest; then she hears what sounds like laughing, like the ravens think it's all a joke. Her sisters used to laugh at her, tell her she's a stupid girl; she puts the can down quickly to throw snowballs at the ugly birds. She turns to see which raven's making all this awful laughing noise; instead she sees one of the men, standing outside by a wall: pissing brightly in the snow, displaying frontal nudity. He's the one who's laughing, and it only makes her anger worse; she aims her snowball at the man, wishing it would strike him dead. His hands are busy with himself, so that he can't move fast enough; she hits him right against the hip, and this isn't just a game for her: she wishes it had been a rock. She picks the can of water up and listens as he curses her, joining all the ravens that have lined up on the kitchen roof.

Inside it's starting to get warm, she puts the can down by the door, and she opens up the tandoor with a poker she keeps by the stove; she throws another stick inside and warms her hands up near the flame. She puts water on to boil the rice, another pot for lentil stew; her hands have gotten cold again from handling the water can. She squats down near the tandoor and at first her hands refuse to warm, then slowly start to tingle as the blood begins to flow again. She rubs her hands together, her good fingers rub the ones all scarred: several fingers fused together, made her worthless as a bride. Once her hands are warm enough, she scoops the rice out of a bag; she pours it in a wicker basket, picks out bits of dirt and stones. All her life she's taken beatings for the stones that get cooked in the rice, but there's nothing more that she can do except sort through like she's always done. Her father was the worst because he'd lost already half his teeth: every time he chipped one he would beat her more than usual. For all she cares about these men she hopes that all their teeth will break, or that they'll rot right in their heads—but then they'd beat her up again, just like her father always did.

Carefully she picks out stones and throws them out onto the floor; the tandoor is so fired up that the water's almost to a boil. Before she puts the rice in, she scoops water out to make some chai, hoping that none of the men come earlier than usual. Once the snow is here there's no more work to do out on the road; the men will sleep through half the morning, get up in a couple hours to eat their morning rice and dal. By noon they'll start to drink again, they'll sit inside and play at cards, and every now and then someone will drag her back into her room. She's hoping that the man she threw the snowball at went back to bed: she'll have to give her chai to him if he comes before she's finished it. She loves the smell of boiling chai, she wishes she could get fresh milk—instead she pours milk powder in with cinnamon and cardamom. She brings the pot up to her nose to fill her hungry lungs with steam, the only part of life she has that even hints at luxury. While her nose is in the pot, she's startled once more by a voice; she forgot about the hippie boy after the raven scared her in the snow.

"'Ello!" is all she understands, although he shouts a lot more words; she doesn't know which language this young hippie man is blurting out. She curses underneath her breath at Antone for his gift to her; instead of taking her away, like he had promised months ago, he only brought more work for her: another awful man to feed. She doesn't want to answer him because she wants to drink her chai in peace, but she's afraid that all his shouting will wake up the other nasty men. She gets up off the floor where she's been squatting sorting out the stones, and she pulls the chai pot toward the front where the tandoor isn't very hot.

"'Ello!" he shouts again, then for a moment he is quiet; the door is open just enough so she can see him lying on her bed still strapped down to the narrow board. He is covered with the sleeping bag so just his head is sticking out; one arm is up and pulling at the tape that keeps his head strapped down. The sun is finally up enough to come in through the window; it's shining on his dirty hair, a kind she's never seen before. It's like a sadhu's matted curls—it reaches past his shoulder blades—but it's golden, like her milky chai, not black like other holy men's. His eyes are not the dark brown every other normal person has; instead his eyes are colored green, like apples sunk inside his head.

She thinks about the bottle that she helped the boy fill late last night, anticipates the bruise she'll get when someone takes a drink. She plans, instead, to hide it now, then bring it out when they're all drunk; she'll see how long it takes before they notice something's wrong with it. The hippie boy squirms back and forth, he says 'ello a few more times; she's not sure why he's on the board, why Antone left him stranded here. Antone didn't say too much, she didn't understand his words; except he had forgotten that he'd promised he would rescue her. By then she couldn't give a damn, her life just made more miserable: another man to feed and clean, another asshole in her bed.

She pushes on the door and it squeaks loudly on its rusty hinge; she doesn't step inside, so the hippie doesn't know who's there.

"'Ello?" she hears him say again, then he maybe asked about some tea; she figures he is hungry since he hasn't had a thing to eat since Antone dumped him yesterday.

"Oos-dehr?" he calls out next, and she's still standing just outside the door; she doesn't understand his words, but detects a note of fear now that she hadn't noticed earlier. For an instant she feels sorry for him, lying helpless on his narrow board; she wonders why he doesn't just get up and order her around: he's only held down with some tape, he'd only have to pull it off. One time she saw a sadhu sitting on the road outside of town, his legs bent in the lotus style and wasted down to skin and bones. He'd been that way for fifteen years, his legs had not been uncrossed once: nothing wrong with either limb, he hadn't had an accident. He just one day decided that was what he was supposed to do, to travel using just his arms, a way to mortify himself. She'd seen him coming off the pass, an alms bowl tied around his neck; his hands were wrapped in dusty rags, his arms as big as someone's legs. He said his holy pilgrimage was to walk like this into Lahal, to a temple on a mountainside, where a spring flows out between two rocks and the water would assure a better station in another life. His duty was to drag himself five hundred miles to get a drink, to refuse to ride in people's cars or crawl into some dusty bus. It strikes her that perhaps this boy is also on a pilgrimage: he really is a holy man, a sadhu lying on a board, a pilgrim heading for Lahal. He's mortified by lying still, he's not to move himself an inch: providing merit to those few who stop and help him make it there.

# The Vision

The only clue that Antone has he's lying flat out on his back is when he opens up his eyes he's only seeing timber beams, all black with soot and spiderwebs that hold the roof above his head. No one is around, and he can't tell if it is night or day; it isn't very long before the nausea kicks in again. His vision blurs and though he doesn't suffer mortal agony, he closes up his eyes and wishes he could sleep a few more days. He's swimming in a vat of sand, he cannot move his arms or legs—he's not sure why this is but knows he needs a dose of heroin.

When his eyes are closed it starts again, a vision he has had before: a raven falling through the air, its wings stretched out to catch the wind. It's falling down on top of him, deep inside a narrow hole: Antone feels his shoulders trapped, he can't tell if he's hot or cold. The raven's falling toward him, backlit by the bright blue sky above; he sees its feathers rustling, its talons stretched to grab his flesh. But it doesn't ever reach him, as he's falling equally as fast: tumbling backward straight into the fiery-

frozen pits of hell. Then the raven with its widespread wings becomes a crucifix of Christ, still falling with him through the
hole, an arm's length up above his head. He sees the wound in
Jesus' side, the spikes run through his hands and feet; the blood
is dripping from them so he wants to keep from being splashed.
The wounds are bleeding down on him, and he looks up into
Jesus' face; he tries to see if he is dead when the face becomes
the boy he took. And yes, the boy looks like he's dead. Antone
opens up his eyes and once more sees the blackened beams, and
faces of some village men.

   He cannot move because they've got him tightly by the arms
and legs; these village men have got his hands and feet stuck into
boiling pots. The pain is getting more intense as Antone's limbs
begin to thaw, and he doesn't have the strength to fight, can
barely turn his head to look; he's not sure what they're doing if
not trying to cook him up to eat. His nausea is stronger now, he
really needs another fix; he's never felt this kind of pain, like big
nails driven through his flesh, not even when his foot was
crushed when he was just a boy of six. He's sure he had more
heroin left over in his lacquered box, and suddenly he's scared to
death they've stolen his last ounce of smack. He needs another
fix *right now;* he struggles with the village men, trying to look
around the room to find his box of heroin. The last time that he
had his box was in that filthy little shack—the last thing he recalls is when the angel lit the match for him. He doesn't want to
close his eyes, afraid of what he'll see this time; the men have got
him held down fast: helpless to defend himself. The only thing he
does is spill the water from their cooking pots. Why don't they
cut him into bits and cook his parts up all at once?

   The men speak in a dialect that only sounds like Kullui, and
Antone's understanding just a word from every two or three.
Though they speak in calming tones, they never loosen up their

grip; he feels as if he's going to die, and these men act like they're having tea. He calms enough to watch a village woman with another pot, and she pours the boiling water in the bowl where they have got his feet. The shock streaks up his legs and spine until it slams into his brain; he opens up his mouth to scream, but not a blessed sound comes out.

The second time he wakes up they no longer hold his arms and legs, and the pain is not as bad although he feels a throbbing ache down in his ankles and his wrists. He finds that he can move, except his hands are strangely numb and stiff; he brings them up before his face, sees they're all wrapped up in rags. The rags are clean and tied up neat, like marshmallows on roasting sticks: the outsides turned a golden brown, he's afraid to think what's underneath. He reaches up to touch his face, his nose and lips aren't feeling right; he can't feel through the bandages, but his nose has always been right there. When he takes his hand away, the bandage has a fresh new stain: not bright like blood but brown or gray: the nausea returns again. This time he feels like he might puke, might pass out from this sudden wave; he tries to sit himself up straight, to find his precious little box. He cannot push up with his hands, can't feel beneath the bandages; he struggles up by pushing with his elbows and his shoulder blades.

He can't get up at first because his head spins and he's seeing spots; the nausea gets worse and worse, and he lies back down to wait until the dizziness has gone away. He's on his back and tries to lift his knees up toward his chest, to get the blood out of his legs to feed his crazy spinning head. But his feet are like his hands so that he can't feel anything at all—at least until he's shocked again, like lightning running in his veins. He tries once more to sit up straight, he's got to somehow get a fix or will himself an un-

timely death; the pain is so immense that he is sure he will die
anyway. This time he stays upright until the dizziness has disappeared, and as the spots clear from his eyes he looks down at his
bandaged feet: more bulky than his bandaged hands. He slowly
looks around the room: the fire is lit but no one's there; the tandoor's made of hardened clay, there isn't any chimney pipe. By the
stove he sees his boots with laces spilled across the wooden floor:
the tongues are folded forward so the boots look like they're vomiting. Next to them he sees his pack, his rucksack is still closed up
tight; he's praying that the box is there, salvation only steps away.

The nausea gets worse and worse, he swallows to suppress a
retch; the acid gall burns in his throat but nothing else is coming
up. He's shaking uncontrollably, his need for smack gets more intense—he cannot use his hands or feet to get himself across the
room. He rolls onto his arms and knees, starts crawling like a
one-year-old; his head spins but he'll die if he can't reach his lacquered box this time. Already he can feel the stick of needle sliding in a vein, the pain and then the pleasure wave, the sense that
everything's okay. Voices mumble off somewhere, by now they
must know he's awake; he crawls on even faster, worried that
they'll come investigate. He can't help but bruise his hands and
feet with gentle taps against the floor; the shocks pump up his
spinal cord, blasting through his shell-shocked brain. When he finally gets across the room he hooks his arm in through a strap
then pulls the sack onto his lap, yanks it open with his teeth, the
bag supported with his arms. He spills the contents on the floor:
a jackknife and some underwear, some papers not worth anything, a notebook with some addresses. The lacquered box is
there as well, he shakes it between bandages; the contents thud
about inside: feels like everything is there. It's a struggle opening
the lid, but inside it's like a treasure chest; he's better now just seeing it: the glimmering of gold doubloons.

His glass syringe is still inside, a work of art all by itself: the plunger sliding in so well, now wrapped inside a soft clean cloth. His mixing spoon lies next to that, the same spoon that he's used for years, stolen from some restaurant, the handle bent back on itself. There are matches and a lighter and some needles and some half-smoked joints; a mirror used for snorting coke, half a pack of chewing gum. And there beneath the other things, he finds what he is looking for: the plastic bag of light brown smack, enough to last a couple days.

Just staring at this plastic bag does wonders for his state of mind, but it only takes a moment for his symptoms to come back again. Desperately he starts to chew the rags off of his bandaged hands; the knots were made precisely so he has to rip and tug them off. At last he's got the right side loose, unraveling it with his teeth, until he finally sees his damaged hand; and the electric shocks are all he feels, but this image makes his stomach retch, his hand is just a stubby mess, it's hardly recognizable. Three of the fingers have turned black, the skin sloughed as if they were snakes; his thumb and pointer finger look like rotting summer sausages. His fingers can't feel anything, just the ghost of something terrible; he can't get them to bend or move, his fingers dead as something that a cat might leave outside the door. He starts tearing at the other hand, the knots caught in between his teeth, and these bandages come loose as well: the left's no better than the right: the hand like something flat and dried up lying on a dusty road.

He's staring at his two bad hands, staring at his box of stuff, realizing that there's not a chance in hell he'll make a fix. He tries to grab the heroin, but his fingers won't cooperate; his trembling is so violent that he'd spill it if his fingers worked. With the box down on the floor, he'll pick the bag up in his teeth, then chew a little hole in it and snort the powder up his nose. He is resting on his arms and knees, trying hard to keep the trembling down; he brings his face close to the box until he sees his image in the mirror. It's like someone has been beating him, like he's been bludgeoned with an iron pipe; his nose worse than his fingers with the tip all black and shriveled up, the nostrils swollen like his lips, cracked and split and oozing something similar to tea with milk. He doesn't stop to look too long—with an elbow he holds down the bag; with his teeth he tears a too-big hole, spilling smack onto the floor. He falls down on his side because he's too weak to stay on his arms; he puts his face against the floor to snort the powder up his nose. But his nostrils are so swollen he can't pull in any air at all; his tongue goes out instead, so that he licks the powder off the floor, his mouth as dry as cotton candy swirled around a paper cone. He has to suck to pull saliva out, enough to wet what's in his mouth, hold it underneath his tongue and hope that some of it dissolves. And it's then that he begins to sob, not making any noise at all, too dry to even make the tears his misery would justify. He's curled up on his side there with his face against the dusty floor, his knees pulled up against his chest; he is shaken by his trembling sobs so that he can't inhale the air he needs, consumed now by the horror of salvation right before his eyes.

# The Chai

Amod's hands are full again, and his back's against the kitchen door, swinging out into the dhaba with the sunshine through the windowpanes. The frost is melting down the glass, the tandoor hardly hot at all, and yet it's warm here in the dining room. Everyone's excited because the road is almost clear of snow: a jeep came in this morning all the way from Matri Bagh, the driver saying that the road was clear until they hit Nadar, just a few miles south of town. If the sun keeps shining bright, a bus could be in by this afternoon: the tourists all on honeymoon, all bubbling with the thrill of seeing snow the first time in their lives. Amod's serving cheese nan to some hippies who got stuck in town, so anxious to escape the snow that's all he hears them talk about: the next bus down to Chandigarh, how quickly they can hit the beach, to Goa where the drugs are cheap and beer's the only thing that's cold.

Doctor Mary was in earlier, was there when he unlocked the door—she startled him because he thought he'd see her in the afternoon. His hand was still in bandages, and the pain had started calming down; he had trouble turning back the key to let the doctor come inside. He was afraid that she might hug him when he finally opened up the door, but she only wanged, said *namasté*, and asked him if his hand hurt much, no different than usual. His shoulders started to relax, and he listened as she told him, in her stumbling bits of Kullui, how she'd been confused about the time he had been walking by the riverside; already she had done her rounds: two patients in maternity.

"I could eat a hungry horse," she said, and Amod didn't understand; the doctor's tries at Kullui were often coming out all wrong. She was looking for some breakfast, told him coffee would be really nice: a glass of juice, some buttered toast, a pancake with some marmalade.

For a time it was the two of them alone inside the dining room; just the cook back in the kitchen having trouble firing up the stove. After several pleasantries she finally brought the subject up: she thanked him for his thoughtfulness, the food he left out on her stoop. She said it meant a lot to think that someone thought to care for her, and that she wasn't sure how she should show her deepest gratitude. Then she told him what he's longed to hear: for months now she's been much too shy; she's loved him from the very start and wants to run away with him. But this last was just his fantasy; what she really said was something else: she'd like to pay him for the food—how much would be appropriate? He didn't know how to reply, unsure of how he should respond; pretending not to understand, he wagged his head from side to side. The fact she wants to pay him means she didn't understand at all: the tiffin tins left by her door were offerings left for his god. He was glad when someone else came in, two hippies with their backpacks on, complaining of how cold it's been and loudly calling for some tea.

*　　*　　*

His arms are full as Amod pushes through the dhaba's kitchen door, his tray is cluttered up with teas and cutlets swimming in their sauce. Everyone is talking of the accident they heard about: the driver up from Matri Bagh said an ambulance drove off the road and down a cliff three hundred feet. No one saw it happen but it woke the local people up, exploding like a bomb just half an hour before the rising sun. There wasn't any way to help those trapped inside the ambulance: the whole thing was a ball of fire burning on a ledge a hundred feet above the valley floor. By afternoon some kids climbed up the rocky cliff to look inside; all they saw were two charred bodies smashed inside the forward cab, the ambulance was upside down and the back end crushed in like a can. When this story was first being told, the doctor was still sipping tea, and the driver spoke in such excited tones she asked Amod to translate for her. When she heard it was an ambulance, he saw her face turn chalky white; he could tell that she was thinking of the hippie with the broken neck.

"I'll have to call the embassy," she said while pushing back her chair, and though he knew the lines were down he didn't bother telling her; she'd want to go check anyway. Amod helped her with her coat, then watched as she rushed out the door: clomping in her rubber boots, awkward and unladylike. He wants to understand why she would offer to pay for the food, to know what her intentions were—perhaps it's just some custom that he's never heard about before. Or perhaps it was because she didn't know his heart would ache so hard: it's suddenly been emptied and the blood replaced with sand and dust.

Amod takes his tray of food up to the table closest to the stove, and serves it to some honeymooners who straggled in just after noon. He can tell that these two are in love, not just their parents' business deal; they've been coming in for several days, their weekend stretched out by the snow, still staring in each other's eyes and ordering all kinds of food that sits till it is cold and stale. He doesn't have to fuss with them, they hardly know that he exists; he's not sure how it happens but he spills a glass of lemon tea. It lands right in the husband's lap, the groom dressed in his brand-new suit; he jumps so quickly to his feet his chair falls back and hits the stove. The naked lady on the lid falls down and hits the floor again, and everybody looks around while Amod quickly makes amends. He's nothing but apologies while he's wiping at the man's blue pants; the napkin in his bandaged hand so that it hurts more than it did before. He puts the man's chair back in place, then goes to pick the lady up, to put her back on top the stove, up where she proudly guards the door. He pulls his hand up in his sleeve, but still can feel her body heat; he's not sure why it is, but there's relief there in the added pain.

When the rush is over he tells Ram to cover while he takes a break; he's going home to get some sleep, the buses won't be in till late. He goes out through the kitchen door, into an alley barely shoulder wide; the snow is melting off the roofs so that it's dripping down onto his head. He's got his black galoshes on, like all the local people wear, and his coat is one he'd picked up when some wealthy tourist left it behind. Instead of going home he thinks he'll see what's going on in town, and in the street the light's so bright he can barely open up his eyes. The sun is blinding off the snow, and for a moment he can only stand; he waits until his eyes adjust, his pupils finally slamming shut. In front of him are produce stalls, their wallahs sitting counting change; the apples are in season but all the good ones have been shipped away. The oranges are in season too, trucked in from orchards in the south, and potatoes brought in from Lahal before the snowy passes closed for months. The wallahs sit among their goods, beneath their strung up canvas tarps—the snow is melting down the cloth so that it drips onto their customers. Amod's eyes have coped now with the light, and he starts to go across the street: the gutter ankle-deep with slush so that he's glad his boots are watertight. On the main street there's a sidewalk, and the stores have shoveled off the snow; even though the canvas awnings drip it almost feels like summertime. Along the sidewalk little dhabas have their big stoves hissing kerosene, sizzling little yellow snacks in slightly rancid vats of oil.

Amod's lived here thirty years, yet no one seems to notice him: a little man in someone's coat, a size or more too big for him. His dhaba serves the tourist trade, the food all on the pricey side; the locals eat their meals at home or in dark dhabas off the street where tourists never dare to go. So as he walks through town nobody ever says hello to him, or asks to sit and share some chai, to talk about the snow and how it's earlier than other years. Instead he simply walks along and watches what's all going on, often standing for a while yet no one ever seems to care or pay him any mind at all. Maybe it's because he is afflicted with a lazy eye, and so they're never sure if he is looking here or over there. Today he watches as a man sells hashish to a foreigner, another time a young boy steals a bucket from a hardware store. He's listening to people talk, hearing gossip of the accident: someone's heard there was a Brit inside, a rich one with a handicap, a pampered piece of royalty on tour in some big ambulance. Everyone is speculating when the buses will arrive; they all feed off the tourist trade in one way or another here.

He walks across the street along a path that's trampled in the snow, and there's a free spot on a wooden bench outside a chai shop sitting in the sun; he sits down next to several men, to rest and let his hands warm up. He gives his order to a little boy, then watches as the wallah brews the chai four glasses at a time. Amod listens to the spitting hiss of kerosene that's pressurized, and though the sun is really bright and hurts so much he has to squint, he watches as the wallah does the dance he's done ten thousand times: pouring milk out of a metal can, and spices measured from a box, the angry flame of kerosene that's licking at the blackened pot. There's sugar poured in from his hand, and just before the milky tea starts bubbling up over the top, he snatches it from off the flame and swirls it with a motion that he'd use to flip two greasy eggs: the chai mixed well before he fills the glasses on a metal tray. The boy who took his order is the wallah's son learning the trade, and he passes out the glasses, lets his father make out any change; he sorts it from a little box he hides beneath his wooden stool.

Amod sips the sweetened chai, still listening to people talk, how someone heard that someone found a frozen hippie on the pass. His hands and feet like blocks of ice, they say that he might not survive—they're waiting for the roads to clear so they can send him down here on the bus. Neither of the talking men can think what he was doing there, wandering out in a storm with several kilograms of hash. One of the men lowers his voice, says something about local police, how instead of turning in the man, they'd keep the hashish for themselves because the hippie will die anyway. Amod looks down at his bandaged hand, then gives the boy two rupee coins; he goes across the street in the direction of the hospital.

To his right down toward the river there's a band of old deodar trees: a park that runs right past the town about a hundred fifty meters wide. From the middle of the street Amod can see the tops of all the trees; the coloring is beautiful: the green and white and bright blue sky. As the sun warms up the branches they all start to drop their loads of snow; he can see the clumps drop heavily from the branches twenty meters up. Because there are no trucks or buses racing up and down the road, it's quieter than usual, and he hears the landing of the snow: it sounds just like the deep bass boom of fireworks ten miles away. As he walks up toward the hospital, he remembers when that sound was real: so many years ago he wonders why it should occur to him. The snow drop sounds like rifle fire, heard through the thick walls of his house; he couldn't have been more than five, and his father had been gone for days, his aunt verged on hysterical. His mother wouldn't let him play, not even right there in the yard; and Amod turns the corner from the street onto the alleyway. It surprises him how something that occurred so many years ago can still feel freshly visceral, the deep bass thump of falling snow can make him feel such nausea. He looks down at his hand again as he keeps on shuffling through the snow, and he hopes the doctor won't be there, but trying to call the embassy: he'd rather have his bandage changed by a nurse he's certain doesn't care.

# The Smoke

Phillip can't see how she's done it, but she's rigged his board up like a sled, and even though it's dark out he can see the mountains move along. She's got it gliding pretty well, keeping up a steady pace: the crunching of her footsteps match the rhythm of her labored breath. The sky has gotten clearer since she dragged him from the burning town, though for a while he thought that it might snow, he couldn't see a single star. But now the stars are twinkling and the moon is shining overhead, just a week away from full: he thinks he sees a mouth and nose. All of this is so surreal, but unlike any dream he's had—it just keeps going on and on: he'd like to wake up warm in bed, but he knows he isn't sleeping now.

As the ragged mountains pass him by and the moon eclipses twinkling stars, his thoughts go back to all the sounds and images from hours ago. When the girl came back this morning he was braced to be abused again, for her anger to spill in his lap with just one arm to protect himself. But she doesn't threaten him at all: she brings a steaming glass of chai; and when he cannot lift his head to get the glass up to his lips, she searches through the kitchen till she finds a saucer she can use. She sits beside him on the bed and he watches her spill the chai out of the glass onto the saucer; she blows to cool it off, then brings the saucer to his lips and carefully she tips it in. It's hard to drink while lying down, so he almost chokes himself to death: his tongue as dry as burning dung—but the chai is still ambrosia-like, if maybe just a bit too sweet.

He's not sure why she's being nice, and he's not sure he should trust her yet, but once he's had the drink of chai his stomach starts to bellyache, churning like some beackside spot named "Punchbowl" or "The Devil's Pot." He doesn't have to ask for food because once he's finished with the tea, she comes back with some rice and dal, all steamy in the morning air, the sunshine through the window lights the steam until it disappears. At first it makes him gag because she doesn't feed him with a spoon—instead she dips in with her hand, her fingers webbed and curled, he thinks, like a spastic in a wheelchair. With the fingers she can move she makes the dal and rice into little balls, then with her deformed fingers puts the rice ball up before his mouth. With her thumb she flicks it past his lips, and he's certain she's not washed her hands; he feels a little sick at first, but it really doesn't taste too bad.

"Could you put a little salt in that?" he asks with dal-bhat in his teeth, and she looks at him and nods her head, wags it maybe no or yes. He knows she doesn't understand, just thinks he must be thanking her; and suddenly it tastes just fine, like mother's steak-and-kidney pie. He opens up his mouth so she can flip another ball inside, and as she brings her hand up he is looking at her scars again: her pinkie and her ring fingers are fused and bent off to one side, her hand looks like a leaf that's dried and curled up by the sun. As her hand gets closer to his mouth so that he cannot focus anymore, he looks up at her face and sees she knows what he was looking at. He blushes for a moment, because he knows it's not polite to stare, and still she keeps on feeding him, flipping balls of dal-bhat in, squishing up another as she waits for him to chew the last.

After several balls of rice he gets behind on swallowing, so that she's ready with the next before he has the last one chewed. She puts the next one to his lips, tries to flip this last one in, and he's like a toddler in his chair, trying to turn his head away. But the tape won't let him go too far; the muscles in his neck get tight. Suddenly the pain is back, a thunderbolt shoots down his spine. This jolt goes to his hands and stays, like fire ants or swarming bees, then worse than that his hands go numb, so that he can't feel anything. Once more he's scared to death that he has finally done it wrong this time: from now on he'll be paralyzed. The fear makes all his muscles tense, his chest so tight he cannot breathe; this time for sure he's going to die, and the only thing he's feeling is his pounding heart inside his chest: like it's fighting to get out of there, to take a big fresh breath of air. The girl sits waiting with her bowl, her withered hand up to his mouth: still trying to push a rice ball past his set of clamped and bloodless lips. It's like once upon a time when he was playing in the swimming pool: too young to swim unsupervised, and he's too close to the deep end where the bottom drops off suddenly. It's that very sense of panic when the bottom's not there anymore—he slips and sinks down underneath, and he wants to take a big deep breath but can't even breathe the water in. His violent thrashing doesn't help, and he can't tell which way's up or down; can't open up his eyes because he's afraid that it will hurt too much. Then suddenly some magic force has pulled him out into the air, his cousin has him by the hair, and Phillip's thrashing madly trying to grab the boy around the neck. And with the first breath Phillip takes he sucks a cup of water in, and it's just that same way this time when he finally opens up his mouth: Meena flips the rice ball in because she doesn't know what's going on.

When he finally stops his coughing fit, with the dal-bhat over everything, the feeling's come back to his hands, his free one covers up his mouth: his windpipe isn't clear yet but at least the air goes in and out. He wants to curse this stupid girl for nearly choking him to death, but by the time he's got his wind she suddenly has disappeared, there's yelling from the other room. His neck has not stopped spasming, and he's trying to relax himself; but something's still caught in his throat and he has to cough from time to time, which makes the pain come back again. From the other room he hears the sound of angry people arguing; he wonders what the fight's about, because it sounds like it might escalate.

It must be twelve hours later, and she's dragging him across the snow—all around are mountains that are lit up by the twinkling stars, the moon that shines three-quarters full. He is trying to make some sense of all the things that happened earlier: the shouting from the other room, the words he couldn't understand, the acrid smell of burning dal. But he couldn't see a thing while lying strapped down in the little room, just every now and then there'd be a raven through the window or the dark edge of a threatening cloud. It's eerie now how quiet it is, compared with all the noise before; the only things he hears are Meena's footsteps falling in the snow, the scraping sound his board makes every time she gives another pull. He's scared of what she might have done, of where she might be taking him; she's nothing if not kind now but the sounds he heard were brutal ones. He is trying not to think about the red stains on the sleeping bag: the ones left by her tortured hands when she dragged him through the smoke and ash.

The sleeping bag is all he's got, plus a shawl the girl had thrown on top: the cold is creeping through his bones, coming straight up through the ice and snow. And though she's made his board a sled she hasn't made it waterproof; the snow melts where it's close to him so that he's damp along his thighs and flanks. A shiver sends pain up his neck, which hurts worse since she rescued him: dragged him headfirst off the bed so that his foot end bounced against the floor. He is back inside her musty room: there's smoke collecting overhead; he's starting to suspect that this is more than something on the stove. This is after all the noise had stopped, it seems like hours since he's heard a thing—he is thinking that they all are dead or they ran away and left him there. Then he sees the smoke blow past the only window in the room, and thinks she must be making dinner, that it is quiet because they settled down. The smoke, though, isn't soft and sweet, like woodsmoke from a cooking fire, but dirty like bad city air, the greasy smell of kerosene on things that aren't supposed to burn. When the little room's door opens he sees more black smoke come spilling in, then Meena standing over him, her right eye almost swollen shut.

She whispers something out of breath, then disappears down on the floor; he can just make out the sound of fire and Meena scratching near the wall. It doesn't take her long before she's back up on her feet again; she is tying round her waist what he assumes to be a money bag. He looks up at her face again, her right eye turned off to one side, and even with the smoke and fire she hasn't shown a trace of fear: her look just says *don't fuck with me*. Then she straightens out his sleeping bag and throws her shawl on top of that; her hands are stained with blood and dirt when she grabs the head end of his board to pull him off the narrow bed. When the foot end drops off of the bed he's hammered with a searing pain; he cannot pull his breath in straight; his head is tilted up so that the blood goes rushing to his feet: dark spots float thick before his eyes. All this happens in a flash. She drags him through the dining room: the smoke as thick as Vegemite, his eyes are burning instantly, he coughs with every breath he takes. The only time they stop is when she trips on something on the floor—he drops on something round and soft, he tries to reach and catch himself. He touches what feels like a leg: the skinny part below the calf. At first he thinks the leg is hers, that his board has fallen on the girl—but already she is up again, while the leg is still down under him. He snatches back his hand because the leg belongs to someone dead, and the sounds he'd heard were what he feared: the fight came to a bloody end.

And this is what he heard before the fire in the dining room: the sounds made as the girl fought with the men when they came in to eat. He cannot understand the words, but the inflections are all clear enough; at first it seems like simple stuff, like family fights heard all his life. But then he hears a clattering, like a pot thrown clear across the room, and the girl is in a screaming rage, and by the sounds he hears he knows that it's not one but several men out there. She must be fighting all of them, the chairs are being pushed around, the awful thud of flesh and fist—her shouts of rage are muffled like a hand is clamped over her mouth. He is terrified by what comes next: a syncopated thumping sound, a table scooting inch by inch, the nervous laugh of drunken men. He knows what they are doing, and she can't be more than five feet tall: a small deformed defenseless thing, a gang of men between her legs. His horror's really more than that because he can't risk getting off the board, and even if he could help, he's too scared of being hurt himself. If he had more than one hand free he'd put both his fingers in his ears—he can't stand all the things he hears, the thumping noise goes on and on above her raging muffled screams. When it finally stops he's feeling like he's just been beat and raped himself, and it's then he hears her sobbing cry, and she must have run outside because it's quiet then for hours and hours, just the muffled sound of shuffling cards.

He can't recall the dream he woke from, drenched inside a caul of sweat; just felt something awful happened with his heart still pounding in his chest. The little room was filled up with the ghost of some explosive sound: unsure if it was gunshot or some firecrackers going off. The ringing echo slowly waned, it was deathly quiet in the room, and all that he could hear was cawing ravens walking on the roof, their distant piercing colic howl, like children in another room. He wondered if they'd gone somewhere, perhaps the men went off to work; perhaps they'd left for somewhere warm and thoughtlessly abandoned him. He listened for the shuffling cards, the splash of glasses being filled, the sound of matches being lit, but all he heard was echoing. He was dying for a cigarette, to help to clear his dusty head. It was then that he first saw the smoke: backlit by the setting sun.

He has never cared that much for snow, and he's never gotten used to cold—that's why he came to India, because he'd heard that you could get stoned cheap and live in huts along the beach. But all the freaks in Goa said they wanted to come here instead: *It's too hot down here in the south and the mountains have these mineral baths.* At first the scene seemed pretty cool: a stick of hash cost fifty pence, a room for just two pounds a week. But then his so-called friends all left, which happens every now and then—he's not surprised to wake up late to find he's left behind again. And now he's lying on a board, dragged off by some poor deformed girl; the sleeping bag keeps slipping off so he's having trouble with the cold. He's still not sure what happened in the town that's burning to the ground, but Meena dragged him through the fire, past the body lying on the floor, and no one tried to stop her since there wasn't anyone alive. He didn't hear the shouts and screams you'd hear when something's caught on fire, but just the sound of fire itself: the snapping of old burning wood, the wind sucked in by rising flames, and Meena coughing in his face.

As she dragged him from the town he saw a picture that he won't forget: the sun was setting so the sky had turned a lovely purple-blue, and a scattering of clouds up high were colored on one side in red: like ink in a correcting pen, like candies flavored cinnamon. Under this he saw the jet-black rolling plumes of smoke and ash: the greasy dust of nasty men, so dense it covered half the sky. And from these churning clouds he saw the ravens suddenly appear, as if the birds were born of fire; they circled high above his head: they'd lost their only place to rest.

# The Prince

Ravi's in the bathroom washing up before it's time to eat: Mary's trying once again to cook a box of macs and cheese. Her water's kind of simmering, and it has to reach a rolling boil to kill the bugs and parasites: the hepatitis viruses. In the seven months she's lived in town she's been sick half a dozen times—can't always keep her own advice to let the water boil awhile. But cooking now for someone else, she can't afford such sloppiness: she doesn't want to be the one to treat her guest for tummy ache. She gets up from the wooden box she keeps close to the tandoor stove, measures out the milk and butter bought down in the marketplace. She lets the pot sit on the stove, tin plate balanced for a lid—glances at her watch to see how long she has been cooking it. She's thinking of Prince Charming, how she couldn't get through on the phone; couldn't reach the embassy to let them know the awful news. It must have been his ambulance that burned up halfway down the cliff; there's not another ambulance for at least a hundred miles or more. Mary's feeling awful, like the accident was all her fault: if she had been awake she could have told them not to drive too fast. But the timing lets her off the hook: it was dark out when they heard the crash; she wasn't over-sleeping: she'd been up all night in surgery. The driver must have raced like hell to make it here before the snow: the ambulance ran off a cliff, the driver maybe fell asleep.

She is so glad Ravi came tonight, she could barely stand to be alone, sitting with the ghosts of all the people who are haunting her. She can't stop thinking of Prince Charming sliding off a mountain road, or that dead baby dangling from the screaming mother's strangling womb. The scenes keep playing through her head, the crash ends in a ball of fire; she sees her gloved hand sorting through the tray of vicious instruments. She always feels her husband's doing something in the other room—she can't quite shake the sense he'd come and kiss her if she asked him to. But she knows that she can't call his name, that's something lunatics would do: asking for the tender kiss of someone dead a year ago. She hears the squeaking bathroom door, the footsteps of a solid man; Ravi comes into the room and checks the water on the stove.

"It's boiling. Should I put the noodles in?" and he takes the box of macs and cheese; puts his thumb into one end and tears the cardboard off the top.

She watches as he tends the stove, adds another stick of wood; cautions him how last night they had almost caused a chimney fire. He's squatting on his haunches as he pokes the wood inside the box—his head is tipped to one side so his neck and nape are well exposed. He had his hair cut earlier by some-one down in the bazaar: harshly trimmed around the ears, but overall she thinks it's nice. He stands up from his squat and goes to reach inside a bag he brought: a scrawny tandoor chicken wrapped up tightly in a plastic sack.

"I brought this just in case," he says, "and I found this in one of the shops." He pulls out of the bag a slender bottle with a cork on top. She hasn't had a drop of wine since well before she left the States; she's never been a drinker but she wouldn't mind a little taste.

"Maybe just a half a glass. In case there's an emergency." She searches on the counter for some glasses clean enough to use.

From his pocket Ravi pulls a handy multigadget pocket knife; she listens to the pleasant squeak and pop of cork on bottle glass. Ravi reads the label to her, translating the Hindi script: aged for maybe eighteen months, a winery south of Madras. He sniffs the cork with both eyes closed while lifting just a single brow; tastes the wine he's poured into a teacup quickly rinsed and dried.

"Pleasant barnyard finish, with a subtle kiss of vinegar." She has to smile at his attempt to lighten up her somber mood. He tells her just to sit and drink, that he'll prepare their evening meal; she watches as he deftly drains the noodles without getting burned. The roasted chicken's painted red with a spice that looks like turmeric; he carves it at the counter with the sharp blade of his pocket knife. He does a running monologue that finally makes her laugh out loud: perfect imitation of how Chidda pulled his bandage off. Mary's on the wooden box, the tandoor stove is nice and hot; the wine is not too pleasant but the alcohol is strong enough. It only takes a couple sips before it starts to take effect: a warmth inside her stomach and her shoulders dropping down an inch. She lets her eyes close lightly and for a moment she is back at home: sitting in her living room with dinner in the microwave. The chicken smells delicious and the wine has piqued her appetite; she smells the tangy powdered cheese he's mixing with the noodles. Her shoulders drop another inch, relaxing muscles in her neck; she's breathing in the smell of someone finally taking care of her.

She opens up her eyes to find she's staring at his solid hips; he's standing right before her with two plates of steaming noodle dish. The fire has burned down a ways, so they both sit closer to the stove, and the cheesy plate of noodles looks much better than the night before. The chicken spice is mildly hot, and she lets him fill her cup again; she can't drink any more than this in case the nurses call tonight. She finds that she is ravenous, she's eating with abandon now: knowing there is nothing in the noodles to surprise her mouth. Ravi keeps her laughing by describing how his hair was cut: he didn't know the treatment ended with a violent neck adjustment. She finishes her plate of food and sips through half her second cup—she's more relaxed than she has been since climbing off that dreadful bus. As their chuckles fade away, she takes a long, slow breath of air; holds it for a moment, then exhales a satisfying sigh.

"We used to eat this all the time, while Rich and I were paying student loans," and she tells him how they lived so cheap while they both were doing internship. She describes for him one winter break, they had four days off in a row, and all they wanted was a chance to go off somewhere all alone. Richard pulled a road map out and picked a town up in the hills; they found a mom-and-pop motel that charged them what they could afford. Richard made her laugh when he explained the sounds heard through the walls; they spent their time just walking down the snowy backroads of the town. She loved the fact that no one in the world knew where they were just then: outside some Pennsylvanian town, in a room without a telephone.

Suddenly she cannot help but tell him how her husband died; how it wasn't all that long ago, how she misses him so terribly. She knows that this is all defense, she's trying to put some roadblocks up: the mention of a loving spouse should splash some water on them both. But it doesn't seem to work that way,

Ravi just sits silently; in the light he looks like he might cry, and after several moments he reaches out and puts his hand on hers. He knows how lonely she must feel, how the universe can be unjust; all she wants right now is just to climb up on his solid lap and snuggle close into his chest: have him touch her hair and back, the way her father did when she was sick and needed comforting.

Her impulse isn't sexual, her sudden urge to hold him tight—she isn't sure what she should do and so she bends to kiss his hand. And there she finds a wedding ring, a simple rosy-yellow band; surprised that all this time she didn't notice he's been wearing it. He tells her how he's sure he couldn't bear the pain that she's been through; he's always thought that he would die if he ever found himself alone. He's been married over seven years—the first time that they've been apart; his wife could not come with him here: she just began a brand-new job. Then suddenly he's quiet, and she senses something change in him; he takes his hand away from hers and stands to pace across the floor. He says he should be going, it's a long walk back to his hotel; he's sure she'd like to get some sleep: no telling when they'll call for her. He's putting on his coat to leave, and Mary's totally confused; his hand is on the latch when he declares there's something he must say. He turns to her and says there's a confession that he has to make: years before he vowed he wouldn't lie about it anymore. He tells her that he felt with her an instant camaraderie, and that he meant each word he said about his wife in Canada. But for years he hid behind a lie, afraid of living openly—he doesn't have a wife at all: a *husband* is a better term.

Mary's flooded with relief, she very nearly laughs out loud: the tension in the room was his discomfort with his simple lie. Her training as a doctor makes her good at unexpected news, and all her life she's been the kind of person people come out to. She

knows he's watching carefully for signs that she's rejecting him—
so she doesn't have to hide her smile, she gives the man a tender
hug. She tells him that he doesn't have to worry about what she
thinks; half her friends in college had come out as gay or lesbian.
He bends down now and kisses her, a quick one soft against her
cheek, and she thanks him for the macs and cheese, her first good
laugh for weeks and weeks. She asks him to drop by again, and
he steps out into all the snow; she watches him walk off a ways
before she shuts her creaking door.

It isn't very late yet, so she takes the dishes to the sink; she hasn't
done much cooking so she isn't used to washing up. The plates are
thick with chicken fat, coagulated cheesy streaks; she'll have to heat
some water if she doesn't want the grease to stick. She is thinking
about Amod, how the poor man brought her all that food; how she
never thought a local person might be watching out for her. She
feels stupid about earlier, when she told him that she'd like to pay;
as soon as she said anything she knew it was a big mistake. His face
went stony blank as he pretended not to understand; she knows his
English isn't good, but *she's* the stupid idiot. She'd like to go apologize, to let him know she gets it now: he brought her food because he knows there's no one taking care of her. She dismisses in
a flash the thought there might be more to it than that: it's not that
he's not nice and sweet, but the image is ridiculous.

   The tandoor has lost all its heat—she'll have to build another
fire—but all she's got are two big logs and nothing small to light
them with. Tamding leaves the wood outside her door when he
remembers to, and she goes to check if he had filled the box up
for her earlier. She's shocked to find him right outside, an arm
full of deodar wood: carefully he's putting down each stick so that
she doesn't hear.

"*Namasté*," she says, and Tamding wangs his only empty hand.

"I'm bringing wood," he tells her, with a pleasant smile across his face.

She tells him that his timing's good, she's just come out to look for some; he says he'd gladly build a fire: an expert at that kind of thing. She stands back so he can come in, and asks him if he'd like some tea: she's never had the time before to socialize with anyone. She knows he should go back to work, but there isn't any work to do—they've only got two patients left, and the nurses all know where she lives. And without his coat on Tamding doesn't look so terribly absurd. He's got a sweet and gentle face: his smile can go from ear to ear.

# The Visit

Amod doesn't lock up until almost quarter after twelve, when the last of all the honeymooners leave for their unheated rooms, to snuggle in their freezing beds: unused to having someone else to rub their freezing feet against. He goes out through the kitchen door, a set of tiffins in his hand. The temperature has dropped so that the roofs aren't dripping anymore. He is careful as he walks along the alley out onto the road; the slush is frozen solid and the snowbanks have an icy crust. He thought about it all day till he almost had himself convinced: Doctor Mary didn't mean the things that he thought she had said. It was just some strange expression, just a way to show her gratitude; she often speaks to him so fast: he probably misunderstood. So many of the foreigners say *thank you* for the strangest things, like when he brings their dinners out, or puts their checks down gently with a little bowl of anise seed. He's argued with himself all day, that he's the one who acted rude: it's all misunderstanding and it's *he* who should apologize. He wishes mostly that he hadn't fallen in the schoolyard snow, that Doctor Mary never saw who left her all those tins of food.

For years he's been invisible, living here in solitude—a man whose eyes can look both ways so no one dares look back at him. His family has been dead since he was barely five or six years old; the sound of falling clumps of snow still triggers ancient memories. It's midnight with the power out, the moon has already gone down; but the stars are so amazing that he doesn't need his torch to see the pitfalls in the ice and snow. The doctor is the first one to acknowledge him in all these years; the hippies and the honeymooners barely see that he is there, caught up in their little worlds of drugs and sex, respectively. His boss will sometimes speak with him, though Ram Percash is much too shy, and sometimes even Tamding doesn't stop if he's got things to do. But Doctor Mary looks at him when she asks him for a lemon tea, and she seems to know which eye is good, not bothered by the lazy stray. That isn't much, but still it's more than anybody else he knows—*so what* if she says *thank you* for things no one should say *thank you* for? He watches so he doesn't fall, a repeat of the day before; his black galoshes don't provide much traction where it's slippery. He wonders if she'll be awake, or if that man is there again; he assumes that they had sex last night: the man stayed until two o'clock and half the candles had gone out. If she hadn't wanted sex then she would not have let him in alone; Amod's trying not to think of it, because the thought can make his stomach hurt. She's being much too indiscreet; he's sure that there will be some talk; at least the man is not from here, so she's not sleeping far beneath herself.

It isn't all that far to walk from the dhaba to the doctor's room; with care he climbs the short stone wall that marks the boundary of the school. The snow's been trampled flat here by the hordes of screaming playing kids, and even though it's slick with ice, the surface has been roughened so there's a little bit of traction here. For years he's trained the big black dog that she shouldn't ever bark at him; he barely sees her in the dark, but hears her little Kali whine. She follows Amod's hand signals for simple things like sit and stay; he's trained her since she was a pup, by giving her small bits of food. When he finally sees her silhouette, she is standing underneath a tree—even in the dark he sees the tangles of her matted fur. He signals that she can advance by patting lightly on his thigh, and Kali starts to wag her tail so violently she almost falls: she's having the same trouble with her footing on the icy snow. She slips and wags and wiggles with such overflowing love and joy that he can't deny a smile for her: she's a little on the stupid side, the only friend he's got in town, always eager to behave, although he knows she's just a slut who wags for almost anyone. His smile becomes a muffled laugh, the first one he's had in a while: her tail has got a lot of mass, with snow all clumped into the fur. She's wagging it so violently that it makes her slip from side to side; she's trying to spread her hind feet wide, to keep her balance on the ice.

He walks across the schoolyard to the tree the dog is underneath, and she postures down submissively until he scratches her behind the ear and tells her she's been very good. She squirms to lick his hand and sniff the still-warm stack of tiffin tins; he pats her on the rump and wonders if she's not with pups again. He knows that if it weren't for him she'd probably have starved by now, with litter after litter she has trouble keeping up her strength. He wishes he had extra food to give her something good tonight; tomorrow he'll make sure she gets the scraps off all the dinner plates.

From the tree they're standing under, Amod clearly sees the doctor's rooms; he can tell that Ravi's there because the candles are all lit again. He wonders what he should do next: just wait until they finish up? He can't believe that she's in love; she must be only using him. Amod's never had the nerve to ask about her family: he knows she had a husband once, a nurse said she was widowed; she must have had some children, though its hard to say with foreigners. The only reason he can guess for why the doctor's all alone is that her family must be dead, with no one left to keep her home. That's why she stays and works so hard, she's keeping herself occupied—perhaps that's all this romance is: someone to help distract herself.

Kali sits down next to him, no longer underneath the tree; her large size makes it easy for her to nudge or lick her master's hand. Amod isn't sure if he should come or go or leave or stay; he looks up at the dazzling stars, at the band of white across the sky. He doesn't know a thing about the planets or the Milky Way; as a child he thought the stars were dull, obscured by smoke and dusty air. His mother never let him out to see them without all the lights, but here he's high above the plains; the snow has washed out all the dust. The power has been out for days, and the stars are clear as window glass, like rhinestones dangling from the lobe of some young honeymooner's ear. No one's ever told him what they think the stars are doing there: could be the gods all staring down, a million little beady eyes, or scratches in a big black dome, or diamonds floating in the air. The only explanation that he's ever thought of for the stars is that they're only what they seem: just little lights above his head, and when the sun goes down at night their dimness shows up brilliantly. This explanation doesn't make the stars seem less mysterious, but he's never had a friend to ask the reason for the moon and stars, what happens to the sun at night. He reaches down and pats the pregnant dog about its bony flank, then absently he pets her head, pulls softly at her long black ears; he stares back at the doctor's rooms to see if anything has changed.

Her windows are the last ones on the compound showing any light, all the rest are black and blank as feathers from a raven's wings. Maybe that's what makes the stars: the gleaming eyes of ravens as they fly up in the midnight sky. Often he has wondered where the ravens go to sleep at night; he's never seen them in the trees, and they're not out making any noise. He's standing out there all alone and no one knows that he is there; it could be that they're watching him like he's been watching all the rest; suddenly he's really glad that Kali came to sit with him.

He looks back at the doctor's rooms, hears someone coming out the door—he recognizes right away the person's moving quietly. Even with the brilliant stars, the night is dark as Kali's fur, and Amod's certain that he won't be seen there shadowed by the tree. He listens as the latch is pulled, as the door comes open silently, with just the hint of squeaky hinge and then the shuffling of rubber boots. Amod's stomach starts to hurt, a low-grade gnawing nausea; whoever's coming through the door just took something away from him. It's not just something sexual, his hopes have never gone that far; but Amod suddenly feels more alone than he has felt before. Worse than when he was a kid, when his neighbors had to take him in; they didn't treat him like a son, but at least they shared their roof with him. Even though the doctor can look straight into his crooked eyes, talk to him like he's a friend, and treat him like she really cares; he knows that there's no place for him to fit inside her lovely life, and that he couldn't sit there in her rooms and make her laugh at night. This man who's sneaking from her rooms proves Amod's played the hapless fool: but the doctor's been his only hope, though for what he's never known for sure.

Her door is twenty meters off, and he's squinting to see in the dark, but it isn't very long before her lover stealthily comes out. At first all he can tell is that the figure wears a bulky coat, that he closes the door quietly; this shadow moves off careful not to make too much noise in the snow. He thought Ravi was taller, that he had a different kind of coat; but no one else has ever been inside her rooms so late at night. It isn't till the dog stands up and tries to run off toward the man that he recognizes who it is, still looking like a mangy bear: the first time Amod's ever seen him walking without whistling. And Kali wants to run to him, one of her many favorites, but Amod's got her by the neck, a handful of her furry hide. Afraid she'll give them both away, it isn't till she starts to bark that he has to let go of her scruff, hoping if he doesn't move that Tamding will not notice him. He watches as the dog wags off to make a fool out of herself, and this time it isn't funny as she slips and slides across the ice, her tail still clumped with balls of snow and flailing like a wiper blade at work out in a thunderstorm. Tamding turns around to see which dog is running after him, so he's looking back while running forward, rushing on to save his life. Tamding's always been a fool, and Kali's too promiscuous, and Tamding almost falls and cracks his skull there in the frozen snow. His big coat makes the skinny man look even more ridiculous: some adolescent vulture with its feathers molting all at once. Amod can't look anymore as the big dog finally greets the man, as she goes sliding forward on the ice, and tries to jump and lick his face, without another thought for Amod standing lonely in the dark. He turns away from all of them, hears Tamding try to calm the dog, and he knows Kali will go with him because he lets her in the duty room. She'll eat a few chapati scraps, then sleep down by the fiery stove—she doesn't have to get out till the nurses bitch about the smell.

For a moment Amod's thoughts go unchecked whirling through his pounding head; he thinks of Tamding in her rooms, and how could he have had the nerve. Or did she get things going first, now she's got a taste for it: perhaps she reached down in his pants, or helped by lifting up her skirt. And how could she have kissed him when she must know Tamding is a fool; how could she have sex with him: a moron with a stupid grin. He wonders how long Doctor Mary's opened up her door for him, and he knows he's been an idiot for bringing her these tins of food. He's still holding his tiffin tins, still standing near the big tall trees—he's feeling waves of nausea, the smell of food now makes him sick. He takes apart the tiffins, drops them listlessly into the snow; his only friend's deceived him and he's been a stupid imbecile. He needs to get away from here, and he doesn't want to go back home, and he doesn't want to walk through town, and even though it's icy, he turns to walk down by the riverside.

# The Fire

With every step that Meena takes, the tumpline makes her forehead hurt; she's used to dragging heavy loads, but this one's more than usual. It isn't till the moon has gone behind the mountains to the west that she feels that she can take a break, dry her chilling forehead sweat. She's not afraid of all those men, they can't abuse her anymore, but she wants to put a lot of space between herself and all the smoke they make. Like any road in India, there's a chai shop every couple miles, but because the road is full of snow, the shacks they pass are dark and cold. It's midnight when the moon goes down, and she's been dragging him for several hours; she comes across a shop she hopes will have some cakes of dung to burn. She pushes on the flimsy door and pulls him in the empty shack; she hesitates a moment, though there's not a living soul for miles.

Hardly any snow has blown in through the cracks around the door, and the only window's boarded up so it's darker than the night outside. She leaves him strapped down to his board; tucks his sleeping bag in all around; the bag has gotten damp so that her holy man is shivering. Her sadhu hasn't said a thing since she dragged him from her little room, since she tripped over one of the men—she knows he knows the crime she did. She'll have to make a fire because there's nothing else to keep him warm; she has matches in her little bag, mixed with the coins the men tossed on her bed. There are usually some candles left for travelers caught in the snow; she's hoping that the wallah left a scrap of something she can burn. She takes the purse off her belt and pulls the box of matches out; she lights a match cupped in her hand and quickly glances round the room. The chai shop is a basic shack, with a dirt floor and a wooden bench; along one wall a shelf hangs with three stubby candles in a row. She quickly brings her match up to the tallest candle on the shelf; the light spills from her hands like water scooped to wash her hands and face. The candle only fizzles first, then flares up to a four-inch flame; the light is dazzling since her eyes have grown accustomed to the dark; her shadow spread across the room could nearly cover ten of her. As the candle settles down, she gives the match a dainty shake; the room's become quite dim again, lit by a tiny one-inch flame.

She finds a tandoor near one wall, an oven made out of mud and stone; there's a little pile of kindling wood, a couple loaves of dried-up dung. This type of stove's not warm enough unless it's lit for several hours; she looks about to see where she can light a fire right on the ground. She hears her sadhu shivering, the nylon bag rubs when he shakes; she makes a stack out of the kindling, and takes the candle off the shelf. Careful not to put it out, she holds it underneath the wood; she imagines where they're going: to a temple on a mountainside. She remembers what that other sadhu told her when she filled his bowl—he'd seen this temple in a dream, where the water bubbles from the rocks, and those who wash and drink from it are guaranteed a better life. He'd said there was a holy man, a master who would teach him things; all he had to do was get there walking on his callused hands. He said the water gushes from the rocks, and the rocks have turned a golden hue: like the sunlight on the Ganges or the shimmer off a temple dome. No one can explain why there aren't other rocks that look that way: a god performed a miracle, so even in the winter there are ripe fruits hanging from the trees; the snow just melts upon the ground. She wonders if she'll meet him there, the sadhu with the shriveled legs; she wonders if she'll have to wait till death to throw this life away.

This holy man she's helping now says that he has to pee again; she doesn't understand the words, but his hand signal is clear enough. She's brought a few essentials in a bag she's carried in her hand: the saucer he can drink from and the cup she needs to help him pee; a bowl she hopes to use if they should ever find a place to beg. She knew she'd have to care for him, because he can't do anything himself, and she's glad the tumpline hurts her head, and the snow makes walking difficult: if all of this were easy, then it wouldn't be worth very much. It's the only thing that she has left, with the bag of coins tied to her belt, this duty to this holy man, this sadhu lying on a board: to drag him to this temple so that he can drink the water there.

He fills the cup up several times, and she throws the urine out the door; when he's empty he asks for a drink, just tips his hand before his mouth. She doesn't have a drop to give, she didn't think to bring a jug; she's got a metal pot so she can melt some snow above the fire. The fire is going beautifully, the room is starting to get warm; she doesn't know what she'll do next, when the little bit of kindling's done. She goes out through the door and gathers snow up in her cooking pot; she has a little bag of rice, some lentils for a bit of dal. But she doesn't have the fuel to keep the water boiling long enough; she's worried because he's shivering more, and his hands and feet are pale and cold. She wishes she had mittens she could offer him to keep them warm; she'll go out in the snow and get some rocks to warm them by the fire. Out back she might find wood to burn, or a few more cakes of dried-up dung, and later when the rocks are warm she'll place them all along his board. Maybe they should spend the night and start off when it's light again; she'd rather put more distance, though, between herself and what she's done. Since the fire isn't in the stove, she has to hold the pot herself; she's put in just a little snow so it won't take very long to melt. The kindling wood still snaps and spits, and the snow sizzles inside the pot; it isn't long before it's warm. She swirls the water till it steams. The pot is just a big black hole, with the fire flaring underneath—its shadow dances wildly round the stone walls of the little shack. This motion isn't strange to her, she's watched this dancing all her life: the children of the mountain gods, who flit around the room, then tell their mothers what goes on inside.

She pulls the saucer from the bag and pours some water into it; she takes a careful sip herself so that she doesn't burn his mouth. The warmth gives her a little chill, she feels it going halfway down; she tries to let him drink but he is shivering so much that when she puts the saucer to his lips it half spills down his cheeks and chin. After he has swallowed it, her sadhu gives the faintest smile: the kind seen on the face of someone tolerating suffering. While she fills the man with melted snow, careful not to get him wet, she is looking at his face and hair in the flicker from her little fire. She's wondering how old he is: his skin is like a little kid's. It's covered with a film of dirt but smooth as if it's slick with oil. His hair's a mass of matted curls, thick and tangled everywhere, so in the dancing light his locks are snakes that wiggle from a hole. Her sadhu would be horrible if it wasn't for his strange green eyes; she cannot hold his gaze for long, although she'd like to stare at him awhile. In the firelight his eyes seem like they're made of semiprecious stone, much darker than they were before, all emeraldish and faceted. She cannot guess his age because he doesn't give the standard clues: the wrinkles and the length of hair, his language and his style of clothes. And as she's standing up to see if she can find more fuel to burn, he reaches out and touches her, his fingers brush against her arm; she jerks it back instinctively, her arm raises across her chest. She's ready to defend herself, she fiercely turns to glare at him—but only finds his eyes are closed, ready to accept her blow. She's horrified she came so close to striking her poor holy man, whose only crime is lying down and giving her this chance to help, to suffer through her present life.

She stands and walks out of the shack, into the snow that's halfway to her knees, and the night's so dark she can't see more than different shades of ground and sky. She wonders if it's clouding up, preparing for another storm, or if the dimming of the stars is from the smoke of Koksar's funeral pyre. She wraps her arms around herself and sniffs quickly at the freezing air; there's a faint sweet smell of drifting smoke, a little on the oily side. For a moment she thinks she'll be sick, that she is breathing something awful in—but it dawns on her the smoke is coming from her pile of burning dung. She's not sure what her feelings are, or how much of it is her fault. Has she done something wrong, or was she just supposed to take it all? It could have been a punishment, bad karma from some prior self: for all the rocks she missed while she was sitting sorting through the rice. She can finally see enough to walk around the shack and look for fuel; she knows she doesn't have a prayer, there's nothing left for her to burn.

★    ★    ★

In the morning she remembers fleeting snatches of the dream she had. She's drinking from the temple spring, scooping water up with both her hands, and it shimmers with a golden light that's nothing like she's seen before. She knows the place is beautiful, even though she hasn't looked around: the rocks the sadhu told about are reflected in the little spring. They are bigger than she thought they'd be, and their color is more glorious than anything she's ever known, and the water tastes a little sweet: it satisfies her thirst, but she can't stop herself from drinking more. She hasn't yet looked up from scooping water to her greedy mouth, when she notices a miracle: her fingers are completely healed. The calluses and scars are gone, they hold the water beautifully: her cupped hands are as perfect as the petals of a wildflower. She's still bent over, looking at reflections of the temple grounds, when a piece of shit goes floating through the water right in front of her. She looks up to see the Koksar men are squatting in the holy spring, their left hands splashing water up to wash their filthy private parts. Her hands are in the water when there's suddenly a flash of light and crashing thunder all around—this instant lasts forever as the lightning reaches from the clouds. A single bolt spreads fingers to touch each one of the Koksar men, and the water is electrified, and it tears up through her perfect hands—she pulls them from the golden spring to find that they are scarred again. She wakes up then because one of the rocks that she placed by the fire has suddenly split straight in two by gas expanding deep inside. The crack was like a pistol fired, waking up her holy man; the shack was lit by just the coals, and her sadhu's scream was horrible. The overwhelming feeling that she had was that it's all okay; her burned hands are a sign that what she did was only destiny: what happened to the men was just revenge sought by the mountain gods.

# The Snake

His whistle doesn't sound quite right—it's like the watch-man's out of breath—and Tamding's never run before, so she's not sure what to think of this. So Mary meets him at the door, she's dressed up in her working clothes: long underwear be-neath a skirt, her feet in eight-inch rubber boots. Tamding says to hurry while he does this funny little dance, his eyes rolled back inside his head with arms held up and quivering. He speaks to her in Kullui, so Mary's slow to catch the words—then suddenly she understands, enough at least to start to run, not bothering to close her door. The wet snow turned to ice last night, but the air is now so balmy warm that things are dripping everywhere; some buses rumble off in town, the road has finally opened up. She's glad at least it didn't rain, the sky is still an aqua blue; her feet sink down into the slush so that she almost touches ground.

This morning rounds took half an hour, a fraction of the usual; the young man with the broken hip still lying in his trac-tion bed with blankets half a meter thick: a pleasant smile across his lips, his family gathered all around to help him on and off the pan. She discharged both her labored moms, though only one took home a child. The other almost made her cry when she sat up in her bed and smiled, then took both Mary's hands in hers and pressed them there against her head. Mary wasn't sure just what it meant to have her hands pressed such a way: Was this woman giving thanks or was she now forgiving her? After Mary left the moms to gather up their things and leave, she went down to the children's ward to see her little three-year-old. The child was still all bundled, with her head wrapped up in snow-white gauze; she slept right through the dressing change, a thing she'd never done before. The child felt slightly warm although her chart read ninety-eight-point-six, so Mary took it as a sign she was catching up on needed sleep.

Mary's thinking as she runs that she should always take the temps herself, the girl had felt a little warm, and they'd stopped her medicines last night when the IV clotted off again. She's yelling at herself for being such a stupid little wimp: she should have stuck another IV in, but the girl has such a trusting smile that she didn't have the heart to hold her down to find another vein. Mary's way ahead of Tamding, who seems determined not to run too fast, and she almost twists and slips and falls when Kali thinks she wants to play: the dog comes bounding through the snow, she's yelling at the dog to stop so she doesn't stumble over it. All the staff has fallen for the charms of this poor little girl, who woke up from her ether dreams to ask if she could have a drink: a smile across her little face, the gauze around her head so thick she looks just like a turbaned Sikh.

The windows of the children's ward are steamed so Mary can't see in, and she's worried that they won't be there: the nurses and the nursing aides off sterilizing rubber gloves or sorting wads of cotton gauze, because they can't stand watching

helpless as their younger patients die. She's imagining the scene
ahead: the child seizing in her bed, the wailing of the mother
with the father standing stoically, his fear now screaming from
his face as silent as a candlestick drips burning tears of melted
wax. She'll have to get some drugs in her, perhaps she'll need
the cutdown tray—the nurse will hold the little arm while
Mary stabs to find a vein. And if the girl should live that long,
she'll have to do a spinal tap, and even though she's not aware,
she's thinking of another time, the very day that she arrived, a
shriveled little three-week-old, it's mottled body hardly with
the strength to take another breath. The only thing she knew to
do was what she'd been taught in the States: to draw some
blood and do some tests and intubate her little chest. *And isn't
there an ambu bag to help this little baby breathe? Why are all these
nurses standing staring at me helplessly?* She'd spent the family's
savings in the week before they went away; but Mary's not convinced they really took the girl to Chandigarh. So there's a
burning pit inside her gut as she runs into the children's ward,
her patient on her mother's back, tied there with a woolen
shawl: Mary told them they were free to go as soon as all the
roads were clear. As she's trying to figure out just what the hell
is going on, the little girl wangs gracefully: her little hands before her face, the mother beaming broadly that the doctor came
to say good-bye.

Mary turns when Tamding calls, still struggling through the
icy slush; breathlessly he tells her *that is not where you're supposed
to go!* Mary looks across the courtyard to a small crowd in the
dressing room, the place where they were calling her, with
Tamding pointing there as well. She somehow got things all
mixed up, anticipating something else; she can't help feeling
charmed again, relieved the girl is truly well. Mary feels a flash
of pride, her skills have saved a life this time: this bright-eyed

smiling three-year-old is anxious to be home again. She backs out of the children's ward, smiling at the mom and child, and instantly she's caught up in somebody else's urgency. She rushes to the dressing room where everyone is crowded round, talking faster than she understands. The crowd is not the nursing staff, but people from around the town; Tamding gets ahead of her and pushes everyone aside. On the table lies a little man who's soaking wet from head to toe; she's not sure what the story is but she knows they'll have to get him dry. It's hardly more than freezing out, and she figures it's a suicide; that's how they like to do it here, by getting drunk then jumping off the bridge to wash their cares away. She sees one every couple months, so far no one has killed themselves—they come in like a burst balloon, all limp and barely sputtering: all she does is get them warm and dry so they can go back home. It's not like there's a crisis line, or a place she can refer them to: no mental health professionals to meet with them three times a week. All that she can do is dry them off and let them rest awhile, perhaps observe them overnight, but this time it's so cold out she's concerned about his temperature: a case of hypothermia.

"Tamding, get these people out," and "How long has he been wet like this?" and "Did anybody see him jump?" She's asking all these questions with her stethoscope pressed to his chest, trying to listen to his heart and hear what water's in his lungs. The nurse today is Chidda, almost worse than having none at all; she'd be okay if only she could keep her mouth from running on. Mary tries to tell her that they'll have to get these wet clothes off, but Chidda's trying to tell her how her aunt had tried to kill herself:

"She onetime drank a glass of bleach, but that just gave her awful gas. And once she tried to hang herself, but the chair slipped and she broke her hip."

"Chidda, check the blood pressure." She hands the girl her

stethoscope, hoping that will shut her up enough so she can think things out. Mary finds the scissors that they keep for cutting bandages, and she starts to cut his trousers off when Tamding puts a hand on hers, reminding her it's likely these are all the clothes the patient has. She's worried that he broke his neck, that they'll hurt him taking off his clothes, though Prince Charming's X-rays were the first she'd ever seen with something wrong. She didn't see this man brought in, but she knows they didn't have a board: carried like a bag of rice so if his neck is broken then he's already been paralyzed.

The man is in a uniform, with a black stripe down along his pants; she's glad that he's so small because she has to lift his hips herself. Chidda's kind of helping, but she's hesitant to touch his pants; she pinches at the fabric like she thinks she'll burn her fingertips. She's only twenty-one years old and hasn't been a nurse a year; perhaps she's just embarrassed by this crowd of people standing here. As Mary pulls the trousers down, the nurse can't help but smirk and laugh, the way young nervous people do: she starts by sucking in her breath so everybody turns to look. She jumps about a foot or two, startled by the naked crotch: the penis an enormous snake that looks about a meter long. Mary's also quite surprised, expecting something shriveled up, his testes in his abdomen, his temperature so low he shouldn't have much hanging there at all. Then Mary turns around to find that everyone is trying to see, with Tamding standing right in front, his eyes as wide as deviled eggs. Someone makes a joke—she's got the vaguest clue what it's about: everybody laughs out loud at Chidda's nearly purple blush.

"Tamding! Get these people out! And get some blankets from the duty room! And tell someone to go and get the suction from the theater!"

Chidda now won't touch the man, she'll never hear the end

of it: the nurse afraid of being bit, the snake inside the patient's pants. Mary's on her own again, her hands are full of cotton gauze; she's trying to dry his torso off, and it really is remarkable. It stretches halfway to his knees, the thick end of a baseball bat; it's all the more astounding seen attached to such a little man. The total time he's been exposed is maybe half a minute, yet half the town by now knows of the drowned man with the giant schlong. Mary yells at Chidda, who's been motionless and mesmerized, to get some water on the stove, to warm up some dextrose-saline: Mary's worried that he'll vasodilate if she warms his arms and legs too fast.

She's asking where the family is, if anybody saw him jump, but no one in the crowd wants to take credit for a suicide. She's got him wrapped in blankets that are smelly warm straight from the stove, and his heart rate's still at fifty-two, his pressure ninety over palp; there's not much water in his lungs so she's thinking he might do okay if Chidda gets some saline warm. Mary rolls him on his side to check his rectal temperature—to find the hole she's looking for she has to move his testicles. She's amazed again how big he is for such a skinny little man; she's thinking in the wilderness how they would strip and climb in next to him, warm bodies pressed on either side: no one here would dream of it. The thought itself is horrifying: snuggling up with such a snake; how awful it would be to have a lover like an elephant. She has to hold his scrotum as she's waiting for his temperature; his testicles move in her hand; she wonders why they're hanging there instead of keeping warm inside. Chidda brings warm bottles of the saline Mary asked her for; Mary looks at the thermometer, which doesn't even register. She's dealt with this just once before, a woman found in Baltimore: she's doing all she knows to do but crawl in naked next to him.

She thinks she'll run two bottles in, an IV stuck in both his arms; she wonders since he's not awake if she should try a warm gastric lavage. She knows she'll have to work fast if she's really going to save this guy, but she's feeling much less anxious since she thinks she knows what's going on. Mary stops and takes a breath, glad the crowd is thinning out, the morning's entertainment for the town has gotten boring now: they've all gone off to be the first to tell each other what they've seen. No one says they're family, no one's claiming to have seen him jump—the only thing she's learned is that they found him just below the bridge, clinging to a great big rock. Chidda's slapping at his arm, trying to raise a vein to cath, and Mary tries to think if there is anything that she has missed.

She's remembering the woman that she treated back in Baltimore, an ancient thing who nearly froze after the gas man turned her meter off. Her past-due was a hundred bucks, and it was pay it or buy groceries, which makes Mary think of blood sugar, or if the patient had a stroke. She takes this poor man's other arm, with Tamding as her tourniquet: his hands around the patient's arm to help her place a second line. It's then she sees the bandage, while she's trying to find a decent vein: his skinny arm is cold and smooth, the size of a large ten-year-old's. There's wet gauze wrapped around his hand, the burn she dressed two days ago; she looks up at his face, his eyes are closed from his unconsciousness. The feature she'd most recognize is lost behind the frozen lids; his hair, of course, is tangled wet, and he's not the same without his clothes. He's wrapped in woolen blankets now, but he hadn't always been undressed; she pulled his pants and jacket off, and she should have realized then she was pulling off a waiter's suit. Chidda just keeps slapping since the veins are all so cold and small; Mary's not sure what to do: this man half dead in front of her brought all those tins of nourishment. The inside of her chest goes numb, she can't afford to lose control—seems every life she touches heads off straight into some tragedy. She's supposed to have a healing hand, instead the gloves she wears are black; how's she going to save his life if she's the one who made him jump? She looks up then at Tamding, because she's seen them talking late at night; he says he hardly knows the man, that he doesn't socialize too much. He's not sure even where he lives, down near the Post & Telegraph; he hasn't got a clue why little Amod tried to kill himself.

# The Pew

It seemed at least a half an hour before they got him through the folding door, the bus fumes made him feel so sick he wished that they had left him there to finish freezing in the snow. He's only done the job halfway, his hands and feet and face destroyed; now they've got him on the bus, nearly dropped him on the slippery stairs. Antone's lying in the aisle, resting on a narrow board, so every time they hit a bump he smacks his head against the floor. He's in and out of consciousness, not sure what is and isn't real, although he's certain there's a pain like someone's stripping out his arteries. He's trying to remember how he ended up in such a state: his hands and feet all wrapped in rags, he can't get air in through his nose. He's confused because of all the birds, his hands and feet in boiling oil: the ravens flapping laughing while he tried to fill his glass syringe, and everyone is smoking and yet no one lights one up for him. He'd give anything for just a drag, to fill his lungs with acrid air, to feel the surge of energy while soothing his excited nerves. It isn't helping him at all to breathe in other people's smoke, it's just a goddamn-fucking tease, like when you think you're in a vein but all you do is infiltrate. He opens up his eyes to see the dag end of a bleating sheep, and up above its shit-thick tail a child is leaning over him: hanging from his mother's lap, a bus-sick–looking two-year-old.

The rusted rooftop of the bus is the color of bad marmalade, and the aisle is thick with passengers, their last chance to get into town before the winter snows begin. Every time they round a curve, something rubs against his side—Antone doesn't want to look, afraid he might be sick again. His eyes close and he finds he's back inside the home he grew up in; someone's ironing his clothes and humming something horrible. The woman is his mother, though he's never liked the way she looks: there's something not quite right as if her nose is slightly out of place. He used to bump his head against the wall while watching her do chores; it didn't hurt but helped to ease the ache caused by his loneliness. They must have gone around a curve and hit a pothole in the road; his head bangs on the floor and it's exactly how it used to feel: a semi-pleasant memory, though now he's wishing he was dead or passed out from some uncut dope.

He opens up his eyes and sees the woman sitting near the aisle, the third one crammed into the seat, busy knitting winter socks: the shocking brilliant colors of acrylic mixed in with the wool, her ancient face there juxtaposed, her mouth missing the two front teeth, her fingers clicking, flashing like his grandma praying the rosary. He thinks his eyes are open but he's seated in a wooden pew with candles glowing distantly, some ancient seated next to him is fingering her shiny beads. The place is so enormous that it almost takes his breath away, so dark and full of echoed sounds, the dim light through the colored glass, the flickering of candles shows the bodies far up on the walls: the blue robes and the bleeding wounds, the faces gently suffering, the smell of something burning sweetly caustic in his little nose. They've sat for maybe hours and hours, his grandma's whispered chanting joins the others floating through the air, a chorus that sounds like Kullui now echoes through the atmosphere: a pounding beat above it all, his head against the wooden chair.

What is he to do now with this agony of memory, lying bouncing on a board, his face an oozing open sore? He's staring at the butt end of a sheep he's sure will defecate; or is this great cathedral just a place for keeping lunatics? It's a snake pit made of leaded glass, the chanting voices that he hears are people who have gone insane, answering the questions asked by creatures no one ever sees. He's conjuring an image up against the ceiling of the bus, the rusted metal canopy the canvas for a masterpiece. He sees a skinny sacred cow, a red mark right between its eyes—it's standing underneath a cross and blood is dripping everywhere. The sky above the cross has turned the color of the Virgin's robe: powder blue with foaming clouds like bubbles in a bubble bath. Something's nursing from the cow, a teat in each of many hands, its skin the same blue as the sky, its nose long like an elephant's. The sun streaks through the clouds above, shines upon the wooden cross, illuminates the crucified: a figure with a woman's form except for male genitals. The face is shrouded in a beard, with two eyes where they're supposed to be, a third above the tortured brows: all three eyes are closed like those of infants gently slumbering. This creature's hair is long and braided, piled up like the Buddha's crown; golden hoops hang from the ears, a halo frames it from behind. At first he thinks the creature's skin is sloughing off the nose and chin, but the skin is flapping leaves of gold that pilgrims press upon their gods. At first he's not sure what it is that's crucified in front

of him, some monster or an alien, so hideously beautiful, its
third eye opens up to stare like no one's ever looked at him. He
feels the warmth of dripping blood that's vomit from a bus-sick
child; it all comes clear to him at once: this creature crucified
above is Antone looking at himself.

# The Shakes

There's not much she can do for him but sit and watch him getting warm, and they've moved him to the duty room to put him near the smoky stove. She has the book out on her lap, she's reading up on hypothermia, but all the therapeutics involve measuring electrolytes and cardiac arrhythmias; she only has her stethoscope, her finger on his thready pulse. His heart beats out a rhythm like a slow dance at her junior prom: she's wrapped up with a sweaty boy she doesn't even like that much. She's not sure what she'd do right now if suddenly his heart should stop: she has her little box of drugs, an IV in both of his arms, but she doesn't know his blood pH, can't measure his potassium, the EKG is broken so he's not hooked to a monitor. The book gives two sets of advice, she's supposed to guess which one is best: to use peritoneal dialysis or let him warm up by himself, some blankets and blood gases and a warm room in intensive care. She can't do any tests at all, so she's driving with her headlights off; she doesn't want to leave his side, no telling what might happen next. It's half-past noon and timid Chidda's on till eight o'clock tonight.

As she's reading she keeps getting stuck on the section about what might go wrong: poor little man is facing sudden death from cardiac arrest. His blood pressure could take a dive, his blood sugar could bottom out, electrolytes go up or down, his lungs become edematous. A clot could cause his brain to stroke, or he might start having seizures soon, and if he makes it through the night, the list of ills gets longer still: sepsis or pneumonia or a hole burned in his stomach wall. Mary's never had to treat a friend who very well might die, this little man with crooked eyes, the only one since Richard died who's given anything to her. She keeps a finger on his wrist, measuring the silent tick, and Chidda walks by outside with the catheter she sent her for, a Foley freshly sterilized: she'll have to put it in herself, as Chidda couldn't possibly.

She's feeling slightly claustrophobic sitting in the duty room: Tamding has walked off somewhere, but Padma's sitting knitting socks, her short legs dangling off her chair—she's talking in her singsong voice to Manu sitting silently. The duty room is stuffy warm so when Chidda opens up the door the cool air flows in from outside feeling fresh on Mary's tired face. The catheter's set in a tray, a sterile drape across the top; Chidda forgot the rubber gloves, must trudge back through the snow for them. While Mary's waiting for her she checks Amod's sluggish pulse again; she listens to both of his lungs, afraid she's overloaded him. His breath sounds are still fine, perhaps a crackle every now and then, and the book says start him on some meds as soon as you can get them in; she sent Tamding for the box of drugs she brought from home in case she needed them. Once more the fresh air wakes her up: Chidda stomps in through the door; the noon sun melting all the snow.

Amod is still comatose, a wool cap on his head for warmth; Mary folds the blankets back, exposing legs and genitals. His feet and calves are still like ice, but his thighs have got a little warmth; she's trying to be nonchalant, pulling on her rubber gloves, wondering if the catheter could possibly be long enough. Chidda gives another laugh, a burst of nervous energy, as Mary pulls the foreskin back, her gloved hand round his flaccid shaft. It's like she's trying to cath a horse, her fingers barely reach around; she has to wash the smegma off with cotton dipped in alcohol. The tube passes quite easily: could drive a Tata truck up there; but she has to pull his penis straight because the tube gets hung up in the kinks. The damn snake's halfway to his knees, and his prostate gland must be enlarged, because his urine should be draining out; she's only got an inch or two more tubing she can shove up there. But sometimes if the prostate's large, the catheter gets stuck inside; she has to push it back and forth to try to get it past the gland. This task absorbs all Mary's focus, with one hand around his penis shaft, the other moving up and down to get the catheter to pass. Mary doesn't see that she is putting on a little show, with Manu, Chidda, and Padma staring at her fancy handiwork, and people passing by outside all pressed up to the window glass. To get a different angle she holds his penis straight up in the air, and everyone is quiet as she's trying to the get tube inside: they're open-mouthed and all amazed she even has the nerve to try. It hurts to pass a catheter, and even though he's comatose, Mary's trying to be gentle as she struggles with the rubber hose. As the cath slides past his gland, poor Amod lets a moan escape— Chidda jumps back with a scream, the people outside point and laugh, and urine's spraying everywhere, his kidneys working overtime. There's a balloon up in the tip to keep the catheter from sliding out, and there's a port down on the other end used to fill it with a clean syringe. Mary's trying to get the urine in a basin placed between his legs, while trying to squirt clean water in the port end of the catheter. The laughter is distracting her, and she's ashamed she let them look at him, but she's glad he made the little moan, a good sign he can still feel pain. She pinches off the rubber end, then hands the basin to the nurse: Chidda's face has turned so red she looks like she's delivered twins.

"Chidda!" she has to call her twice, "take this out and measure it. And tell these people to get out of here. And where's the extra length of hose?"

When she finally gets him hooked up to a bottle underneath the bed, she puts the blankets back in place, then checks his pulse at wrist and neck. She rolls him over on his side to take his temp another time; the book says he should warm up about two to three degrees an hour, and it's been a couple hours since she rushed into the trauma room. She wishes there were curtains to provide a little privacy—she has to hold him on his side five minutes with the probe inside. When she takes it out he moans again, his temperature reads ninety-three, and suddenly he's shaking from a seizure storming through his brain. His arms and legs are quaking and his shoulders are hunched up and back; quickly Mary reaches up and opens both his eyes at once. They're not rolled up inside his head but both are staring back at her, and for a moment she is paralyzed, a terror grabs her from behind: the first time she has seen both eyes look at her simultaneously. She's got to get some drugs in him to calm the static in his head; when she turns around to ask for help she finds that she's alone again. The only person with her is the woman from the laundry room, poor Manu spinning yarn for socks, the only one who sticks around when things aren't going very well. Manu drops her spinning stick to help the doctor handle this, and Mary's not sure what to do but give him some diazepam.

What she fears the most is that her patient's damaged mentally:

that even if he lives, Amod won't be the man he used to be. Maybe all she's doing now is trying to save a vegetable: the man may never walk or work, a burden to society. No one has stepped forward yet to claim that they're his family, that they're the ones who'll help him to relearn the chores of daily life: to put on socks and wipe his butt and chew things before swallowing. Maybe she should let him die, this could be the kindest thing to do; allow her friend to rest in peace, to burn him where two rivers meet. All of this she's thinking as she's reaching for the Valium, to fill a 3-cc syringe and stop the seizure in his brain. She's tipped the drug vial upside down, she's stabbing through the rubber cap, and she knows all of a sudden that she'll be the one to care for him. She knows that's what he'd do for her, and maybe this is all her fault: for denying him the right to care by trying to pay him for the food.

She turns back to her patient, to push the Valium through his IV line, and Manu's sitting by his head, her hand stroking his trembling brow. Mary's own hand steadies his, so she can get the needle in; she's worried what the drug will do, his breathing isn't very strong. She's having trouble with her aim when suddenly his trembling stops—she doesn't have to look at him to know that he has passed away. The tears are ready in her eyes, and she knows she can't do CPR: can't kiss the breath back into him, can't go through all that pain again. A sob is welling up in her, she hardly has the strength to breathe; a spasm crawls across her chest as if she's had her wind knocked out. But when she finally looks at him she knows that she has been a fool: her sob breaks out hysterically, her vision blurred with streaming tears. She watches as his chest expands, as Amod takes a big breath in; he wasn't seizing after all: the shaking was just shivering. She's laughing as she checks his pulse: a slow but steady fifty-eight; his brain has finally warmed enough to stimulate his other parts.

She can't stop laughing at herself, the tears are dripping off her cheeks; she knows she can't take any more, this being so emotional. She must look like a lunatic, her laugh is inappropriate; this fish bowl of a duty room is not the place to be right now. Manu still strokes Amod's brow, her touch helps calm his shivering; Mary wants to go outside, she's lost all of her self-control. Chidda comes back stomping in, and Mary can't stand to laugh in front of her; she has to push the nurse aside to get out to the cold fresh air. She tells Chidda to keep him warm: she'll be back in half an hour or so.

Mary takes the path to town to keep from being all alone; her tears have started drying and she isn't laughing anymore. She goes around a corner and sees Ravi walking up the path; he's just what she is looking for, a shoulder soft and leanable. He doesn't smile to see her, though; five men are following behind. They've got something between them that they're having trouble carrying.

"My cousins found him on the pass," he says, but Mary isn't listening. They've got Prince Charming on his board, he's all wrapped up in bandages; it really is impossible: she thought that he was dead for sure. The accident was days ago, with everyone burned up inside, and now they've brought him back to her, so she can try her CPR. She's close enough to see the boy, his face is now an awful mess: his eyes and mouth are swollen up, his nose has started peeling off. He has aged at least a hundred years, his hair is charred an ugly gray; her heart skips several beats because she feels that she's responsible. She glances up at Ravi for the message written in his eyes: expecting some kind of reproach, *How could she let this happen here?* But she only sees anxiety, he wants to know what they should do; it's then she sees the boots and bag, the track marks on the upper arms; this isn't her young man at all, but some fossil found out in the snow.

"Tell Chidda she can deal with him. I'll be back in a little while."

# The Kiss

He can tell the girl is next to him, still lying on the hard dirt floor; it's dark inside the shack but he is certain someone else is there. The stench of smoke still in his clothes recalls the awful day before: the black clouds of the burning building, the body Meena tripped over. The cracking noise that woke him is still echoing around the room, but there isn't any light to see so he can't tell what or who it is. The girl sits up beside him, but neither of them say a word; he listens for the girl to breathe, to hear if they are still alone, for the sound of stealthy tiptoeing. It's torture not knowing the time or what is in the room with them, and all that he can do is keep from closing up his eyes: afraid he'll fall asleep again, afraid that what had made the noise is waiting next to murder him.

At least a couple months go by before the morning finally comes, and Meena doesn't build a fire, doesn't make them any tea, just tucks his sleeping bag around and drags him back out through the snow. Everything is white and blue, the sky is like an iris flower; so glad that they have left the shack he doesn't mind the hunger pains, the light so bright it hurts his eyes, the fact his bladder's full again, or even that he hasn't had a chance to shit for several days. At first he's glad the sun is out, with its penetrating arms of warmth—they sneak beneath his sleeping bag and calm his constant shivering. But after just an hour or two he has to push the bag away; he begs the girl to stop and set the pee cup in between his legs. She understands his sign language, she gets his cup out of her bag; she helps him open up his pants: her expression always serious. There's a raw mark on her forehead where the tumpline cuts across her brow, and once his bladder's empty he can ask her what he's dying to know.

"Where are you taking me?" he asks, while she's helping button up his pants, but she only nods her head and quickly says something in Kullui. He doesn't understand a word, but that she's being friendlier, though she doesn't dare to smile until she's done the buttons on his fly. He cannot help but think about the sounds that he heard yesterday, her muffled cries of agony, the table pushed across the floor, the syncopated thumping of the men as they were raping her. He doesn't understand how she can stand there smiling down at him: how she can stand to live at all, as if their raping hadn't murdered her. Then he wonders if the smoke and fire, the dead man lying on the floor, was just revenge she brought to give some justice to her tortured soul.

As she drags him farther on he thinks about the day before; the light and heat and rhythmic pull all work at hypnotizing him. He sees the men standing in line, their dirty pants around their knees; their penises are stiff and hard while one by one they damage her. Then suddenly he's next in line to take a turn between her legs, and it isn't sexy in the least, he knows how she is suffering. Disease is dripping from her crotch, but the men behind him egg him on; physically they're pushing, and it's horrible but sexual. He pulls himself out of this trance when he feels the urge to push inside; he wants to fling the bag away but realizes that he's hard. And what is he supposed to do next when she helps him pee again? She'll bend to open up his pants, he'll think about her lying there: his penis will point at her chest, she probably should cut it off, these thoughts have so disgusted him. All day long she drags him forward through the blazing sun and snow; all that he can think about is how these men had treated her. Had they raped the girl before? And had she really killed them all? Or did the men just run away? He tries to think of other things, like where she might be taking him, or how long till he can go home, and what became of Antone who had driven off to who knows where? But every time his guard comes down, the images come back to him: the men still standing in a line and he stands right in front of them. The girl is on the table and they hold her legs spread wide apart, but that's not what's arousing him: for her he's feeling horrified, a sickness deep inside his gut— it's the power that he's feeling in the penis pressed against his ass, the men all pushing from behind, the snarling throbbing pack of dogs each aching to be next in line.

The last thing that he wants to do is rape this poor defenseless girl—he wants just to be nice to her, to hug her close and let her know it doesn't need to be this way. But someone keeps on pushing an erection up against his leg, he feels it shifting to one side, the pressure of this throbbing pack now rubs it up between his crack. He feels a pressure in his groin, his penis now fully erect, and they're trying to push him toward the girl, and he's trying to step back a foot. The sun's so hot he can't breathe in, he's caught between atrocities: he's mortified he's feeling such a pulsing pressure in his groin, the urgent need to push like all these animals he's holding back.

He wakes up from this horrid dream and throws the sleeping bag aside; he flings it off into the snow; the sweat has soaked through all of his clothes and he cannot fill his lungs with air. Meena stops her pulling and comes back to see what's wrong with him: kneeling down into the snow, speaking in her Kullui. She dips her hand into the snow and brings it out all wet and cold, then puts it on his forehead like the sweetest kiss he's ever had. He wants to get up off the board and run away as fast he can: unworthy of such loving care; *what is he to her anyway?* As she's cooling off his brow, her fingers dipped into the snow, he realizes what he's done, he's dreamed of rape and sex with men; his semen soaks his underwear.

From then on he can't find the nerve to look straight into Meena's face; he doesn't want to ask to pee so he refuses anything to drink. Still she's being nice to him, she stops and tries to cool his brow; she cooks and feeds him rice and dal, tucks his bag in when it's cold, and drags him closest to the fire. He's uncertain how much time's gone by, it all goes on and on the same—maybe it's a day or two or maybe several weeks have passed. The sky has stayed pure azure so he keeps his arm across his eyes, the sun like acid on his face keeps dripping down and burning him. Only every now and then he lets her tip some water in: his mouth feels like he's eating salt, or ashes from a funeral pyre. His lips are chapped and cracked, his tongue's become a swollen sack of dust; he sucks on little bits of snow to try to keep from suffering. Maybe it's the next day but eventually his bladder's full, and he's terrified of telling her, of asking her to help him go. But it's a rough ride going through the snow, and there's no clean change of underwear; she helps him get his pants undone and holds the little cup for him. He's certain that she's noticed the dried semen in his pubic hair, but she doesn't let on that she's seen, her face is still a pleasant mask now starting to look worse for wear. He is so concerned he'll stiffen up and that she'll glean his darkest thoughts that it never does occur to him to think about her being raped, to feel what's pressed against his crack: he's too concerned with what it's like to have his bloody cock cut off. And he's not sure which is more relief now that she's got him buttoned up, to finally let his bladder down or find his penis still attached and tucked back in his underpants.

A young boy helps her drag him in; the house is only one small room; they put him by the tandoor that is leaking smoke into the air. The girl speaks with an older woman, their words sounding like gibberish; he can't see what she looks like but her tone of voice is comforting. Besides the kid who drags him in, he only sees the ceiling beams, and one small snot-nosed little girl no bigger than a three-year-old. But after half an hour or so he can tell someone is by the stove: the shadows moving on the walls, water poured into a pan, a practiced steady chopping sound. For a long time no one speaks or sings, though he can tell the room is full of souls, of many people's unwashed clothes, that musky smell of sweat and dirt he knows from riding buses here. After what seems several hours he hears somebody's quiet speech: a woman talking to a child, asking her to do something. Of course he doesn't catch the words, but the tone does not need translating; it is not an awful angry sound, but one that holds room for respect, a simple straightforward request. It's quiet for some time again, then someone else speaks quietly, like *Is there more that I can do?* or *Should I chop the onion now?* Then conversation picks right up; somebody lets a laugh get out, a slightly stifled chuckle like they're laughing at the little one, not wanting her to notice it. The smell of cooked food fills the room, the sound of something being fried, the biting scent of onion is enough to make his stomach growl. Then someone comes in through the door, the cold air passes across his face; he knows the last one has come home: a husband or an eldest son. The whole house seems to breathe a sigh with everybody safe inside. There are only sounds and smells for him, the ceiling up above his head, a sense of life inside this room like he's never really known before.

Once they finish cooking, Meena brings a plate of food for him: kneeling down beside his head she flips the little rice balls in. The taste of dal-bhat on his tongue, he listens as the others eat, their fingers on their metal plates, the chewing done with open mouths. He is looking up at Meena, but his thoughts are of his family: his parents with their silverware, the crystal on the table-cloth. How would he be different if he'd been born to this family? His skin would not have been so fair, his dreadlocks wouldn't have been blond. This girl is squishing balls of rice to feed him with her fingertips, and a feeling takes him by surprise. She looks at him so patiently that he wants to kiss her cheek and run his fingers through her long black hair.

# The Eye

Antone hears the doctor's words, but isn't feeling too concerned: she's talking about things that really aren't important anymore. The doctor has examined him, she's pushed and probed him here and there, unwrapped the rags from hands and feet, then slowly wrapped them up again. She's telling him what parts are dead, too early yet to amputate, how really it's just watch and wait to see what will be left of him. But it's hard for him to concentrate on things so insignificant, with the image of himself as God still floating through his consciousness. He's trying not to blink, he's so afraid to interrupt his stare; he doesn't want to take the chance he'll lose what he has finally gained. He needs to understand his role: what things he should and shouldn't do; he always thought that God was both all-knowing and all-powerful. Someone pulls a blanket up and tucks it underneath his chin, fluffs the pillow for his head and asks if he wants anything.

He cannot make any reply, can't move his still-unblinking eyes—he's staring stone-like into space where everything makes perfect sense. His face and hands and feet are not as painful as they were before, though shocks stab through these parts like being zapped with electricity. But if he doesn't move at all, and if he doesn't blink his eyes, then all he sees is his own face draped on the body of a god. It's horrible and comforting to see this image of himself; he's not sure what it means yet, but he's trying hard to concentrate. Then someone comes and sits with him, to feed him little bits of food; he doesn't taste the rice and dal, although he chews it thoroughly. He only has to open up and more gets placed inside his mouth; if he should spill or drool, somebody gently wipes it off his face. And the image keeps on haunting him, the message that it's offering: this figure with his awful face, a god of pain and suffering.

When he's finished what he wants to eat he only has to close his mouth, then someone cleans his chin and lips and dabs his nose with medicine. These people who attend him speak respectfully in lowered voice; every couple hours they come and kneel around his metal bed. They bathe his hands and feet for him, in water warm as baby's breath; they take his excrement off in a special blue enamel tin. His skin is rubbed with scented oil—their touch so light and delicate—then carefully he's wrapped up into long white lengths of swaddling cloth. Through all of this he keeps on staring off into the other world: this image of himself as God, as Buddha hanging crucified. He's not sure what to make of it, the third eye staring back at him: a look of so much pain and grief, the source of so much suffering. His blood drips from his hands and feet while other gods present to him: a pantheon of deities with heads bowed down and worshiping. There's Shiva with his trident staff and Vishnu trying to kiss his feet; Kali with her tongue stuck out, her skin black as his lacquered box: she's holding out her cutoff heads like sacrificial offerings. All around are servants ministering to his every care: pilgrims come from far away to pray before him on their knees. Every now and then a pain will sear across his arms and legs: enough to bring tears to his eyes, the opposite of heroin. But suddenly he understands the nature of these awful shocks: it isn't something wrong with him, it's the power of Almighty God. What's stored inside his hands and feet are signs of his omnipotence: at his command, for life and death, are Zeus's raging thunderbolts.

# The Change

The tumpline's cut into her brow, and Meena's feet are soak-ing wet, but at least she's had something to eat and spent last night in someone's home. The father of the family said her des-tination's still a ways: the temple with its flowering trees, the golden spring and holy man who's offering enlightenment. Even though it makes her bleed, the tumpline is her sacrifice: the only chance she's ever had to influence her destiny. Every time she takes a step she thinks about the dream she had, her hands wet from the golden spring as strong and smooth as just-picked fruit. She walks along a valley floor now, glad there's snow still on the ground: she'd never get him there without the snow to help him slide along. She's wearing black galoshes, but they've finally sprung a leak; she's thinking that tomorrow she might start out a lot earlier, before the sunshine hits the ground, when it's colder and the snow is hard.

The valley is magnificent, with the sky as blue as lapis beads; the snow up on the mountainsides is caught between the cliffs and peaks. The wind makes all the sound there is, a light breeze whispers in her ears; because the tumpline hurts so much, she tries to concentrate on this: the breath of Shiva on her neck, that maybe he is saying that she doesn't need to be afraid. She's taking an example from the sadhu lying on the board, who hasn't said a word in days and hardly even looks at her. It's as if he's in some kind of trance, enduring all this sun and cold: eating what is offered him but never wanting any more. She knows that if he keeps it up he's certain to discover truth, to exit from the cyclic path of birth and death and birth again. It's karma he's avoiding now by never doing anything, just tied there to a skinny board to fast away and meditate. And when they reach the temple she might be the one to help him drink: her damaged hands dipped in the spring, she'll put them to his swollen lips and let enlightenment drip in.

Since she started dragging him the weather hasn't changed at all: the air as dry as uncooked rice, a breeze like ice against her face. She stops to rest and catch her breath, to look for landmarks once again—unsure she'll know the way by the directions that she heard last night. The father of the family squatted by the smoky tandoor stove; he held a stick in his right hand and dragged it through the hard dirt floor. He said to just stay to the right, to take the second valley north; she'll know the place because the rocks look like a pair of humping goats. It's two days more from there, he thinks, though he hasn't yet been there himself: so many pilgrims stop to ask he's certain that he knows the path. He said he'd seen it in a dream, the sheer rock cliffs and rushing spring, the two rocks with their golden hue, all year the trees are vivid green. It's just like what the sadhu said, the one who walked there on his hands: he'd told her of the golden stones and how they would enlighten him. She's trying not to be afraid, to convince herself that she believes; she looks up at the mountains that have been her constant company, their peaks all dipped in powdered snow like greasepaint on a baba's nose. The first clouds she's seen in a week accumulate off to the south, all billowy in shades of gray and resting near the mountaintops. Aside from clouds and rock and snow, there's nothing else for her to see; she's glad the sun is shining still to keep her holy man from cold. She puts the tumpline back in place, then starts off with another step, and her forehead is so scraped and raw that tears spill from her tired eyes.


There isn't any dung for fire, no kindling leaning by the stove, and the smell inside this little shack has almost reached unbearable. The only light is from a stub of candle she found near the door, and even though the smell is bad she has to keep the door pulled closed: the wind is whipping round outside, the snow collecting on the floor. If it were September other pilgrims would be staying here, with someone boiling milk for chai, with rice and lentils on the stove. Warmth and laughter would come from the pilgrims so close to their goal, bubbling with excitement like so many little two-year-olds. But now the snows have closed the pass and the pilgrims went home long ago; she's alone here with her holy man, a burden growing heavier. Even with the door closed, a cold wind blows through the leaky shack—the stone walls full of unstuffed chinks so that the candle threatens to go out. The only wood is what is used to hold the roof above their heads, and she'd gladly pull a timber down if she thought that she could manage it.

She's not sure what she's going to do now, huddled in this little shack: much better than out in the storm but worse than any other night. She's squatting in the near dark of a candle barely staying lit, thinking what to do now that she's found the awful source of the smell. She's not sure how she'll keep him warm without snuggling up right next to him, but now he's finally moved his bowels and she's not sure she could get that close. She dragged him in this drafty shack before she smelled his excrement; he could have been this way for hours, and she'd wondered how they'd manage if he ever asked to defecate. But after several days had passed, she thought perhaps they didn't go: that sadhus kept themselves so pure their bowels didn't have to move. Now she's found out otherwise, protected from the rushing wind: the smell that seems so terrible is coming from his holiness.

The day had started beautifully, like all the other days before, with bright blue sky above the peaks and sun enough to keep them warm. But later in the afternoon, the clouds she'd seen off to the south had suddenly obscured the sky, the wind came slapping in her face, the snow stinging her eyes and ears. She checked that he was tucked in well, his sleeping bag nicely secured, then leaned into the tumpline so they could get out of this sudden storm. She'd asked if he was all right, but her sadhu wouldn't say a thing: just stared up past her face as if he was in some form of Tantric trance. Several hours passed before she came across another shack, and at first it wouldn't open up, she had to nearly break the door—her shoulder now is feeling sore from pushing on the door so hard. She lost all hope of comfort when she saw there wasn't any fuel, and the smell inside the shack was foul, like something bad had died in there. It wasn't possible to go back out, to pull him farther through the storm, and she squatted by her holy man to make sure he was warm enough. The stench was awful next to him, and he turned his eyes away from her; she thought he might be angry that she'd found him such a place as this. So she tried to make him comfortable, by fluffing up his sleeping bag, but the stink came out from underneath so strong she had to close her eyes.

She's not sure how to clean him when she's wearing all the
rags she owns, and all the water's made of snow, and the only
thing she has for fire is the board that he is resting on. She can't
just let him rest this way, so she takes the scarf from round her
neck; he isn't helping her at all, won't even raise his bottom up.
His pants and underwear are fouled, the filth has run down to his
knees; the vicious stench makes Meena gag: she's not such an un-
touchable. It's not like cleaning up a child, whose business never
smells as bad: a thing you can forgive them for until they learn
some self-control. Instead she wants to smack him one, then let
him suffer in his shit—she should put him back out in the storm
to blow away the stink of it. But she takes his filthy trousers off
and throws them outside in the snow, then wipes him down the
best she can with one half of her woolen scarf. Then she takes a
small handful of snow and gently rubs him down with it, like
scrubbing pots with mud or sand to get the metal nice and clean.
It doesn't take too long before he's shivering from bitter cold;
there's still filth stained across his board and in his cracks and
crevices. She takes the clean half of her scarf and dries him off the
best she can, then throws it, too, out in the storm: the wind blasts
ice and snow inside.

The last thing that she wants to do is touch another stinking
man, but she knows what she will have to do, or both of them
will freeze tonight. As she's taking off her clothes she's thinking
of another pain, when filthy parts of filthy men kept sliding in
and out again. But this sadhu's not made of this earth, he's gone
beyond the needs of men: the hateful lust of pounding flesh that
drives them to be born again. She is hoping that all of those men
will be reborn as sickly pigs, as insects on a piece of shit, as ravens
flying overhead. She wants them all to cycle through so many
lives they'll never stop, they'll just keep living on and on and
never find enlightenment.

The stench is still strong in the shack, and her holy man is still a mess; there's nothing less her own flesh wants than what she is about to do. The wind is blowing through the stones, and snow spills underneath the door; the storm is sounding worse and worse, the mountain gods at war outside. She lays her pattu over him, then tucks it in along one side; she only hesitates a bit before she blows the candle out: her own flesh puckers up with cold as she climbs in naked next to him.

# The Cliff

The chief stands with his deputy, his shoulders hunched around his neck—he hates the cold worse than the snow, so bitter he can see his breath.

"He's there, sir," says the deputy, and the police chief looks up at the wreck, the ambulance up on the cliff, the local fellow he convinced to climb up and investigate. This whole thing's put him in a mood, and he'd like to climb up there himself, but there's no way he could reach the cliff with snow and ice on everything.

"He's looking inside, sir."

"I can see that," he says to the deputy, trying not to snap too loud while talking with his teeth clenched tight. Though the heavy snow's an obstacle, it's the cold that gets into his bones, like music on the radio: a bad song played too many times. He hasn't felt warm since back in September when the monsoons stopped: for two weeks it was almost hot, like Bombay in the winter months. Before his boss promoted him, he thought he'd like a cooler clime: a posting in a hill station above the hot and dusty plains. It was a step up to be district chief, so he couldn't pass the offer by; he's thinking where he'd be now if he'd kept his job in Calcutta: back where he had been for years, investigating homicides, the knifings of the faithless pimps and whores that no one cares about. But at least he would be warm enough, and he'd have his wife in bed at night; she moved back to his parents' house as soon as the first snowflake fell. He misses all his children and his feet are always blocks of ice; his deputy's annoying him by chattering his teeth too much.

When he first heard of this accident he didn't give it too much thought. The snow had come the night before, the roads were slick and treacherous; someone's bound to drive too fast and wind up sliding off a cliff. Some kid climbed up to see the wreck and said that every one was dead: the driver and a passenger were crushed and burned strapped in their seats. It didn't make much sense to him to try to get the bodies down, until the snow was melted and the job could be done properly. He sent one of his deputies to go out for a second look; the deputy said that it was an ambulance from Chandigarh. The chief thought for a moment what an ambulance was doing here; he would notify the hospital when the telephones were on again. It took two days to clear the roads, though the wires were still down somewhere, so he didn't get the telegraph till three days after the accident. It was from his boss in Chandigarh, they were looking for some stupid Brit: a tourist who had hurt himself, that's who the ambulance was for. He's thinking it's his karma, that he should have stayed where it was warm—even with the best excuse he won't be able to explain.

"How many bodies did he say?" he asks, because the man up on the cliff is yelling down to them in Kullui. That's part of why he hates this job, the language is so terrible; he can't make out a word of it when people speak the dialect. He faked it when he first arrived, and he must have done too good a job: now everyone he works with thinks he understands the local tongue. He's too proud to admit he doesn't catch what local people say; half the time he's in the dark about what news is going round. Language is his nemesis, he isn't any good with words: even with his English he has trouble being understood.

"He says there's just the two of them. Nobody in the back at all."

The police chief takes a deep breath in, to think about what step is next: the telegraph said they had sent a doctor in the ambulance. He's looking at the wreck again, above where it went off the road: the angle of trajectory implies that it was driving north. If the Brit was in that tourist town, that's still two hours farther north; they must have never picked him up: he's still waiting for the ambulance.

"It's too bad the Brit's not in there," the chief says to his deputy, and he's calculating from his watch if it's worth it driving up this late. He hates the drive up north from here, it's always twice as cold up there: a little town with cheap hotels and poor Nepali refugees. The heater in his jeep broke, and the twists and turns can make him sick: it's not safe driving late at night with all this snow still on the road. He's got a list of reasons why he doesn't have to go tonight, but mostly it's the doctor there, a woman dressed in baggy clothes, whose English sounds American, who speaks to him in Kullui.

"We'll go up in the morning. In the meantime, get the heater fixed." He turns to go back to the road, a hundred meters through the snow.

# The Twins

*T*hat's *what life is like,* she says, *lots and lots of people die. No one ever said that it was up to you to save them all.* Mary stops to buy some chai, to drink the calming sweetness in; she stops to watch the chai man counting change out of a dented can. *You can't do everything yourself! You've got to be more organized! Tomorrow you should make a list of Kullui to memorize.* She buys a few samosas from a wallah near a produce stand, then eats them slowly as she takes the long way to the hospital. *If you could just learn to relax. Don't be so damn hard on yourself! If I had been a man, the nurses would have shown me more respect.* She stands outside the gate to think, *you've got to get a better grip.* She takes a couple breaths in deep; *the poor man tried to kill himself. And there's nothing that you could have done to save that little British twit, and lots more would have died if you had left and closed the hospital. Just stop this stupid roller coaster. Get a handle on yourself. Every time you turn around you think you've killed somebody else.*

She goes back in the duty room to check on Amod's steady

pulse, then spends half an hour checking out the frozen drug addict. She thinks this might be just the time to get off the amusement ride: she lets all her compassion drain while staring at his blistered hands. His arms are scarred from years of use: a million little needle sticks; she wonders how he got up on the pass strung out on heroin. *He did this to himself,* she thinks, *you cannot feel responsible. It's not your fault this man's not smart enough to come out of the cold.* She does the least that she can do, she tells him what she knows for sure: that this is just a waiting game to see which parts will fall off first. She asks the nurse to clean him up, and to let the Christians in this time, figuring it couldn't hurt to let them care about this guy.

It isn't long before the doctor's conscience gets the best of her, and she cannot stand not being there while Amod's temperature is raised. All she does is baby-sit, a finger lightly on his pulse; she rolls him every now and then to check his body temperature. Nothing else goes wrong with him, he doesn't hemorrhage or seize; his pressure doesn't bottom out, does not inhale his vomitus. But while she sits she cannot stop the conversation in her head: the argument goes on and on: *Am I supposed to care or not?* The voice keeps on berating her, accusing her of being a fraud: *Richard never seemed to mind when he was up all night on call. And everybody knows that doctors have to deal with life and death. So why'd you take this job if you're not strong enough to handle it?*

She watches Manu knitting socks; she hasn't said a word in years; the clicking of her needles is like water flowing over rocks. It is such a calm, hypnotic sound that Mary has to close her eyes, but in her head she still can hear the arguments that will not end. *So why don't you just go back home? Stop worrying yourself to death. You've got a couple million; could devote your life to spending it.* She opens up her eyes again to watch poor Amod's shallow breath; his chest rising half an inch, then slowly falling back again. The voice she hears is not her own, but the nagging of her evil twin: the one filled with self-loathing, who has lost all her self-confidence. *You might as well go kill yourself if you can't do this anymore. Go find the place where Amod jumped, and fill your pockets up with stones.*

She opens up her eyes when she hears Amod move or make a sound; Manu puts her knitting down to stroke his forehead with her hand. Finally after hours and hours, his temperature reaches normal range; she tests all Amod's reflexes, pokes the bottoms of his feet, listens to his lungs and heart, and pinches for his pain response. Everything seems normal; she is getting ready to go home when Amod opens up his eyes, both staring off in different ways. His eyes aren't open very long, but his good eye focuses on her: Mary leans close to his head so she can hear him if he speaks. He doesn't say a word, but lets a smile turn up his trembling lips—a subtle sign that shows her that her patient's brain is working right. She feels a huge relief from guilt, a sense of total weightlessness; the voices that she heard all day at last stop all their bickering.

Now it's the next morning and she's stumbled to the children's ward: that's where they've put the only patients checked into the hospital. The windows in the children's ward have curtains over most of them, to shut out the staring curious from horrors done to little kids. So when she pulls his catheter, this time there is no audience—she knows it's better her than Chidda, but Amod is still mortified as she pulls the woolen blankets back. It only takes a second to let the water out of the balloon; Amod's staring off in space, just like the patient next to him, until the hose is pulled out and his crotch is covered up again. He is propped up in his bed now, and he's even had something to eat: Manu came in early so that she could feed and sit with him. Mary had to ask her to step out while she removed his cath, and she saw how darkly Manu blushed when she understood what Mary said.

Amod's looking pretty good considering what he's been through, but Mary's feeling numb and cold as if she'd been the suicide. They didn't call her all night long, but still she didn't sleep at all: she tossed and turned and waited for the sounds of an emergency. The generator didn't cough, there was no haunted whistle-tune; instead she listened all night to the nagging of her other side. *You should have checked in with the nurse before you tried to go to bed. You should have made sure that they emptied out his Foley catheter. You should have fixed the EKG: sent Tamding down to Chandigarh; you should have thought to start poor Amod on a drip of lidocaine.*

In the morning she felt like she had been beaten with a baseball bat; she couldn't get the blood to pump out to her frozen feet and hands. Amod doesn't seem to hold a grudge that she has spoiled his plans, to the point where she believes him, almost, when he denies that he tried suicide. She's just glad that he looks so good, woke up when she came on the ward; but still she's thinking that she should have handled something differently. From what she understands, Amod's claiming that he slipped and fell—what she doesn't understand is why he was walking out so late at night. He had gone down by the river, and the rocks, of course, were slick with ice, the incline of the bank too steep.

"I'm sorry I caused such a fuss, but can I go to work tonight?"

She chuckles when he asks because he barely holds his head up straight; she has to help him forward when she asks to listen to his back. His heart and lung exam is fine, his blood pressure has normalized, and his chart shows that his temperature is holding around ninety-nine.

Some officers come on the ward, the police chief with his

deputy: both in formal uniforms, both their faces rather stern. She had forgotten all about this part: that suicide's against the law, and they have to fill out special forms when travelers are hospitalized. She stands up when they come inside, the thin door slams against the jamb; she's dealt with both of them before, they act so tense and serious, like everything's a homicide. These meetings have been difficult, because they don't speak English well, and they won't speak Kullui with her; when they shake her hand they squeeze until her carpal bones collide. But her hands are still so cold she doesn't feel the crushing grip this time; she wishes they would leave because they both seem so uncomfortable.

She strains to understand the broken English of the chief; she's fighting with a feeling they should take *her* into custody. He's stumbling around for words in a convoluted sentence form, and his deputy keeps helping him with words she's never heard before. She's trying to explain that Amod only slipped and fell, he hasn't broken any laws, he wasn't trying to kill himself. She quickly realizes they aren't interested in Amod's plans: couldn't give a damn that he went late-night swimming in his clothes. It's unclear, but they seem to want to know about the foreigner: the addict on the wooden board, something about an ambulance. But the only ambulance around is the one that crashed the other day: Prince Charming with his broken neck burned up inside an awful wreck. She's nearly certain that's who they mean, but they keep pointing to the other one: the man brought down from off the pass, his face and limbs in bandages. She tells them he's a mystery, she doesn't even know his name—his passport wasn't in his pack and he still won't speak to anyone. Mary isn't certain if the officers both understand; she tries again in Kullui, but only gets blank stares from them. Their heads wag back and forth as they are rifling through the hippie's bag: she wonders if she broke the law by tossing out his bag of smack. The police chief asks his deputy to write things down in Hindi script, then asks her, please, to sign some forms; she's clueless as to what they are. They bow to her, say *namasté,* and crush her frozen hand again; she understands there'll be another ambulance sent for the man. She wonders what it's all about. Is he someone they've been looking for: an antisocial psychopath who should be in a lockdown ward?

Mary realizes that she's waiting for the door to slam; she's staring at the hippie while anticipating something loud. But the timing of the slam is past, she turns around to see the door: Manu's got her foot inside, her hands are full of tiffin tins. Mary can't help wondering that something must be going on; Manu's turned dark red again, her eyes cast downward to the floor. The room fills with the smell of spice as Manu takes the tin lids off; there's more than food enough for twelve, but this picnic is for only two.

Mary makes excuses, has the feeling that she's been left out; she backs out through the door and shuts it slowly so it doesn't slam. This morning there were just a couple patients in the OPD: an old man with a cough and then a woman with some dental pain. So Mary's finished with her chores, there's just the two men on the wards; she's not sure what she's supposed to do now that she's got some time to spare. For the first time since she came no one is calling for her services; she crosses through the slush to find out what's up in the duty room. She can see in through the windows that her favorites are all eating lunch: Padma with her angel face, knitting yet another sock; clumsy Sushila eating dal-bhat with her fingertips; and Tamding with his broad round face and eyes so filled with merriment: the night she asked him in he just sat quietly and drank his tea. All three of them are laughing at some joke that Tamding must have told—she realizes that they never laugh like that when she's around. She wishes she could join the fun and follow all their gossiping; she'd like to just relax and laugh and turn this into normal life. But the voice comes back into her head, the lectures never ending now: *They'll never let you play because they think that you're incompetent.* She doesn't want to listen but the voice has reached a fevered pitch: *Now that there's so little work, they wish that you'd just go away.* She pushes on the door and sticks her head into the duty room; and, yes, their laughter stops. Poor Sushila drops her dinner plate. Their silence fills her head, like they're expecting her to bark commands; she wants to come inside and sit but hasn't got the courage now. She looks at Sushila, who is scooping up her fallen rice.

"I'm going for a walk," she says. "I'll try not to be gone too long."


She's walking down the sidewalk, past the dhabas and the sweater shops; she knows that she should eat some lunch but hasn't any appetite. Everyone seems happy with the sunshine and the melting snow: tourists walking past her look delighted by this miracle. But her other half keeps pointing out how things aren't really as they seem: she's seeing dirty piles of slush that make the sidewalk slippery. Water's dripping off the roofs so that she wants an umbrella; it smells like all the griddle snacks are being fried in motor oil. *This town has got no charm at all. These hotels all look miserable. I'll bet there's not a single one that's got a halfway decent shower.* She's noticing the dirty water running down the guttered streets: rushing little greasy rivers thick with floating garbage bits. Half the signs have misspelled words—the English parts that she can read: *You'd think they'd find a painter who got further than the second grade.*

Mary's reached the edge of town where the wool shops and the sidewalk end; she's come full circle from the day she first stepped off the tourist bus. She's staring at a gravel lot that's filled with shoveled piles of snow, blackened by the diesel fumes of buses idling away. The smell at first reminds her of the long ride up from Chandigarh: eighteen hours of bumps and curves and screeching music videos. She realizes that to leave she'd have to climb back on a bus: a day without a toilet stop, the elbows in her pancreas. *And just where do you think you'd go? You sold your house in Baltimore. Your loving husband isn't there; your mother moved to Florida.* As she stares she doesn't notice teardrops running down her cheeks; doesn't notice someone standing close enough to hear her weep. *And if you run away you know they'll have to close the hospital. Everyone who dies will come and haunt you for eternity.*

"But all I want is someone to appreciate that I am here."

*All you want is someone who was killed about a year ago.*

A hand touches her shoulder then—she jumps as from electric shock; expecting to be asked for change, instead she sees her husband's face.

"I should take you home," he says. "The hospital will cope somehow. If we get seats together we'll both have someone to lean against."

She looks up at her husband's ghost, whose eyes are filled with deep concern.

"We can't go home," she tells him. "We haven't got one anymore."

# The Spring

The farther Phillip's dragged along, the narrower the canyon gets; he's looking up at icy cliffs that block out half the sky above. For days he's wished that he were dead: the humiliating accident; this girl is such a fucking saint; he still can smell his excrement. But he's gone beyond that incident, he hasn't thought of it all day: the waves of cramping nausea, the loss of asshole muscle tone. It helps that he can see the walls, instead of just the sky and clouds—the canyon is so narrow he could spit across the thin divide. The air feels slightly warmer, and the sky is filled with birds today: the ravens black against the clouds, like pepper on his scrambled eggs. They had a meal the day before, a tiny bit of rice and dal: enough to fill a raven's craw, to drink she had him suck on snow. Every night she tortures him by taking off all of her clothes; she drapes them over both of them, snuggles to him really close. He doesn't have on any pants, she tossed them out with his underwear, shit-stained in the snowstorm, which was miles and miles and days ago. So when she snuggles up to him he feels her hip against his own, so warm against his frozen flank it almost feels uncomfortable.

He hasn't had a hard-on since the day he dreamed of raping her, by virtue of not trying to think, a kind of self-hypnotic trance. He's found that he's quite good at it, at turning off his tortured mind. It started with his belly pains, the cramps and awful nausea, the alternating hunger pangs from eating so infrequently. He thinks about an ice cream cone, a vision from his younger years: he's walking on a sunny day when the scoop falls off his sugar cone. He's looking at it on the ground, the ice cream was mint chocolate chip; he's focused on it lying there, the broken cone is next to it. The pavement is so hot the ice cream's melting instantly, and that is what he thinks about: the ice cream with its chocolate flakes, a nauseating stream of green; his treat turned so inedible he wouldn't eat it on a dare.

At first he kept reliving all the disappointment he had felt: the injustice and his burning rage, how it should have been some other kid. It took him several days to let those angry feelings fade away, to let them simply pass along as something only trivial. But today the image simplified, he doesn't need to close his eyes: the dusty pavement's disappeared, the ice cream floats up in the air. If he concentrates enough, the ice cream doesn't melt at all, he keeps it frozen if he keeps his focus on this single task. Anytime his mind wanders, the ice cream melts and drips on him, but all he has to do is bring his concentration back: the ice cream freezes up again.

So now when she lies next to him, to keep his cock from getting hard, he takes himself away from her by staring at the ice cream cone. He does it other times as well, to get some distance from his pain: sometimes the scoop is chocolate chip, and sometimes it's rocky road, and when the pain is really bad, like when his guts are cramping hard, the ice cream's plain vanilla with a dash of sprinkles on the top. He can do it so consistently, he no longer feels the heat and cold, or that his backside's forming pressure sores, that he's so starved he isn't hungry though his belly is in constant pain. He seems to have forgotten the whole reason he is lying there: if he should sneeze or laugh too hard, he'd cut his spinal cord in two.

Today he's looking at the cliffs, the ravens flying overhead; he wonders why one-half the sky has gained a gorgeous golden hue. Meena's pulling hard today, as if they've got somewhere to go, and last night there was dung to burn, the chai shop got a little warm, so when she crawled in next to him she still had on some of her clothes. She's got to be half dead by now, he's hardly seen her eat at all; yet hour after hour she keeps pulling him on through the snow. Last night she fell straight to sleep, he listens as the rhythm starts: the way she breathes when she's asleep, the change when she begins to dream. Her breath is like a mantra, like the sound his board makes in the snow: the steady effort and release, the air goes in and out so slow. He doesn't sleep much anymore, he drifts off in the day sometimes—but all night when she's next to him, he's staring at his ice cream cone, the flavor changing now and then, but all the rest stays the same.

Today, though, things are different, a strong sulfur smell has filled the air, and all the ravens overhead are flying only round and round. Today they don't make any noise, not like outside that little town: the racket of the cawing was like the wailing of a beaten child. Phillip watches ravens fly, the sun not too intense today; his arm is resting on his head to give his eyes a little shade. Then Meena stops her pulling, tromps around him through the slushy snow—she's got the biggest smile that he has ever seen across her face. She looks like she's lost thirty pounds, her cheek bones sticking out too far, and the tumpline's made a scar across her forehead that looks permanent. He's always wondered about her hands, how her fingers became scarred so bad: the fingers webbed and crooked like a freak's under a circus tent. But even with the injuries of someone in a prison camp, she suddenly looks radiant: a sparkle in her night-sky eyes, a lovely smile from ear to ear.

He's not sure why she's happy, since her stomach's emptier than his: a mouthful of cold dal-bhat and a bite of snow to suck upon. The ravens fly on silently in circles high up overhead, and for some reason he's scared again: *Who is this woman anyway? Where does she think she's taking me?* Maybe she's stark raving mad, some bloody psycho lunatic: the place she took him from some kind of special, cut-rate hospital. That's why Antone brought him there, so they could take care of his neck; instead, this loony burned it down and killed the patients in their beds. Now she's standing by his head, she's reaching underneath his board, and with a grunt of effort she is lifting so he's vertical. He's sure that's what her story is, some kind of cultist kidnapper; she's tipping him off a cliff: a special virgin sacrifice. His feet remain against the ground, she's only lifting up one end— his heart is somewhere in his throat—and he's scared because his neck is broken. Suddenly the pain his mind's been trying so hard to deny comes flooding through his spinal cord, his brain stem barely big enough to handle all the impulses. It only takes a second, like a circuit breaker overload; all at once his mind is blank: he's staring at the ice cream cone. He isn't even conscious of the relief this vision offers him, he's only staring off in space: an instant meditative trance. She's tipped him up enough so that his blood drops down into his feet, and the scoop of ice cream fades out when he briefly loses consciousness.

His head is still taped to the board, and she's pushing him up from behind, so when he comes around he's looking out over a precipice. Maybe fifteen seconds passed, though it could have been a thousand years: the scene he's looking down at is enough to take his breath away. Meena's still behind his board, holding him so he can see, but he's not aware of her at all, absorbed in what's before him now. They're standing on a rocky ledge that's halfway up the canyon wall, there's snow right to the cliff edge which drops straight a hundred feet or more. They're at the canyon's narrow end where terraced on the canyon floor are scattered steaming pools of gold like yellow paint pots filled with oil. There isn't any wind at all; a golden mist hangs in the air; a temple in the midst of this is suspended like a submarine. Its single spire of rusted tin is pointing at the cloudy sky: the building made of ancient wood, the stuff God might have practiced on. The spire's an inverted cone, ascending from the mist below, and as the mist envelopes it, he sees the skulls of animals mounted round the second floor. The sulfur air and boiling pools make him feel like he's been dragged to Mars, and all around the temple yard the snow has melted from the ground. Trees are growing here and there, many of them still with leaves, and at the canyon's very end is the beginning of a golden spring: huge boulders with a saffron glow, the water gushing over them.

Her breathing went to double time as she dragged him to the canyon floor; the trail switched back and forth beneath a couple feet of soggy snow. Now Phillip's looking upward at the strangest man he's ever seen: a sadhu with his hair so long, his dreadlocks hang down to his knees. His skin's an awful ashen shade; he isn't wearing any clothes; from where he's lying on the floor, Phillip's looking up at testicles. The penis is uncircumcised—the man can't have a gram of fat—and his legs are like thick broomsticks bent to fit into his bony hips. His abdomen is so flat that his belly button's sticking out, his breast bone's sunk into his chest, so skinny Phillip counts the ribs. His beard is long and braided in a spiral reaching to his waist; his face is streaked with something red, like scratches that are oozing blood. The baba's leaning over him, babbling some gibberish: the smell of hashish wafts down, and his eyes look like he's stoned for sure. Phillip should be terrified of such an awful-looking man, who's holding up a three-pronged spear, a drum and ribbon dangling. The baba's trying to say something which Phillip doesn't understand; Meena speaks some babbled words the baba nods his dreadlocks to. There's something strange about this man, more than just his nakedness: behind the bloodshot eyes there is a sparkling intelligence. Phillip's feeling more than calm, they've pulled him through the temple doors: the sulfur smell is twice as strong, the humid air is nice and warm. There's hardly any light inside, but after being there awhile, his eyes adjust so he can see the ancient beams above his head. Everything is crudely carved, with Hindi script and animals; the temple's built around the rocks; he hears the water in the spring. Suddenly the baba points his trident behind Phillip's ear, the jagged tip against his scalp. Phillip doesn't feel afraid. He's certain that this naked man is not about to do him harm; all the sadhu does is cut the tape that's held his head so long.

The rice spills from the plastic bags the doctor packed around his head; the baba smiles and picks some up and wags his dreadlocks back and forth. Then, like he does this every day, he pulls the tape from Phillip's face, stuck across his brow so long he's certain all the skin's come off. The pain is like an acid scald, a torture over instantly; it leaves him with a burning sting, a less than pleasant memory. What Phillip doesn't realize is the change that has come over him: the pain he felt was not his own, it happened to somebody else. The baba wags his head again, then smiles an apology; he disappears and Meena is there helping Phillip sit up straight. She grabs him underneath the shoulders, doesn't give his head support, and just then for an instant Phillip's terrified about his neck. But like the pain across his brow, his instant terror doesn't last—he takes a leap of faith that nothing bad is going to happen now. Meena has some purchase and she almost has him sitting up; again he nearly passes out, the blood is pooling in his butt.

The dizziness fades slowly and the clouds he's seeing disappear; before him in the semi-dark the baba's squatting on a rock. Between them runs the golden spring, a stream about a foot across, which casts a strange reflection on the baba's exposed body parts. The baba squats with knees apart, his buttocks resting on his heels; it's like he's showing off what hangs beneath his curly pubic hair. The baba makes a lighter flare, one of those plastic throwaways; he brings it up above his beard to light the pipe that's in his mouth. The room fills with the smell of dope—a sweet and potent cannabis—and the baba almost disappears inside a cloud of golden smoke. He takes a few drags on the pipe, then passes it to Meena, then he takes the drum off his spear and starts to swing it back and forth. Phillip watches Meena puff, then hold the pipe before his face; Phillip doesn't do a thing but put his lips around the stem. After just a single hit the room begins to spin and dip—the noise the baba makes is like he's swinging half a dozen drums. It goes like this for hours and hours: the baba beating on the drum, the sweet smell of the drug they smoked, the sense that he's outside himself, it's just his body sitting there. He forgets that he's not lying down, no longer on his wretched board; he watches Meena cross the spring holding the baba's metal begging bowl. She bends and fills it at the spring, then kneels before the baba-ji, her head turned to the side so that she doesn't see his genitals. And the baba lifts one of his feet, and she pours the water over it, and the water drips into her hand and dribbles down onto the stone. With what's collected in her palm, she comes across the spring again; Phillip's back and neck are straight: it hurts if he relaxes them. Meena comes up close to him, her cupped hand leaks around the scars; he sees now the significance of what she is about to do. She brings her hand up to his mouth, he sees the baba swing his drum: the baba looks across the stream, his red eyes meeting Phillip's own. Phillip opens up his mouth; she brings her scarred hand to his lips; he's not surprised how sweet it tastes, what's washed across his baba's feet.

# The Bridge

The doctor told him he should walk, that he should get up out of bed, and Amod's still a little sore—the widow woman helping when he needs someone to lean against. He's not used to attention, but he's thinking he could live with it; she brings him three big meals a day and helps him limp to the latrine. It's only been a couple days since they pulled him from the river-bank, but he's feeling so much better now: his strength is starting to come back, he isn't always shivering like he did the first day and a half.

He's staring from his narrow bed at the hippie they've got next to him, the only other patient checked in to the mission hos-pital. It's amazing how still he can sit; the hippie hasn't moved for hours—the nurses propped him up in bed to see if he'd respond, but he keeps staring straight ahead as if he's in some kind of trance. The man must have his dressings changed, they're doing it three times a day; the hippie's hands and feet are black, his wrists and ankles swollen up. But his face is where he's damaged most:

his forehead is completely raw, his nose about to fall right off, his lips are twice their normal size. The poor man has no features left that anyone could recognize, just needle marks on both his arms and gray streaks through his dirty hair; Amod wonders just how old he is: he's twenty or he's seventy. The man's long hair is pulled straight back, his chin is covered with a beard; the Christians have been feeding him and kneeling by his bed in prayer. Amod wonders why the doctor hasn't tried to run them off again, for trying to convert someone unable to defend himself. Last night there were three of them, spaced evenly around the bed: their heads all bowed down with respect, their arms raised high above their heads. The only thing he understood was when they all would say *Amen:* a tension in their voices that implied a sense of wistfulness.

He's trying not to think about who's been inside the doctor's room, and he's trying to forget what he was feeling a few nights ago. The doctor's been all kindness, and he's truly glad she saved his life; but he felt such terrible despair that he couldn't stand it anymore. He remembers what it felt like when he threw the tiffins in the snow: the sense of being all alone, a waiter in a monkey suit, a man without a wife or kids, who no one ever thinks about. The night had been so beautiful, the slick world thick with icy snow; he walked off through the marketplace, empty at that time of night and void of artificial light. He crossed into the forest where the brick wall has been broken down, and the snow was softer in the trees, protected from the melting rays. He walked for what seemed hours and hours, alone with just the quiet snow; the starlight filtered through the trees, the forest mostly black inside. When he came down to the riverbank he heard the muffled pounding sound of the water rushing through the rocks covered with an icy crust. He walked high up along the bank, to where the rivers meet upstream, where the Manalsu joins the Beas in their journey south down to the sea.

The local people burn the dead here, where two rushing rivers meet, a place he'd never seen before, no friends or family left to die. There was a platform where the bodies burn, the ashes buried under snow, and the trees had all been cleared away so the bright stars lit the area. He wondered who would bring him here, since everybody dies one day; he wondered who would burn his pyre and let the river wash him down. He was certain that nobody cared enough to pay for all that wood, and he guessed that they'd just toss him in: let the river take his corpse away, let the ravens tear apart his meat, let some downstream village smell his stink. He walked up to the platform and he broke apart the crusty snow; he reached down to see if he could feel the ashes left by other men. The snow was dense and heavy, but he reached down through it anyway, and his fingers came out smeared with ash, a bit of gravel in his hand. He thought about the holy men, who rub these ashes on their skin: dance naked while they're smoldering, a way to mortify the flesh. He wondered if he shouldn't just give up the world he's living in, join with an ascetic sect and kiss some baba's dirty feet. In the light cast only from the stars, he looked down at his finger smears: the greasy ash was wet and cold; he dropped the gravel in the snow. He brought his fingers to his head, then smeared the ash across his brow; he was trying to imagine how these naked babas stand the cold. He knew he couldn't do it, couldn't walk around without his clothes: his long hair hanging to his knees, people staring at his genitals.

He put his hand back in the snow and tried to wipe the ashes off; the sky was somewhat lighter so he stood to look around again. There were mountains on both sides of him, it must have then been close to dawn; above the mountains to the east the moon was finally coming up. It seemed that just a day before the moon was like a shiny coin, but as it passed the mountaintops he could see it was a sliver now: the clipping from a fingernail. He wanted to cross the river, to the road there on the other side; the new light from the tiny moon enough to show the icy path. It led up to a walking bridge: two cables strung between some trees, a string of skinny boards suspended by short lengths of fraying cord. In the dim light from a distance it looked like it would be safe enough, but up close he was not so sure: it was at least a hundred feet across. Somebody had been over it, the snow had been brushed off the boards; he thought, *What have I got to lose? No skin off anybody's nose.* He wished he had both of his hands, the left one was still wrapped in gauze; the cables had no tension left, they sagged as he started across. Even without any weight, the boards out in the middle dropped to inches from the silty drink: the river raging icy with the snowmelt from the day before. The first few boards were clear of ice, the footing not too slippery, but as he neared halfway across, the foot boards had an icy crust. He felt the spray come off the rocks, the cables had a solid glaze; several boards were missing from a section of the other side. His weight made both the cables sag, so the boards dragged in the rushing stream; the bridge deck swayed and bucked each time the river rose an inch or two. He had his rubber boots on and was not afraid of being splashed, but the current made him dizzy and he only had his one good hand.

He stopped, unsure of what to do: to go back or continue on—he had at least a half a chance of getting to the other side. For a long while he kept staring down, the water right in front of him: the color of an old man's hair, the long beard of some wizened sage. The cold was seeping through his boots, the spray was freezing to his pants; his fingers started to go numb from hanging to the sagging wires. He wondered what would happen if he fell into this icy storm: his body would be swept along, it wouldn't take too long to die, the water was so bitter cold he wouldn't start decaying till he drifted down onto the plains. But that was just his body, it was his self he wondered most about: would he come back as another man, or come back as something worse than that. The morning looked like six o'clock, the eastern sky was aqua blue; the dawning light enough to make his situation obvious. He stood there for the longest time just staring at this raging stream: dividing Amod's life in half, the future from his dreary past. He wasn't paralyzed with fear, but deciding if he really cared; that's when he fell off the bridge, his mouth filling with liquid grit. He started forward thinking that he'd let the mountain gods decide: Should he go off to some new life, or make it to the riverbank?


He's staring at the other bed, the one the frozen man is in, and he hears the skinny door slam as the widow woman brings him lunch. It must be almost one o'clock, and he hasn't seen the doctor yet: unlike her not to make her rounds unless there's an emergency. Manu sits down next to him, starts opening the tiffin tins; the other day she fed him, but he thinks now he should help himself. He sits up straight to be polite, and she really is a quirky one: years now since her husband died, and still she hasn't said a word.

"Did you really make all this yourself? The biryani's spice is excellent." There are potatoes stuffed with curried cheese, a tender dish of eggplant stew—smiling, she looks at the ground, embarrassed by the compliment. He tries to guess how old she is, her life's not been an easy one; he's looking at her blushing face, the fine lines at her eyes and mouth. She couldn't be past twenty-five; her cooking is incredible; he's looking at the tins she brought, the one that he is eating from. She notices him fingering a small dent in the tiffin's lid; he's startled when he hears her voice, a little on the husky side.

"I found them buried in the snow, beneath the big deodar

trees. Don't worry, they've been sterilized. I put them in the autoclave."

He realizes that he's being fed from his own tiffin tins: the ones he'd thrown into the snow the night he fell off the bridge. Her explanation startles him, he's never heard her voice before; it opens up a flood of words that sweeps all other thoughts away. She tells him in a whispered voice how terrible her life has been, she ran off with a man she loved, too young then to know anything. His caste so far beneath her own, her parents wouldn't speak to her; they had to join a Christian church to find someone to marry them. But she didn't love him very long before he started beating her: a chore he did when he got home, like chopping wood for kindling. She learned to cook when she was young, she loved it more than anything; but no matter what she made for him he'd beat her for the slightest flaw: the stew served just a little cold, the eggplant not cooked long enough. He beat her nearly every day, on body parts that she could hide; then one night he lost control and beat her face all black and blue. That was when she lit the fire, she'd rather burn than show herself: the women in the neighborhood would talk of her behind her back. She thought her husband had gone out; they had no children in their home; she soaked her bed with kerosene and climbed onto the stinking sheets. But she couldn't get the matches lit, her hands shook from her shame and fear; the matches only smoldered when she dropped them on the kerosene. She went to get another match, when suddenly the bed was on fire: it wasn't doing any good if she wasn't burning up with it. She tried to beat the flames out, but her salwar sleeves had caught on fire; she panicked when she felt the flames, and couldn't just jump on the bed; running screaming from the room she didn't see him lying there: her husband passed out in his chair. The house was gone in moments, with her husband still inside of it; when the neighbors saw her face they thought she must have done it to herself, assumed she was distraught with grief, had beat herself with suffering. His death was called an accident, these fires happen all the time: she hasn't said a word since so she wouldn't have to tell a lie.

The ward door opens suddenly, one of the missionaries comes inside: a plate of something in his hand to feed the frozen hippie man. Manu puts her head down, flips a ball of rice into her mouth—she doesn't want to say a thing while someone else is listening. Amod's so astounded by the story that she's told so far, he's not sure what he's supposed to do: report to the authorities, or take her in his skinny arms and tell her she did nothing wrong.

"The doctor said I'm supposed to walk. Perhaps you'd help me with my boots." She puts the tiffin tins aside and takes him out around the block.


She doesn't say another word as they walk across the slushy yard: big piles along the building's edge; the snow is sliding off the roof. Manu's got him by the arm, so firm her grip is bruising him; not since he was three years old has someone worried he might fall. They're walking past the duty room, it looks like nobody is there; the tin pipe sticking from the wall has got a dripping icicle. The courtyard is deserted, with no local people hanging round; he has to think what day it is, there are always people milling here, the outpatients and nursing aids all running to and from the lab. He's thinking it must be the snow, the sky still threatening a storm; everybody's rushing home to get the goats back in the barn. The walk is feeling very good, he's steadier than yesterday; he's stepping with more confidence that he's got the strength to stay up straight. Manu's grip lets up a tad, though still she's holding plenty tight; she's the one who's steering them: they're heading for the marketplace. They walk along the sidewalks where the shopkeepers have cleared the snow; he's back inside his waiter's clothes: she's washed and dried and pressed the crease, he's looking pretty dapper with a clean shirt and his Nehru suit. At first he's looking at the ground, careful where he puts his feet, until his confidence has grown enough to let him look around.

The shopkeepers are all out in their doorways looking at the sky; in little groups of twos and threes they're speculating on the clouds. Manu still is holding on, but she's dropped half a step behind, and as they pass each group the men all stop their talk and nod their heads. At first he's not sure what to think. *Who are these men acknowledging?* They've never noticed him before, it must be Manu next to him. But then he hears them speak his name, somebody saying *Amod-ji.* He looks up with his one good eye: an old man's looking straight at him. His heart begins to race and thump, to find this man has greeted him—he's still not sure it's meant for him, but no one else is walking by. So he nods back to this gentleman, who says he's glad he looks so well; walking farther down the street, the greetings come from everywhere. The nodding heads and *namasté*s are clearly being sent his way; he feels the guiding pressure of the widow's hand against his arm. He doesn't have a clue what might have brought this notoriety, what makes the women that they pass flush red and turn their eyes away. He and Manu reach the corner, turn back for the hospital; he's so confused by all the fuss he wonders if his zipper's down. So with a subtle gesture he makes sure his fly is done up right, afraid he let his secret out, but his pants are safely zipped shut. He's not sure what to make of it, but he's feeling a foot taller now: the town finally accepts him, with a woman hanging from his arm. He's thinking that he must have drowned when he fell off the icy bridge. He's cycling through another life: he's come back as another man.

# The God

Antone's sitting up in bed, some pillows pressed behind his back—his hands and feet still loaded up with Zeus's deadly thunderbolts. He can almost see the sparks fly, though his hands are wrapped in miles of cloth: they come and change it frequently, the power so incredible it's charred his skin and turned it black. He's lost the gnawing pit of fear, no longer feeling so confused: the pain is easy to endure, knowing he is truly God and therefore he's invincible.

He's not paying much attention to what's going on around him; he opens up his mouth at times and food gets gently placed inside. And every now and then his faithful pilgrims come and pray to him, kneeling all around his bed with arms raised as an offering. The prayers go on for hours and hours, but Antone doesn't mind the noise: the droning sound is comforting, the sound of Mass when he was small, the soothing stimulation when he banged his head against the wall. Sometimes he will raise a hand, mark out a big sign of the cross, being careful where he looks and not to point at anyone. It's going to take some time to learn the secrets of his awesome power—the forces in his legs and arms can change all mankind's destiny. He gets a certain pleasure when the women come to change his robes, unwind the yards of swaddling cloth that insulate his thunderbolts. He's not surprised to hear the raucous fanfare of a trumpet's blare, an undulating siren's song, a high-pitched lyric frequency announcing that they've come for him. He's seen the fuss the locals make each time they move one of their gods: with everybody in the street, the shuffling of callused soles, the god up on a platform carried high above the dusty ground. The god sits stoically unmoved, with features that seem carved in stone.

A parade comes in to take him to a temple or a festival: two men dressed up in long white coats, their necks draped with black stethoscopes. They stand around and talk with all the pilgrims who have tended him: gathering instruction on the dangers in his feet and hands. Antone isn't listening to anything they have to say: he's certain they're discussing him, the center of the universe. They put him on a platform, then they take him to a waiting coach, with colored lights flashing around, confetti flying through the air. They let the music blare again, and Antone keeps his stoic face; it's colder in the open, he can feel it in his arms and legs: the lightning and the thunder reassure him of his potency. He's lost all sense of time and space, he's living in the here and now; as they put him in the coach, the faithful gather all around. He'd like to touch and bless them, but he's too god-awful powerful, afraid even the slightest touch could instantly destroy them all. The chariot they've put him in has started moving down the street, he feels the sway from side to side, the rumbling of his faithful crowd.

# The Devi

Meena's back in Koksar hiding from the hated men she shot: crouching in her little room, waiting for the door to explode open with a violent kick. Someone's slamming from outside, she's squatting back behind the bed, and every time the door is kicked the hinges almost separate. She knows the door will open, that it's never kept them back before: eventually they'll break it down and lift her pattu up too far. It only happens when they're drunk, but they get plastered every night; that is how this dream goes on, she's watching as the hinges strain, knowing any moment it will let them in on top of her. Her dream goes on for hours and hours, the door always about to break, and every time she hears a kick the terror rises in her throat. She wakes up in a drenching sweat, too hot against the temple rock, so dark she cannot see a thing to tell her where on earth she is.

She sits up from the heated rock, and feels a cool breeze circulate; she sees the outline of a man go outside through the temple door. The moon is shining just enough to show the man in silhouette: it's the baba with his skinny legs and tangled hair down to his knees. Feeling totally confused, she slowly moves to follow him, crawling past her holy man out cold against the thermal stone. She still feels the adrenaline from her dream about the banging door—her mind is not quite right from all the charas she and the baba smoked. She still can feel the baba's drum, the sense of otherworldliness: the smoke so thick she couldn't breathe, the drum beat echoing her heart. The baba had been nice to her, instructing her on what to do; she hadn't felt a bit afraid when she dipped the bowl into the stream, when she poured the water from her hand between the lips of her young holy man.

She crawls now to the temple door, refreshed some by the mix of air; the light outside is brighter from the clear sky and the brilliant stars. She can see the baba off a ways, the starlight on his skinny rear; the baba walks into the stream, out where the water's boiling hot. It's a horrifying suicide, or she's witnessing a miracle: the water bubbles from the rocks, the steam lit by the glowing stars, the baba walks into the pool and slowly lets himself sink down. She knows the water's scalding, like the flames that seared her years ago; the terror's in her throat at what will happen to his holiness. He's sinking down until his head's the only part that's not submerged—she watches as his hair floats up, the dreadlocks spreading out like spokes. His head is like a spider in the center of a matted web; she's waiting for his anguished howl when he realizes what he's done. But he doesn't cry or scream for help, he's only mortifying flesh: to make it separate from his soul, to speed him to enlightenment.


This morning he pours broken rice into a soggy cotton bag, then lays it in the thermal spring that's gushing from the heated rocks. They're underneath the temple floor, where she had slept so fit-

fully; the rocks too warm but better than the other options that
they had. She somehow can't believe the water's hot enough to
cook the rice, but the temple room is sauna-like, the water scalding to the touch, the baba likes it here because the steam makes
all his joints hurt less. The rice is from her holy man, the bags
packed all around his head—amazed he didn't tell her all those
days they both went without food. The room they're in is small
and cramped, the light comes through cracks in the wall: the
floor a giant sloping rock, the ceiling is the temple floor. She has
to crouch and watch her head to get to where the spring comes
out; the baba says it won't take long to cook the broken bits of
rice. She's too hot in her pattu, and she envies him his nakedness;
the rock that they are squatting on burns through her thickly callused feet. She's squatting near the baba, in a room where she can
barely see, and he's telling her a story as they watch the bag of
cooking rice.

"Those that worship Kali know that she will give them
everything, for Kali is the mother goddess, goddess of destruction
and creation. She is the embodiment of time, time which must
devour all, made from the light that shone out from the eyes of
all the gods combined . . ." She was created when they needed
her, to fight the awful demon king, who had proclaimed himself
the ruler of the earth and all the universe. The baba tells Meena
of the goddess, how her image can be sickening: in one hand she
holds up a noose, in another there's a severed head, around her
waist she wears a string of demons' arms with bloody ends. Her
skin is black obsidian, her eyes intoxicated red, her tongue is
hanging from her head, which makes her that much more
grotesque. The goddess is enormous, and she fights with all four
of her arms, and the baba tells of how she raged with mutilating
fearlessness. The demon army came at her, striking her from all
four sides; she scooped up ten in just one hand, crushing them

and drinking blood, picking up rogue elephants and swallowing them all at once. The armies struck her fiercely, but she laughed at what they tried to do; she crushed their skulls in with her mace and hacked the demons into thirds. Mahishasura was the demon king, and when he saw all of this happening, he flew into a fearless rage the gods had never seen before. But Kali only laughed as she impaled him with one of her spears; the world was drenched in demon blood, with bodies lying everywhere. The stench of death was sickening, the eviscerated bowels of men; she stomped through knee-deep pools of blood, through piles of demons' carcasses. She was drunk from all her killing—she still hacked at bodies on the ground—and the gods who had created her were terrified by what they'd done. The gods pleaded with Shiva, who was the husband of this awesome thing, till he went to lie among the piles of demons bleeding everywhere. Still drunk from her killing feast, her eyes red as the setting sun, Kali thrust her giant sword at anything that dared to move. Then she came upon a body lying lifeless out with all the rest, but this one's skin was beautiful, covered with a fine white ash, his hair hanging in golden curls, his eyes like brilliant emeralds. She placed one foot upon his chest, her black skin stained with demon blood, when she realized that it was him, that she'd touched her husband with her foot. And that is when the killing stopped, when she and Shiva met again: her tongue stuck out to show her shame at what she had just done to him.

When the rice is finished cooking, the baba takes her up a set of stairs, the cooked rice steaming on two plates with scoops of chutney on the side. She knows this is an offering, the meal presented to a god, the deity that must be waiting upstairs on the second floor. The smell of rice is wonderful, her stomach growls impatiently; she knows she'll have to wait until the god has first been satisfied, the essence of the food consumed, the matter turned into prasad. She doesn't know which god it is, she thinks that Shiva's resting here; when the baba opens up the door, she doesn't want to go inside. The passage they've ascended is the way the servants come and go, the pilgrims use the other stairs that open on the second floor. The passageway is poorly lit, but the baba climbs two at a time, balancing both of the plates and calling out in front of him. She thought the place was empty, that there were no other babas here; he's only calling out to let the god know that the food is near. Then he opens up the temple door, its wood so dark it's almost black, and Meena gasps and turns her head: the god that's standing in the room is something black and terrible.

The baba laughs at Meena as he boldly steps into the room, proffering the plates of rice and chutney to the monster-god. At first she doesn't understand, *What kind of holy place is this?* She wants to run back down the stairs but doesn't dare go down alone. She's standing just inside the door, the god has got its back to her—it has four arms and tangled hair, it's holding up a severed head. The baba's murmuring his prayers, kneeling down before the god, setting out the plates of food, his laughter bubbles from his throat. He stands and turns around to let some light into the temple room; he opens up the shutters so the god can see the food he's brought. The brightness takes her breath away, at first because it hurts her eyes, but then because she better sees how horrible this monster is. Its naked skin is black as night, in one hand it holds up a knife, another swings the severed head, the palms all stained with demon blood. Meena circles to the front, she keeps her back against the wall, relaxing only when she sees this god is actually a *she*.

Meena's staring at the Devi, from the story that the baba told:

the figure of the goddess even worse than she'd imagined her. The goddess looks intoxicated, her eyes are rimmed in scarlet red, the third eye in her forehead staring straight back into Meena's own. The Devi's tongue is sticking out, a golden hoop pierces her nose, a garland wrapped around her neck is strung with cutoff heads of men. She isn't wearing any clothes, her dreadlocks frame her naked breasts; around her waist she wears a dangling string of mangled arms and legs. But what's fascinating Meena is the platform Kali's standing on, the goddess has her bloody foot set out on Shiva's naked chest. Her left foot's resting on his thigh, he's lying flat against the ground; he's staring up adoringly, his green eyes seeing only her. His hair is golden matted curls, his skin is alabaster white, and she realizes that this is the image of her holy man. The story that the baba told was that Kali's tongue sticks out in shame, for having touched her foot against her husband and his holiness.

Meena's still not feeling well, she hasn't eaten much for days—she still can feel the potency of charas mixed with lack of sleep, the chilly air and steamy heat. The smell of rice has filled the room from the plates set down before these gods, and she's staring up at Kali who will turn this food into prasad. She knows the baba has it wrong, she sees no shame on Kali's face; her tongue is sticking out in rage, her stance is one of dominance. She stands on top of Shiva, who's believed the holiest of gods, but it's obvious that Kali must be infinitely powerful. And Meena knows what she must do, she's been waiting for this all her life: she takes the pins out of her clothes, her pattu tumbles to her feet, and naked she lies on the floor, prostrate there before her god.

# September

# The Screamer

Doctor Vikram's back again, but he's not the way he was before: he takes time out for morning tea, and almost never yells at her. She thinks it was his year away, or maybe having company. Sushila squarely slaps the clamp into his reaching palm. He doesn't have to ask for it, and he's not so quick to get upset: this surgery went beautifully, just like the three done earlier. Sushila's feeling anxious, with a new mom laboring upstairs, and she wishes she could be there now to coach her through the panting phase. It's taking all her energy to concentrate on what's at hand—she knows that Padma's up there, but that doesn't make her feel at ease, since every couple minutes they hear another bloody awful scream.

"Get some saline on the table, then run upstairs and check on her."

"Thank you, Doctor," she replies. "Are you sure there's nothing more you need?"

"Make sure you check the fetal heart!" Sushila hears the

doctor shout. And she pulls her gloves and gown off and goes running up steep wooden stairs, a shortcut past the autoclave that leads into the labor room. Padma has the curtain drawn, and she's laughing from the other side, when suddenly the mom lets out a scream like none she's ever heard. The husband's standing in the hall behind a skinny wooden door, and Sushila hears him knocking, asking if it's still all right in there. She thinks it's cute the way the husband's being so solicitous—other husbands sit outside and smoke beneath the walnut tree. She peeks behind the curtain to find Padma standing on a box, her ear up to a metal cone pressed tight against the pregnant hump. Padma's laughing at the mom for screaming like she's going to die, perhaps because they're still not used to hearing her make noise at all. Maybe all her screaming is to make up for the years before, when Manu never said a word, since the day that her first husband died.

"Everything is fine!" she shouts to Amod through the labor door, then turns back to find Padma wiping sweat off Manu's beaded brow. Manu's sleeves are pushed up high: Sushila's never seen her scars—the damage that was done the day that Manu nearly caught on fire. Manu finally spoke again when Doctor Mary had to leave: she told them that she was engaged to Amod-the-gigantic-one. Sushila pulls the curtain closed, it's time to check if she's progressed; she pulls the sheet off Manu's legs, can see her tensely trembling knees. Sushila puts on gloves to gently place two fingers up inside; Manu's sweating so much that her pubic hair is glistening. As she spreads the labia while standing between Manu's thighs, Sushila's trying not to think how Amod manages to get inside. Her fingers fit in easily, she's feeling Manu's bulging bag, her cervix is almost complete, the baby's head seems well applied. Then Manu suddenly contracts, her scream so loud it's startling; Amod's at the door again: her shrieking must have frightened him.

Her bag of water breaks and Sushila's shoes get soaking wet; her fingers are still up inside, and she's unsure what she's feeling now. All at once she realizes Manu's baby's coming breech—the part she'd thought had been the head was actually the other end. She doesn't want to seem alarmed, but she wants the doctor up here now, and she's whispering to Padma who is laughing up near Manu's head.

"Padma! Come and look at this . . ." she says to get her to come close, trying to keep her voice calm so that Amod doesn't break the door. She's whispering to Padma that the baby's butt is coming first: she wants her to go down and get the doctor up here instantly. Sushila's never helped deliver someone that she knows: just village women who come in to push and grunt so stoically. Manu gives another scream, her contractions coming evenly; Sushila tells her not to push, that her cervix isn't ready yet. It isn't but a moment before she's hearing Padma climb the stairs—she's calling down behind her for the doctor to come right away. For the first time Sushila has a preference who might come upstairs: Doctor Vikram's nicer now, but he's not the one she wants to see. She quickly scans the table, checking that the ring-clamp set is near; there's a pair of scissors handy and a full syringe of lidocaine. She steps back from between the legs, looks through the curtain's opening; she's relieved it's Doctor Mary rushing up the stairs from surgery.

# The Afterbirth

Mary doesn't say a word, just dons a pair of sterile gloves, then steps into the curtained room and says *hello* in Kullui. Sushila steps aside so Mary gets a closer look; Manu's womb contracts again, her panting turns into a scream. Then Amod barges through the door—he's come in from the narrow hall; Mary says that he can stay, but has to stand near Manu's head. She puts a couple fingers in to stretch around the opening; the baby's butt is first to show: still hasn't passed meconium. She's telling Manu that she shouldn't try to push the baby now—that if she needs distraction she should rearrange her husband's face. This gets a chuckle from the mom, a pause between contraction pains; Mary's quickly making sure she's got the instruments she needs. She is trying to be patient, gently stretching Manu's labia; she doesn't touch the baby's butt, just lets it come out when it wants. Amod's up near Manu's head, whispering in Manu's ear: *Everything will be all right; just do what Doctor Mary says.* Manu seems to have control, she isn't screaming anymore, and Sushila's coaching her to pant whenever she feels pain again. Mary's got the scissors ready, to cut if she needs extra room; Manu's womb contracts again, the baby's butt comes sliding forth—the hips are folded at the waist, so Mary has to work them out. She doesn't touch the kid again, just lets the body dangle there: remembering the time she had to do the craniotomy. This is what she hates the most: she still feels so incompetent; her instinct is completely wrong: she wants to yank the baby out. But fighting every impulse, she lets the baby dangle from the womb: giving nature time to let poor Manu's pelvic floor relax. Then she sees the hair above the nape, it's time to lift the baby up: she slides a finger in the mouth, then pulls its chin into its chest, and Manu gives another push so that the baby's head pops out.

Everybody's quiet as they're waiting for the kid to breathe; Mary holds it upside down while Padma clears the mouth and nose. The baby's skin is dusky underneath the blood and mucous slime, and Padma holds a blanket out, Mary clamps and cuts the cord; suddenly the kid reacts: a scream almost as loud as mom's. Everybody in the room then takes a breath of air themselves, and everyone who sees the kid is certain who the father is.

*"Hoooheee! A boy!"* is Padma's cry: they've made the kind most people want; then Vikram comes into the room, and everybody talks at once. Doctor Vikram's laughing while he's pounding Amod on the back; Amod's grin is ear to ear, and Padma's in a giggle fit. Manu's got the baby snuggled warm against her sweating chest; she smiles at Doctor Mary, who's still waiting for the afterbirth.

# The End

Mary's sitting on a rock after a long hike up beside a stream: the whole day has been beautiful, the sun still shining in her eyes. She's been here for an hour, listening to the restful water sounds, the ravens cawing now and then, the whisper of a balmy breeze. She's glad the summer rains have stopped, September's a delightful time—she's looking all around her at the snow high on the mountaintops. She's thinking about Ravi, how she hasn't written in a while; the last time that she wrote was shortly after Vikram had returned. The sun is so delicious, it reminds her of her time away: how helpful Ravi was in her decision to come back again.

She thought today she'd be alone, with Kali there for company: this hike so far above the town, she'd walked along a rocky trail, she'd forged across an icy stream, forgetting this is India: there are always people everywhere. As she hiked she sometimes passed the Hindu pilgrims from Lahal, so tired-happy–looking since they're nearly at their journey's end. Tamding told about

them once, they're from all over India; they come to seek a better life, their god all dark and terrible: the truly pious pilgrims
walk, the less than pious take the bus. She passed about a dozen
of them, clumped in groups of threes and fours, though every
now and then a single sadhu with a straggly beard. She's taken up
the habit of giving money to these wandering men, since learning that in India this way of life's legitimate: to take off every
stitch of clothes and grow your hair in matted strands, to smoke
dope several times a day, smear ash all over head to toe. She thinks
it is so interesting, that some are truly holy men: that all of this is
just a way to rid themselves of mortal flesh, to keep from coming back again.

The rock she's on is flat and wide and large enough to lie
upon; it's several yards above the trail, and tilted slightly north and
east. She's been hearing just the stream and birds and wind since
she sat down to rest: the panting breath of Kali lying nearby underneath a tree. Mary must have gone to sleep, she's startled by
the growling dog; someone's standing off a ways: an old man in
a ragged shirt, a Kullu hat, and plastic shoes. She's not sure how
long he's been there, but when she looks at him he breaks a
smile: he puts his hands together, gently bows his head and wangs
at her.

"Namasté," she says to him, as a signal that he can approach,
and the old man climbs up on the rock and sits down a few feet
away.

"Good afternoon," he says to her, and she's startled by his
English words; it's obvious he's local and he's practicing this helpful phrase. She's not sure what the man wants, but he's too old to
be any threat: he might be just as tall as she, but he'd weigh in
only half as much. Mary's thinking there's a chance he only wants
to talk to her: often locals like to practice English with the foreigners.

"It's beautiful today," she says, but the old man only nods his head, and so she doesn't speak again: just waits to see what happens next. Her training's made her good at this, at waiting through long silences, when patients shy or lazy want to make her do their work for them. For several minutes all they do is listen to the nature sounds; the old man finally turns to her and says a simple Hindi word.

"Charas?" he asks, and Mary's so surprised she can't suppress a laugh; all summer she's been hearing this, each time she goes out for a walk: she thought it was a greeting first, then learned the word means *cannabis*.

"No, thank you. No charas," she says, trying not to laugh too much; embarrassed at her own surprise: that such an ancient man as this would try to sell a stick of hash. They sit in silence once again, as the old man translates in his head, surprised to find a Westerner who doesn't want to buy his stuff: Why else would she be out here if she doesn't want to score some dope? They sit for several minutes, then he turns to look at her again.

"You stay here. I will go."

He stands up with the greatest care, then cautiously climbs off the rock; he wangs his hands before his face and offers her a sweet farewell. After he has walked away, the dog jumps up and takes his place: she lies down next to Mary, though she always stays just out of reach. Mary now is wide awake, was pulled out of a dreamless sleep; she thinks she'd like to hike some more, but decides she should eat something first. Her bag is filled with oranges, she bought way too many back in town, and she's got a couple chocolate bars from the wallah set up near the school. She's also got samosas and a tiffin tin of rice pullao, and she spreads it all in front of her: a picnic by the riverside, enough to serve a group of four. She breaks up a samosa, feeds the hungry dog the bigger half, and she starts to think of Ravi and her time away from India.

This was way back in November when she thought that kid died in the crash, and she'd lost all her perspective on what was and wasn't all her fault. Ravi happened by while she was staring at an idling bus: she'd walked into the gravel lot to look at them and smell exhaust. Ravi took her to her rooms and made her cups of strong black tea; he told her he'd take care of things: he'd tell the staff and pack her bags. He'd been all set to go himself, discouraged by the pesticides; but really he was missing Tom, the man that he is married to.

His ticket to Vancouver had a stopover in Singapore, and Mary didn't have a clue which city she should go home to. So they bused into Malaysia, found a room to share right on the beach; Ravi was so nice to her, he brought her morning tea in bed, they sat together on the beach and ordered funny-looking drinks. After several days she started laughing at the jokes he made, the laughter feeling different: not so filtered through her suffering. After they'd been there a week, one night they walked along the beach: the moon shone off the crests of waves, they listened to them thundering. Ravi was a gentleman, so soothingly he held her hand; they walked the beach for several miles, till the bugs became too much for them. They walked back to their bungalow, climbed under her mosquito net; they drank a little wine and snuggled underneath the ceiling fan.

They could hear the crash of sand and wave, the quiet humming of the fan, and she had her head against his chest, a mat of hair beneath his shirt. He smelled of salty air and sweat, the way her husband sometimes did; she began to talk of Richard then— the strength of their relationship. Ravi's chest felt strong and broad, she could hear her whispers resonate; he hardly said a word, but gently squeezed her every now and then, assurance he was listening. She talked about the plans that she and Richard had made years before: they'd maybe have a couple kids and someday work in India. At first she felt a sadness as she talked about their spoiled plans, and then she started crying when she thought how happy they had been. But after she had dried her tears, she still felt something ache inside: the accident was a hit and run, he hadn't had his helmet on; they found his bike a block away, the frame completely bent in two. If Rich had gone some other way, or if he'd had his helmet on, then maybe he would still be here and she would not be all alone. This was when she understood the last thing she was hiding from: that if her husband's ghost appeared, she'd want to really belt him one. She's so pissed that he left her, he just kissed her cheek and rode away, insisting that it wasn't late and that he needed exercise. How could he have done it? She had sent him for some groceries, and just like that their plans are gone, her life and happiness destroyed. She wants to slap her husband's face, to make him share her burning pain, to scream at him for leaving her just when the world belonged to them.

She got up off the double bed to pour another glass of wine: the bottle was a little one she found inside the mini-bar. The metal cap was on too tight, she had to twist it with her palm; still the cap won't budge and this was all she needed then to cry. Ravi stepped in front of her and took the bottle from her hand; he brushed her tangled hair back and then wrapped his arms around her waist. Her own arms went around his neck, she wasn't sure what all this meant: one half wanted the comfort from his strong and nurturing embrace; the other half wanted to push him down and have her way with him. She took a deep breath from his shirt, the skin below his velvet nape—was waiting for the slightest sign of sexual encouragement. His musky smell filled up her nose, the sweet-and-sour overtones; but mixed in with his salt and sweat was the long-familiar scent of blood. She opened up her eyes to find his neck is smeared with crimson red; *oh my God, I've killed him* was the first thought that occurred to her.

"Ravi. God. You're bleeding!"

Ravi put his hand up to his neck, then looked at his extended palm; the blood dripped down across his wrist. His eyes rolled back inside his head, his knees both buckled under him—she struggled underneath his weight to get him safely on the bed. Her heart was pounding in her chest, could not imagine what she'd done: just everything she cares about turns into catastrophic loss.

"God oh God oh God," she cried while trying to find the source of blood—every place she touched was yet another place he's bleeding from. She grabbed a wad of cotton sheet and wiped across his bloody nape: *How could I have cut his neck? What kind of god would think of this?* She was watching Ravi's life drift out across the blanket on the bed: absolutely certain if he died she'd have to kill herself. An anger like she'd never known welled up inside her head and chest: *How can you pretend you care, then leave me just like Richard did?* Every place she wiped came clean, his perfect skin intact and smooth; but even as she cleaned him she'd find brand-new spots of fresh red blood. Her hand had become slippery, she wiped it on the pillowcase—this is when she found the source: the blood was coming from her palm. She must have cut it on the cap while twisting on the wine bottle; Ravi'd only fainted from the sight of bloodstains on his clothes. The cut kept pumping blood in time with Mary's swiftly beating heart; the edges of the wound were straight: she must have sliced an artery. Now that she knew where it was from, the blood did not look horrible—was such a healthy shade of red from seven months at altitude. She watched her blood keep spurting out, a gushing little rivulet; she wondered if she let it pump, how long before she'd also faint? All she'd have to do is wait, and she could join her husband's ghost; the only thing she'd have to do is sit until her pressure dropped. But it was just a superficial cut, would close up

with a stitch or two; Ravi would wake up and then he'd take her
to the hospital. She found the idea humorous, that she could be
the patient here: let someone else get out of bed and stumble to
the trauma room. When Ravi came around at last, it was to the
sound of Mary's laugh: she was sitting on the bedside putting
pressure where she'd cut herself.


Now she's sitting on her rock and Kali's growling once again—
she looks up from her rice pullao to find a sadhu standing near.
He's where the old man stood before, a dozen steps back down
the trail; but this one can't be very old, he's standing much too
straight and tall. He isn't fully naked like so many of the sadhus
are: he's wearing an old woolen vest, a loincloth wrapped between his legs. In one hand he holds up a staff, a trident spear
stuck on the top, and from this hangs a *damaru,* a double-sided
wooden drum. His hair is past his shoulders, and his skin is covered thick with ash; the long curls of his dreadlocks have turned
golden from the mountain sun. Mary wonders if she's got a coin
or two to give the man, or better she should give him food: he
looks like he could use a meal. They always have a begging bowl,
some sadhus use a human skull; they stand outside people's
homes and ask to have it filled with rice. But this one's only
standing there, he looks unsure if he should approach; the sun
shines from behind her so he has to squint and shade his eyes:
perhaps the dog has frightened him. She speaks to him in Kullui, to tell him that the dog won't bite, that if he'd come up closer
she would gladly give him half her lunch. He takes a few steps
toward her, till he's standing in a patch of shade, and it's when she
finally sees his eyes—he drops his hand against his side—that
something strikes her funny like she's seen this one somewhere
before.

Then like he's made his mind up that it's okay to share lunch with her, he walks up rather casually, his right hand out in front of him. But he doesn't have a begging bowl, and his hand is not held palm-side up: he holds it like a Westerner, expecting that she'd like to shake.

"Hello," he says in British clip, "I think my neck is better now."

# Acknowledgments

First and foremost, I thank my wife, Beth. Without her love, faith, editorial acumen, and constant support, this work would not have been started, much less finished. My editor, Timothy Sheehan: if he is not one day referred to as the Maxwell Perkins of the twenty-first century, it will be because of my own failings, not his.

This story never would have been imagined if not for our good friends: the staff and patients at Lady Willingdon Hospital in Manali, India. Great thanks to Rekha and Dr. Ooman "Geo" George, Drs. Sheila and Laji Vargheese, Ahmed and Tara Sayed, the Mariammas, Satya, Achamma, Prem, Hannah, Shiv Dassi, Asha Devi, Neelu, Khimi, Tombi, Anju, Kishan, Soma, Sonam, Dr. Philip Alexander, Babychen, Satya Om, Kamla, Takur, Krishna, Ram, Prema, Tikmu, and, of course, Sonky, for bringing the mail.

I thank my daring friends and first readers: Mike Seamans, Shirli Axelrod, Jo Montgomery, Ruth Conn, Ann Lichtenwalner,

Rik Langendoen, Brian Milbrath, Barbara Deppe, Karl Beuschlein, Forrest and Amy Carroll, Martin Farach, Andrew Coltin, Ken Goldman, Kelly Price, Peter Goetzinger, Stacy Panek, Michael Thompson, Sue Fenoglio, and Tracy Willett. I thank the members of my family who were able to get through the uncensored medical scenes of the earliest drafts. Thanks to Jan at Powells on Hawthorne for an open mind and heart; Bobby and staff at Annie Bloom's Books for making this an early best-seller; Judy Ness for excellent advice; Carl Lennertz for a long list; and Trena Keating, David McCormick, and Nina Collins for bringing this novel to a national and international audience. Special thanks to Lauren Danner, Ph.D., for going beyond the call, to Mike Scroggs for his eagle eye, and to all I have neglected to mention, due to my own exhaustion and lack of character.

Finally, I once again thank my wife, because she is always both first and last in my heart and my thoughts.